PRAISE FOR
THE EGGPLANT CURSE AND
THE WARP ZONE

"Rubenfeld's novel is a heart-achingly narrated exploration of how we try to escape both the pain of the past and the absurdity of the future—a fanatical homage to retro video games and millennial angst."
—Jennine Capó Crucet, author of *My Time Among the Whites*

"From the streets of New York to the cornfields of Iowa, Shawn Rubenfeld's debut novel is a joyous romp into the mysteries of love, betrayal, and renewal. I laughed out loud at Joshua's travels and travails as he finds himself, newly divorced and stranded in a small midwestern town teaching with faked credentials at a boarding school. And what a school it is! These pages are full of original characters who straddle the landscape with a stoicism, wit, and strangeness that befuddles a world-weary New Yorker, forcing him to re-examine everything he knows. A cross between Alice wandering the Wonderland and Gulliver discovering his giantism and talking horses, Joshua staggers from one outpost to the next, uncertain about an identity that almost everyone he encounters questions and ultimately shreds. The conclusion is a lovely tour de force that will leave you rooting for our hero to be brave and leap into the unknown."
—Jonis Agee, author of *The Bones of Paradise and The River Wife*

"*The Eggplant Curse and the Warp Zone* is a comedy of errors, much like *Fleishman Is in Trouble*, and it is sheer pleasure to watch the narrator navigate, and stumble, through his predicaments. He's a man of his generation, seeking solace in nostalgia, trafficking in obsession, and resisting adulthood...highly entertaining." —Timothy Schaffert, author of *The Swan Gondola*

THE EGGPLANT CURSE AND THE WARP ZONE

a novel by

Shawn Rubenfeld

7.13 Books
Brooklyn

Printed in the United States of America

First Edition
1 2 3 4 5 6 7 8 9

Cover art by Matthew Revert
Edited by Leland Cheuk

Copyright ©2021 by Shawn Rubenfeld

Library of Congress Cataloging-in-Publication Data

ISBN (paperback): 978-1-7333672-8-8
ISBN (eBook): 978-1-7333672-9-5
LCCN: 2020953033

And roll you tightly like a ball (Isaiah 22:18)

For Ellie

I: THE EGGPLANT CURSE

BEFORE I BEGAN COLLECTING retro video games as an outlet for my grief and self-doubt, most days were tough. I felt jaded, sorry for myself. Trapped in a loop of fail and fail again. I tried talking my way out of it. In bed, I'd hold my phone's selfie camera up to my face so I could see how pathetic I looked. *Come on,* I'd say. *You're better than this. You have a lot going for you.* Was that how Mom used to put it? *In the bigger scheme of things, in the history of the world, of civilization, this is a blip.* It didn't work because my brain wouldn't let it work. No pre-coffee pep talk could change the fact that death had surrounded me, that I was cursed: from my marriage with Heloise, croaking out its last miserable breath, to my mother, buckling to an aggressive stage-four colon cancer. Then I found it hard—no, impossible—to give any heart to my dissertation on Yiddish dialectology, the letters and numbers of chapters and pages collapsing around me until they weren't mine anymore, like my marriage, my mother—atrophying, emaciated, lifeless.

Dead. Like Yiddish itself (well, mostly).

Also, I had just turned thirty, which looks better on some than others. The first time I had faced such emptiness I was told that my life just hadn't started yet. I was fifteen then. What would that same person say now? At least you aren't homeless and living on

the Q train? At least you have all your hair? These were the kind
of things I couldn't stand thinking about.

At some point before Mom died, my ex-wife Heloise laid all
my medical scripts on our kitchen counter and told me to pick
one—Xanax, Prozac, Luvox—and stick to it. *It's not that hard*, she
said. *At least it shouldn't be. Especially for you, Mr. Devotion.* Funny,
I thought. But it didn't happen. As luck would have it, my mind
found its own way out.

Here's how I saw it: I could pop 150 mg a night of a libido-re-
ducing, vomit-inducing, blackout-making, gamma-aminobutyric
acid-increasing, central nervous system depressant that you can't
take with even a drop of alcohol (unless you want your liver to
turn to goo, your insides to melt into your toes—breathing slowed,
heart racing, death) or even grapefruit (yes, grapefruit). Or I could
meet my younger, happier self for a two-hour session of *Teenage
Mutant Ninja Turtles: Turtles in Time* on his yellowing but robust
Super Nintendo. Kicking shell isn't your jam? Not into turtles
on hoverboards? Why not play *Thunder Force? Truxton? Batsugun?*
Hell, even a few rounds of digital pinball can make it seem like
the world around you has faded to black, if just for a moment. It's
bigger than nostalgia. It's transmigration. Rebirth.

It seemed like an easy choice when I put it that way, didn't it?

And that was the point. Choose your wine (you're in New
York, young one—there's plenty of it), choose your antivenom,
and feel as good as new.

Heloise didn't get it, but that was because the only time she'd
let herself touch a controller was for a quick round of *Mario Kart*,
and everyone knows that *Mario Kart* isn't a release the way *Battle
Garegga* is. After nearly nine months of me receiving twice-daily
packages from eBay and hauling dusty living-room-sized boxes of
unwanted games from strangers' attics so that I could sort through
the contents to keep what I wanted and sell what I didn't, Heloise
finally came to terms with the fact that maybe, just maybe this retro
gaming thing wasn't a simple "phase" I'd outgrow. A Year Thirty

crisis (her words, not mine). And so, she went Hail Mary on me, force-feeding marathon-like days at "world-class" museums and $175 operas at the Met, where, after waiting in a line of selfie-snapping tourists, she'd marvel for twenty-five minutes at some Warhol painting of a can or fight off tears of bliss as I fought off sleep and the occasional headache, then roll her eyes when she caught me on eBay checking the latest Sega Saturn listings (the Saturn was highly collectible, so it was best to act fast). Later, on the F train back to Brooklyn, she'd lecture me about disparaging her attempts to help me re-explore the "cultured, refined" world of which I once was part or about spending thousands of dollars "chasing nostalgia like a drug," or about needing to try a fourth or a fifth *actual* therapist or about not talking to my father in the one then two then three months since my mother's death or about neglecting my dissertation on Yiddish dialectology. "You used to be so into your work," she'd say. "Weinreich. Beider. All that stuff about the Nuremberg trials. The far side of the Austrian Alps. What happened to that part of you? Where did it go? I know the last few months have been hard, Joshua, but you've completely abandoned your responsibilities. You can't live like this." Even then she must have seen the inevitable: that I'd accumulate thousands of dollars of debt on PayPal Credit (money I had little hope of paying back) and step away from my PhD once and for all.

The divorce wasn't pleasant. I had to sell a factory-sealed copy of *Panzer Dragoon Saga* for less than market value, estimated at $1,750 (the Holy Grail!), and a complete-in-box copy of *Earthbound* with player's guide, worth $850, just to win the right to lose our ten-year-old cat, Marvin. Heloise said a few things I'd rather not repeat here. I, too, said things I wasn't proud of. But we made it out alive.

At least I did. In Heloise's case, I didn't consider rebounding with a Park Slope hipster who did pottery and made YouTube videos of himself doing pottery "making it out alive," but, you know, that's just my opinion.

I was pretty fucking depressed, which wasn't new, but at least I had my games. Rooms full of them. "You might not like hearing this," Therapist Number One had said when Heli and I were still together, "But I don't think these games mean as much to you as you let on. Do you know the role I see them playing in your life? One that is temporary, makeshift, a coping mechanism. And an expensive one at that. Look, it's good to have a hobby, but ask yourself this: Do these games make you *happy*? Fulfilled? Because fulfillment is important, don't you think?"

Well, people in the rafters, there it is. Turns out what I had needed all along, what I had been so brazenly neglecting, was fulfillment. Please pardon the oversight. I guess we can just end things here then? No? Okay.

Therapist Number Two asked me to pick one: Heloise or video games. I said, "Do you ask a man who has trouble seeing whether he prefers his wife or his glasses?"

"It's not the same," she said. "Please, Joshua, answer the question." So I told her I wanted both. These games, I tried to explain, were games I played for a good chunk of my '90s childhood, back when all I had to worry about were duplicate *Pokémon* cards and being forced to sit through reruns of *Ghostwriter*. I didn't play them with my mother or anything, but with my older brother, Jared, who had run off on a "soul-searching mission" to a kibbutz in Israel mere days after Mom kicked the bucket. (My father, I should mention, wasn't in Israel. Last I heard, he was staying with a "friend" in Franklin Square, Long Island, not far from where we grew up. This "friend" was the second aunt on my mother's side. It's funny the way that works sometimes, isn't it?) The point is, I explained to Therapist Number Two and then Therapist Number Three after Therapist Number Two stopped "accepting" my insurance, I might have been a different person had I not ventured through so many of these games as a kid and it really was comforting to see them collected there, with me from the start of a day to the end of it. Also, I went on, the business of buying and selling retro games was like pressed juice: it was the next big thing. "That's fine," Therapist Number Three had said, "but can't you see how maybe you've taken it too far? A few here and there are fine, but do you need to have so many games? Surely, you don't even have time to play them all?"

"Yes and no. I don't think I needed that Virtual Boy, so you're right about that. I didn't have one as a kid and I was curious. I was ready to trade it for a Panasonic 3DO but the trade fell through. The guy said something about the dust cover being loose. I don't know. Seemed trivial. But I mean, there's Exhibit A. There are plenty out there who are crazier about this stuff than I am. I'm a nothing, a nobody."

The thing I forgot to mention about Therapist Number Three (because there was always a *thing*, you see) was that she didn't know how to spell karaoke. I know this because she asked what Heloise and I liked to do before my mother's first surgery (a loop colostomy at Sloan Kettering) and I mentioned karaoke. I watched her struggle to write it on her little yellow notepad, which, I was pleased to notice, was the color and shape of my Super Nintendo. Then, because she saw me watching, she turned the pad my way and joked that her attempt (kerrioke) was probably off. "Just a bit," I said, eyeing the door. Normally I'm all about clarity over accuracy (a motto I've shared with my writing students for years), but we *were* talking about my doctor here. Expectations were different.

I told this to Heloise but she yelled and yelled about how Therapist Number Three had been trying to nurture the doctor-patient relationship by showing vulnerability herself and how karaoke isn't such an easy word to spell anyway. "We're not paying her to spell correctly," she reminded me.

"Honestly, how can I take medical advice from someone who can't spell karaoke?"

"How do you know that I know how to spell karaoke?" Heloise said. "And you *married* me."

"Heli, please," I said. "Wife. Medical Advice. They're two separate things. I don't care what you can and can't spell. That would be crazy."

She rolled her eyes and stormed out the door.

The one thing Therapist Number Three did get me thinking about (and subsequently got Heloise thinking about, nail-in-the-coffin that it proved to be) was how many other "temporary" fixations had consumed me over the course of my life. She called them Band-Aids. Ways of distracting. A conscious act of avoidance. The pathology is imperfect, she explained. Maybe I looked confused. The Holocaust, I realized, was one such fixation, though it would be hard to conclude that thinking about it provided me any semblance of pleasure. That was back during my freshman year of high school, when I didn't have many friends. I used the money I made babysitting to buy hundreds of books about the Holocaust. I watched dozens of movies. I spent hours at a time on Wikipedia. I convinced my parents to take me to Washington D.C. so I could spend a weekend at the United States Holocaust Memorial Museum. While there, I bought three T-shirts and two magnets. I took the guided tour four times. My father joked that the reason I was so invested in the Holocaust was probably because I had died in it in a previous life. For a time, I wondered if maybe it were true. Then, something changed, and I stowed the books away in the back of my closet and moved on.

The Beatles were another fixation. To this day, people who knew me during twelfth grade, when I had a few too many pimples and hadn't yet figured out how to find a flattering pair of jeans, see me and think one thing only: Beatles. I had a new Beatles shirt for every day of the week (and we Alpha-Beatles fans knew there were eight days a week). I filled file cabinets with fan fiction and surreptitiously snuck the Beatles into every last one of my formal assignments. A history paper on imperialism became a lyrical analysis of John Lennon's "Imagine" (a song, worth noting, that Yoko Ono should have been given songwriting credit for). A PowerPoint presentation about a neighborhood of Manhattan turned into a love song for Strawberry Fields in Central Park with "Strawberry Fields Forever" (obviously) playing in the background. I even used some rare, unreleased McCartney track for the background of an Earth Science presentation about the sun. The song—which was unnamed and known only by its first line and its haunting tonal changes (a signature of most McCartney compositions)—is something I could never forget. Lyrically, too, it was like a landscape painting. And the look on the teacher's face as he realized the loveliness of this little throwaway gem gave me all the incentive I needed to keep that Beatles train chugging along. And so, for the rest of high school it seemed it was my God-sent mission to introduce the Beatles and their catalog of underappreciated solo work to as many of my fellow students and teachers as possible. My mother had once been a Beatles fan too, so we'd often watch the videos and listen to the songs together. It was she who surprised me with tickets to see Paul McCartney at Madison Square Garden. Back then, it was the best night of my life. But now the Beatles are no longer a part of me. Maybe because I stopped needing them to distract me. Or maybe it was because they were taken away from me, ripped out of my life like my mother was.

You know the part that really hurts? I didn't think my mother would die. She told me not to be scared and I wasn't. Even when there were complications after the hysterectomy, even when she suffered systolic heart failure, even after doctors said she didn't have the right body for chemo and that it was too late for alternative treatments, I was sure she'd beat the thing. This was a woman who once took the LIRR forty-five minutes into the city when I had first moved to Brooklyn just to help me fix a hangnail. Cancer? Big deal. She was still standing and laughing and bad-mouthing that kid in third grade who called me a retard and stole the lunch she had made for me. To top it all off, her illness, for a brief, fleeting moment, seemed to bring Heli and I closer as we gained an appreciation for the fragility of life and how short it was. We found renewed meaning in our being together and carried on as if in a bubble, imperfect as it was. We even tried having kids. The initial plan was to wait until I finished school, but then neither of us could remember why we had decided that. Besides, where did waiting ever get you? Dead, that's where. Heli got her IUD removed and we gave it a fair shot. Nothing came of it, obviously. And thank goodness for that.

I was with my mother when she died, on the eleventh floor ICU at Sloan Kettering. My father, brother, and me, silent at her bedside, watching *The Nutcracker* on the tiny box TV (my father's idea). Her eyes had just closed when the monitor let out a dubstep pattern of screeches and beeps like the sound a 56K modem made when it "dialed up" America Online. My brother stood and yelled into the hall until a nurse rushed in. She called in other nurses. They called in a pair of doctors, who asked us to step into the hallway. It didn't last long. When they opened the door again, my mother's skin was blue and her mouth was open. "I'm sorry," one of the doctors said. My father put a hand on his chest. "Just like that it's over?" he said. "But she was just here seconds ago. She was just here." "I'm sorry," the doctor said again. Right then my father ducked his head and performed *keriah*, the rending of garments. He was wearing a black sweater, which he fiercely tore down the middle. He said the Kaddish and I watched uncomfortably as his grief hung there between my mother's body and his own. He had never been one to show emotion, but here it was, cold and shrill. When he came to, he pointed at my brother and me, his browning undershirt drenched with sweat. "Do it," he said. "Your garments. For your mother. You shouldn't let grief fester inside you like a disease." My brother obeyed my father's command—as he often did—but I couldn't. I was wearing a blue Henley that Mom had gotten me as a birthday gift. My twenty-ninth. I knew she wouldn't want me to rip it to shreds. Besides, I still thought then that my Jewishness could be strictly academic, cultural, on the ethnic side of ethno-religious.

"We don't need to do this right now," I said.

His body shook. "Jacob, David. You think they would say such a thing?"

"Dad," I said. "Please."

"Don't do something you'll regret," he said. "Something you can never undo."

"But that's exactly my point," I said.

Back then, retro gaming was still just a skin I was trying on, a "coping mechanism," a way to wash the wound and prevent scars. Just something for those restless moments when I felt like everything else wasn't enough—after I had slipped into the trap that was my own head; after I had fixed myself a cozy spot in the corner of the silent room and heard the buzzing of an invisible fly, then two, then three. That was my life. I couldn't make heads or tails of it. I organized a modest collection with a few of the well-known classics—*Mario, Zelda, Sonic*—most of which Jared and I had as kids and had been left to collect dust in my parents' attic. I widened that net more and more as the days passed until, finally, against all odds (or so it had once seemed), Mom was gone.

★

Here's another thing about video games: they look damn good on a shelf. Especially the Sega stuff. In 1995, Sega started using these uber-enticing (though fragile-as-hell) longboxes for North American Sega CD games and again for the Sega Saturn (since rumor had it they had a warehouse in Anaheim full of leftover longboxes after the Sega CD flopped like a ragdoll). The only time I even remember seeing Sega CD games as a kid was during a day trip to Circuit City at the Sunrise Mall, where my brother and I happened upon a Sonic CD display case near the discounted Super Nintendo carts. "Mini-cartoon!" it said on the box. "Sonic's first CD adventure!" Jared, two years older, yet two inches shorter, grabbed a box from the rack and held it to his ear. He shook it.

"Is this a special edition?" I said. "Why's it so big?"

"It's a CD," he said.

I couldn't hide my confusion. "They're putting Sonic on CD now?"

"Yup. Next is Mario on CD," he said, "obviously," and we both laughed.

"Want to ask for it for Hanukkah?" I said.

"Nah," he said, looking at it again. "You need a whole new system to play it. It does look kinda cool, though."

And that it does. Here, I'll let you in on something: there's nothing quite like being greeted each morning by a near-complete collection of those blue Sega CD longboxes against a brown shelf or those white Sega Saturn longboxes against a black shelf, standing trim and statuesque, the publishers and game titles on the spines like glossy stamps. Or, taking a step to the door, beyond the Sega stuff, to the four shelves of complete-in-box Super Nintendo games in sturdy box protectors, where I can flip through them one by one, recalling, perhaps, how I acquired a game or the memories I had playing it as a kid or reading about it as a kid or seeing it at video game shops as a kid back when I could only dream of owning half the games I have now. There are hundreds of collectors, in fact, who collect retro games purely for their display value, so they can be preserved, I guess, removing millions of desirable games from the supply chain *just* so they can sit on their shelves and look pretty. Whereas I, while certainly an advocate for preservation, collect—first and foremost—so I can play the hell out of them.

They aren't always arranged alphabetically. Sometimes I arrange them by game type—shooter, sports, platformer, racing, RPG, etc. Sometimes I arrange them by publisher—Acclaim, Activision, Atlus, and so on. Sometimes I arrange them by value from highest to lowest or from lowest to highest. Sometimes in the order I plan to play them next. Sometimes by serial number, sometimes release date. A few times I arranged them randomly, merely based on what spines I liked next to each other, what colors I thought popped most. When I was still treading water at the CUNY Graduate Center, my friend Thiago, a comp/rhet guy specializing in the narrative of alternate web spaces, would come over every few days to check out the newest arrangement and play me in a few rounds of *Marvel Super Heroes*. He had the game as a kid, and so he'd usually put in a code at the character select screen to play as Dr. Doom. Then he'd just alternate like a madman between the photon shot and plasma beam. My only hope was choosing Psylocke because at least she could evade the cheap shots by teleporting from one of the screens to the other. Not that it made much of a difference against that stupid plasma beam.

I didn't say these games were fair, did I?

Loose cartridges (meaning they weren't complete-in-box) weren't quite as fun to display, which is another reason I preferred to collect post-95 Sega stuff. I managed to fit some of them onto shelves like the discs, but most were relegated to bins, boxes, and cabinets, stacked every which way (in the corner, the closet, under the desk, etc.). The Nintendo 64 games used to be the most irritating because they didn't come with end labels. It didn't help that the games themselves, while appropriately nostalgic, had textures so blurry that they made me nauseous. Needless to say, they hadn't aged nearly as well as the Saturn stuff, the 2D powerhouse that it was. But, with Heloise's help, I used a label maker to create my own flashy end labels, making them easier to grab in a pinch. *Chameleon Twist*? Here it is. *Clayfighter 63 1/3*? Got ya. *Mario Kart 64*? Sorry, sold it.

Sometimes, when I didn't know what else to do, I asked a question of my games, feigning ignorance, like the question wasn't coming from me: What's Missing? I would say. Usually, the answer was obvious. I would stand with a beer in front of my NTSC Sega Saturn collection, ask *What's Missing*, and start listing off games I couldn't seem to find or just couldn't afford. *Panzer Dragoon Saga*, right. *Battlesport* (here I cursed the two chances I had to snatch this one on eBay before the *same* bidder, *sjruin324* from Harrisburg, Pennsylvania, screwed me in the final seconds). *Daytona USA CCE NetLink Edition.* Or I moved to the desk, where I kept the Atari Jaguar games—those sad, cardboard boxes stacked on top of a few SNES commons—and asked, What's Missing? *Iron Soldier II. Protector S.E. Air Cars.* Etc. The handhelds (kept in the bottom drawer)? Still easy. Neo Geo Pocket Color. Game.com. Turbo-Express. I could even lay my modest collection of *Nintendo Power* magazines on the floor and do it there, too. What's Missing? Issue Sixteen, *Maniac Mansion* on the cover. Issue Forty-three, *Star Fox 2* on the cover (a game that was never released). The inserts for Issues 54 through 59…etc. See? It was nothing, really.

But every now and then, while I was out in the living room or getting ready for bed, caught *just* between my evening rituals, without meaning to, I thought: What's Missing? It started out simple enough. The aluminum-like blue and white MidMod sectional and ottoman with three coordinating pillows, since replaced by a long squeaky futon from Craigslist (I never did have a good eye when it came to furniture). That was missing. The yoga mat rolled up against the door, replaced by nothing. Missing. The forty-two pairs of shoes—Manolo Blahniks, Hermes booties, Prada loafers. Those surprisingly endearing and calming large color block paintings. The Cezanne reproductions. The half-burnt floral candles. Half of the books on the shelves—most notably, *The Black and White of Design, The New Bohemians,* and *The Perfectly Imperfect Home.* The three-piece wooden light fixture on the wall with its spinning discus. The placemats. The plants. The smell, too. Like Earth, lightness, being. Not New York. It never smelled like New York.

And no matter how much I tried to avoid it, no matter how many times I forced myself back into the game room, running my fingers over those prepossessing Saturn spines or those Super NES box protectors (here, too, I was likely to pop in a ferocious Japanese shooter like *Dodonpachi* or *Soukogyurentai,* something that required absolute concentration or else your million-dollar spaceship popped into pieces and you were taunted by the big, black "GAME OVER" screen), at some point, without fail, the one I tried so hard to avoid really hit me (Game paused. Controller down.): Heloise. That unempathetic workhorse. That European beauty. Designer, deity, diva. Heloise. My wife. She was missing, too.

And why wouldn't she be? When my mother was sick, she had given me everything she had—everything she was—so it only seemed fair that in time I would do the same for her. That's how it had been before. That's how it had always been. Heloise was once the most important thing in my life, the biggest fixation of all. But now? Nothing.

What else? Didn't think we were done yet, did you? Well, close your eyes and walk with me here, to the window. Open them. Now. Pretend. Are you ready for me? What you won't see is Bay Parkway, Bensonhurst, a street that has resisted gentrification and evolved from the warehouses of yesteryear to a splattering of ngoh hiang and all-you-can-sing karaoke bars. The wash-and-dry on the corner. The long row of blue and white split-levels with metal fences. The sounds: subways, planes, buses, and people. People late at night. People early in the morning. People being people.

What do you see instead? A big yellow sign that says: "Gone Hunting." There, mounted on a wooden fencepost. Beyond it? Corn. Miles and miles of corn.

Look. There. See for yourself. It really was easier than you think.

Come to think of it, maybe that's where I should have begun.

★

It was my mother who gave me the name Joshua, after her great-uncle Jackie, who, as the story goes, was on the last transport from Hungary to Auschwitz on the eve of liberation in 1945. My father gave me the surname Schulman, which is German-Jewish and literally means teacher (though if one were to remove the 'c,' as my brother did after moving east to Israel, the name instead means 'shul-man,' as in head of the synagogue). When people ask how someone like me can be seduced into teaching three sections of writing at the offbeat Fairbury Academy for Twice-Exceptional Boys, a 600-student prep school in the cornfields of eastern Iowa where a simple cat-and-mouse playground game called Splat "steeped in Fairbury tradition" blew up like a cannonball at close range nearly costing me my entire retro gaming collection (among other, less important things), I say that I don't believe in God, but I do believe in the eggplant curse.

Either that or just dumb fate.

Let me explain. Last May, I attended a frenzied retro gaming convention just outside of Philadelphia with Thiago. We stayed in touch long after I had left the program. After getting the lay of the land (panels to the left, marketplace to the right, game machines in back, food trucks out front), we split—him to where the arcade games and pachinko machines were (all on free play), me to the marketplace to see if I could find someone willing to trade for a few of my doubles. Besides some import stuff, I wasn't after anything in particular. I just thought it would be a productive exercise to scour some of the bins and displays for games that weren't yet part of my collection, which was catalogued in an app on my phone. I hadn't been to a convention before so I was a bit overwhelmed by the crowd. The marketplace was packed to capacity—overflowing. And not just with nerds dressed as Naruto and Sailor Moon, but with men and women in suits, entire families, local news crews. I couldn't help but wonder what Heli would think of the legitimacy of retro gaming had she been there to see it all. Would she still think these were just "stupid kid games?" Would she still think I was just "wasting my time chasing nostalgia?" Me and half the world it seemed.

Still, you could say things got off to a slow start. Because of the crowd, it was hard to get close enough to the vendors to see what they had. Then, when I finally did, all I found was a tub of useless commons and a few offensively overpriced "rare" games that weren't rare at all. Clearly this wasn't the place to find deals. There was one vendor who kept all his games behind a big, lit glass case, none of which had price labels. I pointed to a copy of the underrated shooter *Phelios* on the Sega Genesis and asked how much. Without saying a word, the guy pulled up eBay on his laptop. It turned out that he was pricing individual games by request based on the highest active listing (a misguided practice; it didn't matter that no one in their right mind would ever *purchase* said game at that listed price, mind you). I had dozens of active eBay listings in my alternate life as a reseller, so I understood the impulse to set your price high, but in practice—especially at this kind of convention—the exercise was ludicrous.

At another booth, one of the guys manning the table read my convention nameplate back to me as I crossed his line of sight: "Joshua Schulman, New York," and then said, "We're based in New York." I looked at the banner hanging behind him. *PowerUp Games.* "Whereabouts?" I asked. "Utica." I told him that I had gone to school in Albany, but that I was in Brooklyn now (this was a few months before my move to the Midwest). "Cool," he said. Then he tried to convince me that my spare copy of *Super Mario RPG* was only worth $20 towards something at his table or $15 cash. Useless. I found myself spending most of my time at the Hurry-and-Run booths, where a few lone wolf developers were releasing games for CD-based systems that didn't have copyright protection (like the Jaguar CD and Sega CD), games that had either been cancelled before their initial release decades ago or had been built recently from scratch. "We're making retro new again," one of them said. "Do you want to be part of the new-old future? I bet you do." As I was playing around with one of their prototypes—a *Temple Run*-like game featuring a clone of Chester Cheetah running through suburban streets and collecting gold orbs that resembled cheese puffs—I got a text from Thiago:

Come to the arcade machines asap. You need to see this.

There, an unruly crowd had formed on the dance floor, a few gyrating to the DJ's chiptune remix. I found Thiago, his face flush in the pulsing light.

"Do you see these guys?" he said, pointing. "Mega Man and the Eggplant Wizard. Straight up caricatures of masculinity. I love it. Also, I feel like this calls for a dick joke."

I squeezed in for a better view and took in the scene. The crowd had formed around two cosplay dudes wielding lightsabers. One was dressed as a cross between Mega Man and Mega Man X, his blue tights giving his thighs quite the crunch. The other was wearing a giant purple one-piece beneath a red and white Santa cape. His face was a big green helmet drawn like an eye with a half-open mouth. On the floor beneath him was a long wooden staff. Attached to that was an eggplant. In the middle, Spiderman had taken the role of ref.

"This is trippy," Thiago said.

Their plastic lightsabers hissed and snapped. The two took up a sort of fencing stance and the crowd cheered. A few of the mostly white bros whipped out phones and said, "Oh my God, they're starting," and "Get him, Eggplant Wizard!"

Thiago shook his head in awe. "The Eggplant Wizard. Now there's one you don't see every day. Fandom at its most loyal and obscure."

I felt like I had seen the character before, but it wasn't coming to me. "Where's he from again?"

Thiago was one person who didn't make me afraid to ask dumb questions. For a while, he knew more about video games than I did, even though his loyalties stayed well within the hermetically sealed world of academia. We had entered the CUNY Graduate Center the same year and were both assigned to teach at CCNY. He from Miami, me from just over the Manhattan Bridge. He was the first one who said Heli and I didn't seem built for each other (even though at first he admired her tolerance of my game collecting) and, well, he wasn't wrong.

"*Kid Icarus,*" he said. "Dude, you have it. You showed it to me once. But he's a super secondary character. Tertiary, even. He's also in *Captain N*, a syndicated sitcom from the '90s."

Kid Icarus on the original Nintendo. The NES. Yes, I did have the cartridge and box, but I hadn't played much of it. It was somewhere toward the bottom of my current queue.

"It's a good costume," I said. "I'll give him that."

Thiago pressed his hands to his cheeks. "Just *good*? Are we *looking* at the same dude? It's hand-stitched, man. And the dude has a staff with a fucking eggplant attached to it, and it's good enough to eat. Do you know how hard it is to find an eggplant good enough to eat?" He laughed at the exaggeration.

"Have you never been to Whole Foods?" I said, feeding it.

"I'm just saying. Look at this thing. It makes Mega Man look silly. And Mega Man never looks silly."

A guy near us slid over and yelled above the roar of the crowd. "He's here every year. Comes alone. No one knows who he is."

"Must be a big fan," I said.

"Or he's just a serial killer," the guy said, cackling.

Thiago smiled at me. "I'd love it if 'he' turned out to be a 'she,'" he said.

"It would really unstitch these nerds," I added.

After a few minutes, the match ended with the Eggplant Wizard simulating Darth Vader's neck grab to win. The crowd cheered again.

Thiago grabbed my shoulder. "Can you believe that? The *dick* strangled the *man* to win the match. No joke, you could *easily* write an article about this. You realize that, right? *Masculinity, Monstrosity, and Fandom.* Actually no, you can stay Freudian with the Monstrosity bit, but man, the phallic imagery there. The entitlement of straight white nerd bros. So much material it hurts. What was that Sega CD game you showed me that time? The one with the talking dick pencil? *Wild Woody*? You can throw that in there, too. You'll be set."

I thought it over. "Eggplant delivering the mega blast to Mega

Man," I said. "Cosplay as public performance. One, if anything, that shines a bright light on the realities of sexism and xenophobia."

"Dude, this could be your ticket back in. I swear on it. You have to write it. You've already infiltrated. It can bring you back into academia. *And* with renewed purpose."

"It's all yours, bro," I said, adding the 'bro' ironically. "I don't want to conflate pleasure with work. Besides, I'm just here looking for a good deal."

"And did you find one?"

"I found a few bad deals, but that's beside the point."

He gestured toward the clearing scene. "Well, there you go. As good as you can hope for. And it's all yours."

This "ticket back in" plea wasn't new. Once or twice a month, I hosted Thiago and another department friend, Jordan, who was studying ecocriticism, for a game night. We'd buy craft beer at the local distributor, a few bags of chips, and play anything I had that was two-players, all the while gossiping about department stuff (while I was still in the department) and then about really bad department stuff (as in, *you left at just the right time. You were the smart one.*) after I had packed my office and left. A few drinks in, Thiago would inevitably point to the game on screen or wave to my wall of games and say, "You've gotta write about this shit. Vintage gaming as cultural artifact, man. This is it. It's right in front of you. Modern gaming is mass market copy and paste. Shooter after shooter. Online play. DLC. Microtransactions. Day one patches. But these games. These games are products of their time. They're really *saying* something."

"Like what?" I asked.

"This one here," he said. "Just look. It's *propelling you forward.*"

"Auto scrolling screen," I said. "It's a shoot-em-up. That's the point. That's the genre. What's there to write about? No one wants to read that."

"No. You're missing the point," he said. "Jordan, tell him. Come on. Knock some sense into this guy."

Jordan, holding the second controller first reminded me of the Games Institute at the University of Waterloo, where they publish a critical journal about game studies called *First-Person Scholar*. "Exactly," Thiago said. "Listen to the Canadian. There's a *gaming* journal. This could be your life, man. Just writing about video games. Breaking it all down. If you don't do it, I will."

Then Jordan said, "Okay, I got it. Take this stage we're playing now. Is it saying that space is just more raw material for us to exploit or is there, you know, a greater meaning to the cosmos? Are we just gonna go into the asteroid belts and blow the mountaintops off, mining coal, you know? Patriarchy. Capitalism."

"And all that time you're moving forward towards *intrinsic value*," Thiago added, crunching a chip. "It's pretty self-explanatory, right? You explore the worlds and the regions and now you're in space and the game is propelling you forward. That's an article right there."

"So we're Scrooge-McDucking space?" I said. "I just need to write about it. Then tenure-track jobs will magically follow sans PhD?"

"Yes," Thiago yelled. "That's it. It's easier than you think, motherfucker. What a life that would be. Imagine it."

"*Scrooge-McDucking*," Jordan said. "I like that as a verb. I think I'll add it to my inventory. Thiago is Scrooge-McDucking that bag of chips."

We all laughed. Then I reminded them that all this was moot anyway because the only academic credentials I had were as a linguist, not a theorist (though, like them, I had taken a class or two in literary and cultural theory—not that I retained all that much of it), and we went back to the reason we were all there and the reason I collected: to play.

Near the end of the convention, Thiago and I were resting our legs against the back wall of a big conference room where a competitive gamer was doing a 100% speed-run of the first two *Crash Bandicoot* games live. Word around the room was that he was making brisk pace and was on track to beat the world record. He narrated his progress once or twice, explaining that this trick "saved a few seconds" here and that that trick "saved a few seconds there." When we walked in, he was just getting started with the infamous tower level (the bane of my existence as a kid). The running timer on the screen was at just over two hours. There was a bigger crowd in front but fewer people in back. I was watching the big screen, where they were projecting his face on one side and the game on the other. I couldn't believe that this guy could 100% these games in a few hours when it took Jared and I almost ten years as kids. Just as he was grabbing the final few boxes before his showdown with Doctor Neo Cortex, Thiago elbowed me and pointed to the door, where, lo and behold, The Eggplant Wizard had appeared.

There was a small rustle from the crowd. He lifted his staff as a sort of wave and headed to the other end of the room where there were still a few places to stand and watch the rest of the speed run. As he was passing in front of us, Thiago lifted a hand for a fist bump. I did the same. I saw for the first time that the costume included purple mittens that looked like they had been knitted by hand. I imagined him (or her) sitting in his parents' basement, sweating into the stitches. I tried to make out the face beneath the purple hood but I couldn't. Our hands met, but that's where it all went wrong.

I clasped the mitten, instinctively, and immediately felt his (or her) body tighten. Everything that happened next was in slow motion—the purple Santa cape catching the side of my shoe, the waist hanging forward, the legs buckled back. The weight of the costume fell onto my foot before striking the concrete floor. I went down too and landed with a thud on top. It wasn't a pretty sight. The staff skidded across the room, the eggplant attached to it split open on impact and rolled in two pieces towards the door. Even the back of the suit nearly ripped down the middle. For a moment, everything around us was quiet. Then there was a gasp from the audience as people turned from their seats. Others rose. Thiago took a step back, holding in laughter. Then the collective sigh as the audience realized the speed-runner up front had missed a crucial move to take out Cortex. Then another one. And a third. Someone in the audience screamed, "The fucking eggplant. He ruined the speedrun. He's a troll."

I jumped up as fast as I could, pointing to the disfigured Eggplant Wizard lying on the ground below me—the eggplant mask pulled up just enough from behind so that I could see a patch of pale skin and a few light strands of hair—and high-tailed it the hell out of there, nearly slipping on one of the broken pieces of eggplant in the process. Thiago, the good friend that he was, followed closely behind.

★

Our bus into Port Authority wasn't leaving until five, so we spent the rest of the convention laying low by the imported pachinko machines. There was no sign of The Eggplant Wizard, but once or twice a few people came up to me and shook my hand.

One said, "Hey, you're the guy who tripped the eggplant. Way to go. That dude was freaking annoying." Another said, "Here he is, the eggplant killer. I got you on tape, bro. Thanks for the good time." A third said, "Beware the eggplant curse."

I shrugged it off. Guilt—if you could even call it that—came and went.

Thiago was laughing about it the entire way home.

"Good thing you don't believe in curses," he said.

★

Some weeks later—a Thursday in early August, me at thirty years and nine months, motherless for seven, divorced for four—I woke and poured my usual bowl of Honey Nut Cheerios, brewed my pre-portioned cup of Keurig coffee, and sat on my living room futon with the laptop to perform my ritual eBay searches. I hadn't slept well the night before. As soon as I powered off the TV and climbed into bed, it had felt like my body was rocking back and forth beneath the covers, and I pictured my warped, rusted insides, the blood pumping from my heart being rejected by my major organs, until my lungs stiffened and my brain became a vegetable, until my heart was so overwhelmed with its excess weight, as it felt then, that it ripped a hole in my chest and spilled these gallons of blood onto the bed, drenching me.

I sat up and cycled helplessly through unwanted thoughts and worries. I thought of hereditary cancer, disc rot (the inevitable deterioration of physical media), and the unending shame of having to ask my father for help in case I ran out of money.

The last time I had seen my father, almost six months before this, a cardinal flew in through the window of my parents' house in the Five Towns of Long Island. This cardinal had first appeared in the yard only days after my mother died, sitting on the lowest branch of the spruce tree out back, looking more at the neighbor's yard than at his. But that didn't stop him. "She's here, she's here," he sobbed. "Joshua, shut the windows! Joshua!" I was upstairs with Heli, going through the last of my mother's boxes, but ran down as fast as I could. I found my father on his knees, pointing to the little cardinal on the bookcase, right next to the wooden urn my mother made when she was sixteen. It spread its wings, poised to fly, but then turned its head to face us. "Your mother," he said, pointing. "It's—it's your mother. She's telling us something. What's she telling us? *Ana*, what is it? What is it, Ana?"

He locked his fingers together and started praying. "Barooch attah Adoneiu, eloheniu meloch hayolem..." He limped over to it. He extended a trembling hand. The bird let out a sharp cry, and with a clatter of its wings, fled round and round the house— bouncing off the cupboards, up and down the stairs. "Close the windows!" he screamed. "Keep her here!" But it was too late—it had escaped.

He was still on the floor. He ducked his head. Finally, he

spoke. "You have nothing to say to me?"

I turned away. His movements were slow. Did he think that he was the only one affected by Mom's death? That I wasn't hurting? "Jews don't believe in reincarnation," I said. "The Kabbalists, maybe, but even then the doctrine is pretty complicated. It's not like 'boom, you're a bird. Just so you know.'"

He shuddered. "You're a spoiled, self-righteous brat. Just you so know."

Heloise gasped and disappeared into the hallway.

Here's a fact: I used to envy the kids in school who had fathers who were nothing like mine. Fathers who were kind and thoughtful. Fathers who whispered words of encouragement from every corner of every room. Fathers who were patient and affectionate.

My mother didn't have a great relationship with my father either. Their personalities didn't mix well and they fought all the time, but Jews didn't get divorced so they stayed together. My mother had been born to Yiddish-speaking Galician parents and was the first in the family born in America. (Both her parents had traveled to America in 1930 when they were kids and spent their entire lives learning English). She loved musicals and would take the train into the city for shows on weekends. Occasionally, she would even dance around the couch in the basement, pushing it against the wall when she needed more space. She was a seamstress. She fixed things when they broke. But my father? There was no hope. They were always on opposite poles. It was hard watching them together.

Sometimes my mother would pull me aside and say, "Joshua, you're most like me. Your father doesn't get it. He has no empathy. He doesn't care about anyone but himself. He'd be happy living on an island with only a tape recorder and a toaster. Not you. You know better. You make me proud."

"Thanks, Mom." I told her that we all live on an island, technically.

"That's right," she said. "God, you're just like my father. You would have loved him. He would have loved you."

In bed, thinking of all this, playing these conversations over and over again in my burning head, stuck in place, sweating, I found myself googling Kabbalistic soul migration and cardinals. Intellectually, I knew it was a useless endeavor, but I couldn't stop myself. I never could. That isn't how it worked. I took Benadryl and watched a few YouTube videos on my phone. Tales from Past Lives. The Reincarnation of Anne Frank. Retropalooza Recap. Then, finally, I slept.

There on the futon the next morning, I logged into my email and read a few of the messages I had received from people who were looking for quotes on their kids' old game collections. They were taking up space in the attic and they (like most parents—mine included) were just wanting to be rid of them. Might as well make some cash in the process, they figured, and that's what brought them to me. One wrote that they had a box of Atari stuff, which didn't interest me as there wasn't a ton of trade value there. The other didn't know exactly what they had, but mentioned there was "some Nintendo." I sipped my coffee and messaged back asking for photos. When the photos arrived a few hours later, I saw only a bunch of loose ex-Blockbuster rentals covered with markers and stickers. "Sorry," I wrote back. "I'm going to have to pass for now."

In addition to helping me expand my game collection, this was how I paid rent in the months after Heli left. I combed thrift stores and the internet (Craigslist, Facebook, Letgo, etc) for cheap video game lots (you'd be surprised what people in New York didn't know they had and how many people like me were out trying to grab it first) only to quickly turn them around on eBay for double (sometimes triple) value. My apartment was like a storage unit. In the corner of my living room was a small tub of Game Boys and Game Boy parts. Once they were tested and photographed, I bundled the systems with a game and listed them auction-style one at a time. I had binders full of authentic case art and a desk drawer full of loose discs I'd slowly reunite with their boxes and manuals. "Look at you. You're like a game surgeon now," Jordan had said, watching me work. "Who needs a PhD? Here's a new kind of doctor." Most listings sold within a day or two, but some took as long as a month. It was even possible to find reselling deals on eBay if you were quick. This often involved refreshing "new" listings at just the right time to catch something uncommon posted well below market value. When business slowed for a bit, I advertised my own game-buying services, promising higher "buy" prices than any of the local shops in town. I had just posted for the first time on the local Brooklyn Board and was delighted to see so many new inquiries pop up in the inbox.

It hadn't been a long morning, but it sure felt like one. It's amazing what so much time at home can do to a body. When I was still working on the PhD, I would spend mornings teaching or holding office hours in a glorified closet or doing research or combing through field notes or all of the above until it was suddenly time for dinner. At orientation during the first year, we were warned by the Graduate Chair, an aging academic from Belgium, that one in four didn't finish the program. How could someone make it this far and not finish? Thiago joked that it would be him. "For a department in the heart of New York City," he said, "It sure as hell is *white* around here."

I finished the coffee and took a shower. When I returned, I had three new emails.

Two were the standard Hi, *I just saw your post. Are you inter-ested in my kids' old junk* fare, one slightly more promising than the other. But it was the third that really roused me.

It was from a Dr. Steven R. Kirkland, which I thought might have been a name I recognized, but in the way that any name—especially in the personal space of your inbox—could make you feel like you've seen it before. The subject line said: "Invitation to Apply for Joshua Schulman: Writing Staff at the Fairbury Academy of Roll. Positions Available."

In the email, Dr. Kirkland introduced himself as the Head of School at a place called The Fairbury Academy of Roll (FAR), a college-preparatory boarding school for twice-exceptional boys in

Eastern Iowa. He said that he had been perusing online issues of the *Journal of Language and Linguistics* and happened upon an article I had written three years earlier, still a grad student, called "Reexamining Yiddishkeit: The Secularization of Yiddish Culture and Dialect in Theatre and Film." The article, which sought to broadly redefine the term "Yiddishkeit" amid the secularization of American Jewry through its examination of what the average American knows of "Jewishness" and more specifically, Yiddish, was my first and only academic publication. It was well-researched, and I had once been quite proud of it—seeing it, even, as the start of a much bigger project—but nobody, not even my dissertation committee, had paid it any interest. Dr. Kirkland explained that as a scholar of theatre, he found the work engaging and fascinating and decided on a whim to look me up, which revealed—much to his surprise—that I didn't have a current academic appointment. Or so it had seemed. *I hope I'm not overstepping my boundaries by contacting you in this way*, he wrote. *But I happen to think you'd be a good fit for our school. We're expanding our writing program and we're hoping to reach more folks from the coast. I'm from [near] the coast myself. Born and raised in Syracuse.* Attached was a call for applications. It said: "An education in leadership and citizenship for the best and the brightest. Our mission is to provide gifted and talented boys across Iowa and the Midwest (top 1–5% in their age groups) with the educational opportunities to reach their full potential. Where we provide exceptional C.A.R.E (Community, Academics, Readiness, Expertise). Seeking teachers who know what it's like to be different. Teachers who are flexible, patient, and energetic. Teachers who can contribute to the already rich and vibrant culture at FAR, where no two days are alike. Master's or PhD preferred; no teaching certification required. Room and board included in beautiful Roll, Iowa. Competitive salary. One-year, renewable contract. No holds. Must pass background check."

It struck me as strange. Unsettling, in fact. For all I knew this was just a step or two removed from those Serbian Advance-Fee scams. Weren't all scams mere stories? Claim your payout.

War-torn inheritance. Found family riches. The best one wins.
Was there even a Fairbury Academy of Roll? And if there was,
why on Earth would anyone want me there?

I googled the school, which was when I discovered that not
only was it real, but it was one of the oldest boarding schools in the
Midwest. It was a "Starred Member" of the Association of American
Boarding Schools. According to the website's history blurb, three
governors, two senators, and one President (Herbert Hoover) had
formerly visited the campus as it had been founded as a military
academy but transitioned in the 1960s. One of the pictures on the
site showed students in uniform sitting in a circle on the grass in
front of a blue barn. A lake shimmered behind them. It reminded
me of long-gone family trips to the Poconos, where things felt—I
don't know—simple, under control. Like it felt when I was playing
my games, controller in hand. I wondered: how would all that open
land look at thirty-and-nine-months? Like a fresh start? A blank
slate? Or a new kind of hell? I'll plead the Fifth. I wasn't good
anymore at thinking these kinds of things through.

There was this, though: after a lifetime stalled in one place, the
possibility of packing up and leaving New York suddenly galvanized
me in a way I didn't expect. To give up and give in to the histori-
cal diasporic wanderings of my people. What a trip. But I thought
you decided that you weren't *really* Jewish, Heloise might have said.
So, they're not *really* your people. You're only, what, *academically*
Jewish. *Intellectually*. And maybe I would have sighed and reluctantly admitted what every secular Jew knew already: that you can't
just walk away from your Jewishness, despite the Jewish propen-
sity to, fittingly enough, walk away. It's a part of you that can't
be buried, try as you might. Just look at my father. He had tried.
When we were growing up, he didn't even know what the Sabbath
was. Now, it was his life. I, too, for all my holier than thou talk,
somehow found myself studying Yiddish. No matter what image
I projected on the outside, I would always be a part of that world.
As for leaving, well, Jared had left, and it seemed to be working for

him. Maybe leaving really was the name of the game. But could I seriously entertain the thought of taking my game collection out of this familiar place and bringing it to the *other* Middle East (as in the Middle West of America)? It was hard to say. All I knew was that yes, this place *was* broken, I absolutely needed the money and, technically, I was only trained to do *one* thing (this despite nine years of postsecondary education. Heck, even my last name had me marked as a teacher). Plus, the academic job market sucked. Jordan was new on the market in a burgeoning field, officially ABD, and all he had landed was a phone interview at Penn State Erie. Not a campus visit. Nothing. I read the school's mission statement twice over. It masked everything I know now, obviously. Otherwise, I really would have thought twice. I would have resigned myself to playing and selling video games in my apartment forever, instead of reaching beyond that screen like an imbecile, beyond that (mushroom) kingdom. But no, stubborn self-righteous me thought there was more out there, that I could still—despite every considerable objection—be more than just *this*. Maybe I wanted to live again. Maybe I thought things would work out for once, that I could outrun my doubts, my life. But don't we all believe that?

That night, I wrote back. *Thanks for the email. That was my article, yes. I'm glad you enjoyed it. Too often it feels like our work exists in a space-less void, disappearing into the ether. First, I wanted to make sure you didn't send the job call to the wrong person by mistake. I'm ready and interested to explore new opportunities (such as the one at your impressive school), but I fear that you actually meant to invite someone else. For example, I've never actually worked with kids before, though I'd certainly be open to it.*

Normally I'd sweat over the contents of such an important composition for hours before sending it, but this time, in a startling display of resolve, I closed my eyes and hit send immediately. Then, as expected, I thought of all the things I regretted not including: a shameless quip like "Go Orange!" or "from one Yankee to the next," more pointed interest in the position or the school, a digital signature to make it look like I mattered, etc. Self-sabotage. Nothing new. Heart pounding, I refreshed my inbox and thought like this for all of nine minutes before receiving a response (if only every mind spinning microtransaction was over so promptly). *Hi Joshua, no mistake. You're the guy we want. I really did admire your work. I found it to be a fresh take on an old language. Loved the mention of Solomon the Wise. Here's a little-known fact: I actually studied once under Jacob Adler, albeit briefly. Heard Yiddish quite a bit growing up, too. No one in my family (I'm not Jewish), but when we took trips into the city. Still miss it. Your writing style is superb, and, I don't know, call it blind faith, but something tells me you'd be a good fit here. We're looking to make a diversity hire soon. No guarantees, though! If interested, please submit application materials. The committee will take things from there. If not, no worries!*

"Seriously, this has to be a mistake," I said to Thiago. "This kind of shit doesn't happen. It's too easy."

"Why do you see this as a problem?" he said. "It's all about who you know. The dude read your article—and it's a good one, too. Probably your best work, important work, language preservation, man—and he liked it. Lock, stock, and barrel. That's how this shit moves. That's how the world turns. Tekketay got that book deal because someone read his piece in *Guernica*. You remember that. The dude didn't even have a page of that book written. Then, boom. Book deal. And you remember Roxy. You know what she told me after she got that job at Brown? The chair emailed her and 'invited' her to apply. A directed hire. That's it. That's how she got that job. Hers before she even submitted the application. Dude, just take the compliment and go with it. And before you say anything to put yourself down, plenty of academics work in prep schools and high schools. You'd probably make more than a professor does anyway. Then you can start writing about those damn games and your career will really take off."

"I do need to get out of my head, huh?"

"Kind of, yeah."

"But, dude. *Iowa*?"

"What? Flat redneck cornland? White as snow?" he said. "I don't know. I bet it's not so bad. You can still do your game-selling in *Iowa*. It's not *that* far away. Besides, you'll be king of the hill out there, man. You're from New York. They'll eat that shit for breakfast."

"King of the cornfield," I said.

"King of the cows," he said. "King of the pasture. Anything you want to be, it's yours. Hell, you can be a fucking eggplant wizard."

"Yeah, that'll be the day," I laughed.

I clicked around some more and discovered that Roll had once been named "one of the twenty best places to retire" by *Midwest Today*. On Google, there were pictures of an old root beer stand at the foot of a small lake. I liked root beer and I liked lakes.

Roll, Iowa. I tried saying it out loud. Thiago was right, it didn't seem so bad. It was exotic, even. Maybe there were games there. An untapped market. I pulled open Elaine Chaika's *Understanding Psychotic Speech: Between Freud and Chomsky* and found a chapter I had bookmarked on attentional dysfunction, which referenced clinical research in which a schizophrenic patient was shown a gray color chip and was asked the color of the chip. As evidence of disorganized thinking, a symptom of schizophrenia, the patient said: "Looks like clay. Sounds like gray. Take you for a roll in the hay. Heyday. Mayday." Take you for a roll in the hay, I repeated. Roll in the hay. Roll in the hay. Take you for a roll in the hay. I couldn't explain it. But sitting on the futon in my darkened living room, chanting this line as if it were a song, something suddenly felt right. Like the universe was trying to force me into action. Besides, it was what Mom would have wanted for me. She was always proudest when I took chances. I was the first in my family of accountants to pursue work in the humanities and she really loved that about me, impractical as my dad thought it was. Instead, it was Jared who had taken a chance when she died. Play-it-safe, two-feet-on-the-ground Jared, some 3,000 miles away in Israel. Even Heli was out there parading around Park Slope with a potter. Everyone was trying something new. Now it was my turn. "Okay," I said to no one and yet everyone. "You got me. I'll give it an honest shot. Why the hell not?" In a fury, I opened my CV and threw a cover letter together.

I was invited to a two-hour phone interview two weeks and dozens of new games later, where I explained to a trio of voices on the other end of the speaker how I was still "tinkering" with my dissertation (a quick, but desperate lie I didn't think much about at the time, not entirely uncommon for me when under self-inflicted duress for fear of shame. It was like *slightly* adjusting your character's stats to make him better) but was ready to branch out and "explore a new frontier." They asked about the dissertation, of course, so I recited what I could from the long-ignored first section. "It's similar to that article I published. Sort of like the expanded version. I'm really trying to redefine Yiddish through its tenuous—almost haphazard—place in modern media. Most Americans have a pretty deep relationship with the language, whether they realize it or not. It's been a really rewarding project for me, like a reverse immigration." The sound of my voice was starting to scare me, so I let off the gas. I could hear heavy breathing on the other end of the phone. "It sounds like interesting work," one of them finally said. "Yiddish dialectology. We don't get a lot of people this way doing that kind of work." I laughed, trying to change the topic. "Not many linguists in Iowa?" I said. "Not many who speak Yiddish," they said. "Ah. Well, it all but disappeared as a living language after the Holocaust, but you can find it here and there in pockets," I said. "You've just gotta know where to look. It's still an official minority language in Moldova, for example. And Bosnia." They asked other questions, too. What would you do if you noticed a student was falling behind in the course or seemed disengaged? What would you do if a student corrected you mid-sentence?

"As they often do," I laughed. "And should. Because you know what, I've messed up plenty. Heck, I correct myself mid-sentence. We have a word for that, you know. In Yiddish. *Meyven.*"

They asked for a sample lesson plan appropriate for the age group. After a bit of internet searching, I sent a unit on generating ideas for personal narrative, ending in an exercise where students would linguistically unpack their "names." When they called a second time to discuss the unit, I explained that "writing is about sharing emotion as much as it about sharing adventures and story." Here, standing in my game display room, running my fingers over the spines of my Saturn cases, I imagined, for the first time, a game about me. My sprite, garnished with suit and armor, venturing to the promised land of the (Mid)west. *Heli*, he'd say. *I'm here for Heli. No. something new. I'm here for something new. We, who are about to die, salute you!* "And these emotions can be emphasized through rich, vivid sensory detail, which is stuff, as you can see in the blueprints, we'd discuss ad nauseum during the first half of the unit." I continued, "I'd introduce a few key examples, like Twain's 'First Appearance,' with the expectation that these concepts build off one another. I like that format in a classroom. It's like climbing steps up a much larger staircase. Nothing feels unnecessary or without purpose. For the unit's second half, I chose Cisneros' *The House on Mango Street* because it's a hybrid work and that can lead to some good discussion. But also, at the very beginning of the book, there's a memorable vignette in which Esperanza rejects her name and, ultimately, gives herself a new one. *Zeze the X.* Starting over, so to speak."

Three weeks later, still before I knew what was happening, I overnighted a set of fingerprints to FAR in the care of Dr. Steven Kirkland, Head of School, and, on big glossy paper in the middle of a color packet, they sent me a contract.

I called Heloise.

"I'm going to Iowa, just so you know. I got a job there."

"Come again?"

"I got a job in Iowa. Just thought you should know. They recruited me. Read that piece I wrote on *The Cobbler*. In the linguistics journal."

"Recruited you? For what?"

"For teaching. At a boarding school for gifted students."

"In Iowa?"

"I signed the contract an hour ago. One year, renewable."

"Okay. Well, I'm happy for you, Joe." That's what she used

to call me, you see. Joe.

"People *can* change, you know."

There was some shuffling in the background, like papers splitting in half.

"What?"

"I didn't say anything."

"Are you still dating that pottery guy?"

"His name is Brent. And yes, I am. He's doing a show in Williamsburg on Thursday if you'd like to say bye before you leave. There's a fifteen-dollar cover but you can just say my name at the door and they'll probably let you in."

"That sounds lovely."

"We'll see you there then."

"Great."

"Great."

"Heli?"

"Yeah."

"I miss you."

"I miss you, too."

"I'm not actually coming to the pottery show, by the way."

"I know you're not. I'm not stupid. Are you really going to Iowa?"

"I swear on my mother's grave."

"What part?"

"Of my mother's grave?"

"No, Josh. What part of Iowa."

"Roll."

"How close is that to Des Moines?"

"Des Moines?"

"Please tell me you've heard of Des Moines. Do you even know where you're going, Josh?"

"I'm kidding, Heli. Ha. Ha. Of course I've heard of Des Moines. It's far from Roll, yes. Roll is east. Des Moines is in the middle of the state. Like a belly button."

"Gotcha."

"I'm sorry but you make it seem like you know so much about Iowa when all you really know is Des Moines. It's not like you've been there or anything. It seems disingenuous is all I'm saying."

"Whatever, Josh. It's close to Chicago. I know where it is. Don't you think maybe you should sleep on this one? I mean, who just packs up and goes to Iowa?"

"Already slept on it. But thanks. Truly. Look. It's nothing I haven't done before. They believe in my work. Maybe I do, too. Took long enough. I just wanted to let you know, okay? Common courtesy, that's all. Ex-husband to ex-wife."

"Okay. You do you, Josh."

"That's the point."

"Good."

"Good."

I hung up and signed the contract. Then, because the school would provide me furnished housing, I packed my games, a few books, some clothes, my futon, my beanbag chair, and little else. *Roll in the hay*, I chanted. *Roll in the hay. Take me on a roll in the hay. Maybe today? I'm coming your way! Take me on a roll in the hay.*

Later that week, after the last of my games had been carefully bubble-wrapped and boxed, and after I had checked to make sure the discs were secure and that there wasn't too much weight on the cardboard boxes, and after I had a subletter lined up for the apartment and a U-Haul reserved, I rode the F train to Williamsburg. The empty platforms ran blurry out the window. The light near the door clicked on, clicked off. Standing on the corner of King and Irving, a mere two blocks from the $15 "pottery show" (I didn't dare get any closer for fear of running into Heli or, even worse, Brent) I suddenly recalled something my mother used to say: "Once is never," an old German adage made famous by Milan Kundera (my mother was also a ferocious reader, you see). I made it my Facebook status, hoping, if nothing else, that Heli would like it.

But by the time I was back home and settled into bed, no

one had liked it. Not Heli. Not even my father, who had all the time in the world (it seemed) to post scripture. His post that night: "This is my command—be strong and courageous! Do not be afraid or discouraged. For the Lord your God is with you wherever you go. Joshua 1:9." I waited and then, guided by the light of the morning, I pressed delete. I realized I wouldn't miss this place. It wasn't mine anymore.

But in a way, that had been the story of my life.

I felt small, yet big at the same time. I walked to the window and looked out. Once is never. *Poof.*

II: THE WARP ZONE

AND NOW YOU'RE IN the car. Now the country goes spinning by you like a scream or a laugh. Now the hills roll like a song that once put you to sleep. Maybe it's something you wouldn't remember. The sun comes through the windshield. The day passes in a fog. You feel a hand press the lines of your face. Like a puzzle. A blessing. A command. The buttons of a controller. Jump. Swim. Run. It doesn't stop.

You're two and a half days ahead of schedule, managing a U-Haul with a big postcard of West Virginia on the side door. After twisting your way through the underpasses and overpasses of three boroughs you emerge on a 600-mile long toll road full of truck traffic, which, for all its construction zones, "deluxe" rest stops, and eighteen-wheelers reminds you of the trip in the funeral procession up the hill to Washington Cemetery on Bay Parkway in Brooklyn to bury your mother. You were in a different car then. Your father's silver BMW. Heli was driving. Your father in a too-big suit, sweating in the passenger seat, choosing the constant beeping of the safety alarm over wearing a seatbelt and feeling *suffocated*. You were sitting in back, face against the window. Next to you was your brother.

Months later, Therapist Number Three would ask you to jot down memories from that day, but you decided that you didn't need the added grief. So you told her that all you remembered was the

rain before the rain stopped and the humidity and stressing about a
game you had ordered from Japan that got stuck at the International
Sorting Center at Kennedy Airport for nearly three weeks.

You fidgeted with your wedding ring. On and off. On and
off. "I was thinking maybe it had been opened and mistaken for
contraband or maybe the seller slipped some pot leaves in there or
something. Maybe it actually was contraband. I didn't know. So, I
figured it was only a matter of time before customs agents dragged
me out of bed one morning."

"But it was a video game?" she said, looking up from her notepad.

"Yes," you said.

"And it arrived?"

"It did, eventually, but it was split in half like someone had
stepped on it. I bought another one that night. From Thailand. As
my mother would say: que sera sera."

You said all this and you leaned back in that white linen arm
chair with brass tacks and thought of how good it felt to tear that
package open with your grandfather's pocket knife, but what you
really thought of, what you really saw was your mother's cold,
lifeless body on the hospital bed and it made you question everything you thought you knew about yourself.

"It's okay to be hurting," Therapist Number Three said. "That's
normal."

"I know," you said. "I mean, yeah. I know."

The initial plan was to break up the trip by staying at cheap
motels outside of three equidistant cities: Pittsburgh, Cleveland,
and Chicago, since that would have left you with an *ideal* (according to *Road Trip USA*'s travel blog) seven hours a day of driving
time. But after paying $65 for a smoky room in the non-smoking
section of a Motel 6 in Wheeling, West Virginia and being told
that you had to leave the U-Haul at the very back of the parking
lot where the other large vehicles/trucks were even though there
weren't any large vehicles or trucks there, where there also weren't
any lights, or security, and where you couldn't watch it from your

window, you decided instead to just book it the rest of the way fueled by convenience store coffee, Peanut M&M'S, and the occasional fruit slushie. On and on you pushed until, just after midnight some fourteen hours later, desperate for sleep and with a throbbing headache, you finally passed a big white and yellow sign that read: WELCOME TO IOWA, FIELDS OF OPPORTUNITY.

A big, unmistakable sign off the interstate. It's nice when you get that kind of clarity.

Still feeling the rush, you turned off at the next exit and stopped at a truck stop for a coffee refill and a bar of chocolate. While there, you flipped through a few of the T-shirts hanging by the soda machines. "Iowa: 75% Vowels. 100% Awesome." "Iowa: Corn and Stuff." "Iowa City: All Our Creativity Went into the Name." You took photos. Then, you pointed the van due north, where you drove down a long, rolling gray road surrounded on either side by elephant-high stalks of corn and the occasional white picket fence. No lights, no moon, no one on the road but the millions of gnats careening into the windshield, oozing a film of blood and guts too thick for wiper fluid (Another thought: The Third Plague?). Extra caution was needed around corners obstructed by tall corn. The cabin suddenly seemed noisy. You finished the coffee and then you had to pee, but there was nowhere to pee. Not even a shoulder where you could stop.

You didn't see the deer until it was too late. It just kind of appeared in front of you like some hulking beast. It craned its neck at the sight of the headlights. Its eyes were golden (had you imagined this?). You managed to let out a "what the—" before sending it careening off the passenger side of the U-Haul, deer shit smeared like black blood across the window and door (The Tenth Plague?), and watched as, with a *thud-thud*, it flew over the car and landed fifteen yards behind you.

Your crotch was warm.

You didn't need to think much about deer in New York. Not

that you did a lot of driving there. You just knew this as an accepted fact. That was one way you learned that living in Iowa was different.

The others, well, we'll get to those later.

Because now you're in the car. Now the country goes spinning by you like the memories of something you try not to remember. But you were never any good at shutting yourself down. Not like this machine that stops when you tell it to stop. That goes when you tell it to go. This isn't you.

That wasn't her.

Maybe imagination is what brought you here. Maybe that's why you imagine her in the seat next to you, pointing to your crotch, laughing. Maybe that's why you imagine her someplace else. Maybe that's why you imagine everything you could soon become. Maybe she really is there. Maybe she has been all along. Maybe it's time you tell her something you couldn't say then (scream it!) and lose the moon. Lose the clouds. Lose it all. Lose it all. All of it.

Until it's only your feet on the ground and the miles of waving hills, golden and silent before you.

III: ALONE AGAIN OR

ROLL, IOWA. POPULATION 1,412. I sputtered into "city limits," overwhelmed with exhaustion, and followed signs for the Fairbury Academy of Roll. I searched for downtown but couldn't seem to find it, driving instead through dark tree-lined streets where houses with low roofs and large porches sat like Norman Rockwell paintings. There were no fences. It was as if everyone shared a single yard. After driving out of town again, I found the school's "East" gate tucked in among a grove of trees. It was open so I pulled in and parked in the empty lot. There, I got out to assess the deer damage. The truck smelled like shit. The grille was pushed in and the bumper was gone. It didn't look good, but at least the impact didn't flip me over or anything, which meant at least my boxes of games were okay. I opened the back and forced open a box or two to check on a few of the discs. Everything was okay. See that, I told myself. Look at your luck changing. At least there weren't four deer. At least I hadn't fallen asleep at the wheel. At least the deer hadn't been an elk or, I don't know, a moose. At least I had made it all the way to Iowa in a single piece, the inexperienced driver that I was.

It was late and I didn't feel very good. I got back into the U-Haul, turned on the ignition for some light air, and slept.

Sometime later, there was a knock at the window.

In my dream-like state, I willed my eyes open and saw—you guessed it (or did you?)—the deer. Its head upside down, skull cracked open. Its fiercely golden, bright, sheeny eyes staring at me with all the power of the sun. "Huh?" I said. Then, "Gone. Shoo. Sorry. Wrong place, wrong time."

A knock again, and this time the deer was on its hind legs, forcing its bloody body onto the door. "What did you want me to do?" I said. "You were in the middle of the road! I couldn't see anything."

"You," it said. Its voice high like a squirrel chirping. "What's the matter with you? How could you miss the sign?"

"What sign?"

"This one!"

Sure enough, it was holding a wooden sign. Bright as day. Written as if in shit. "Use Caution. Slow. Roadside Residence."

"This isn't real," I said.

"And neither was the Holocaust."

"Huh?"

"Listen," the deer said. "I didn't follow you out here for funny business, capeesh? I had enough of that beeswax in New York?"

"In New York?"

"Did I st-stutter? New York. The city that never sleeps. The Big Apple. The city so nice they named it twice. Have you ever been? We took a trip there last week, the herd and me. It was awfully depressing."

"What do you know?" I said. "You're a deer from Iowa. Wait. This is Iowa, right?"

He smiled and I could see that his teeth were the color of caramel. "It's a trap, exhausting, suffocating." For the first time, he elongated his o's and over-rolled the r's as if he were Scottish. Suddenly he was standing in a kilt. When I blinked again, he was wearing the eggplant costume from the retro convention.

"It's a what?"

He waved the staff—eggplant intact—as if parting a sea of corn. "Well on the way, head in a cloud. The man of a thousand voices talking perfectly loud."

"Paul?" I said. "McCartney?"

"Dresden," he said, curtsying. He cleared his throat. "Anyway, you're ruining it for the rest of us."

"Ruining what?" I cried out.

He was knocking against the window louder and harder now. I didn't know what to do. Hit the gas? Scream? Pinch myself?

"You're not real," I said. "No. I'm only sleeping. That's it." I thought of Freud. What would he have made of this? Sexual suppression? Wasn't that how all dreams with animals—dead or alive—went? I writhed and grunted and forced my eyes open for real this time, just as I thought he'd flip the U-Haul over once and for all. When I looked out again, I saw a man waving, his face filling the foggy part of the window. It was morning.

"Are you okay, buddy?" he said. He stepped back. He had blue eyes peering out from beneath square glasses and a trimmed red beard. He was wearing a short-sleeve plaid button-up over tight blue slacks. A walkie-talkie was fastened to his belt hooks. His receding hairline, clearly visible from my seat above him, formed a kind of ragged horseshoe.

My headache was worse than ever. The clock said 8:35 but it felt at least three hours earlier. I rolled down the window.

"Hey, are you okay?" he said again.

"Yeah," I said. I cleared my throat. The sun was borderline oppressive. "Thanks. I was just—sleeping, I guess."

"You know you've got broken glass under the tires and your headlights are hanging out. You hit something last night?"

"A deer. A big one. A few miles that way."

"Ah," he said, nodding, flattening his beard. "Yup, that'll do it." His voice was soft and deliberate. Calculated. Like he was recording an audio book. "You sure you're alright? It did quite a number on your hood. Hope you've got insurance. Do you feel pain anywhere? Head? Neck?"

I rubbed my forehead.

"No, no," I said, reaching for the bottle of water I had waiting in the cupholder. "I'm fine, but thanks."

"Where are ya headed?"

I turned to make sure there was, in fact, a school behind me. Then, without really giving it a good look, I pointed at it and said, "Why? Who are you?"

"Steve Kirkland, head of school."

"Oh," I said. "Really?" Like that I popped open the door and was stumbling out of my seat, almost forgetting to turn off the van and grab the keys. "Sorry. I didn't realize. I got in a few days early…obviously. Wasn't any traffic. Ha. Ha. I'm Joshua. Joshua Schulman. The new writing instructor."

"I wondered," he said.

"Quite the welcome committee back there," I said. "The deer, I mean."

I've never been especially good at first impressions. But usually, at least, I'm presentable. In the truck weren't just boxes and bins of video games. There were clothes, too. Lots of clothes. Suits and slacks and polo shirts and T-shirts and sweaters that Heloise helped me pick out. Oil-removing wipes, hair products, a toothbrush. But what good would they do me here? I had driven nearly two days straight with nothing but a purple City College of New York T-shirt and cargo shorts, both of which were now stiff with sweat and covered in stale crumbs. I grabbed my shorts by the waistband and shook them off. They were still damp.

Smiling, I combed my hair to the left with my hand, which, I had learned only two years earlier, was the direction of my natural part. (Yes, I had been sporting a pseudo cowlick for a majority of my adult life. Thiago said it made me look like a badass greaser straight out of *West Side Story*. "But is that a compliment?" I had asked.) "Sorry I'm not a bit more presentable at the moment," I said, shuffling my feet on the warm ground. I had kicked my shoes off during the night—teal Nike high tops—and had forgotten about them. I reached below the seat and grabbed my shoes, falling forward. Stepping into them, I continued, "I didn't expect to be meeting you so soon, in this way. After hitting that deer just about everything was a blur. Didn't even see it coming. It was just...there it wasn't, there it was."

Very articulate, Schulman. You should be a poet.

"Hey, it's fine," Kirkland said, a smile creasing the trimmed edges of his beard. He placed a hand on my shoulder. "Just want to make sure you aren't hurt. What if you have a concussion? That's a liability."

He laughed.

I laughed, too.

With my shoes finally on, I let out a deep breath. "No concussion here," I said. "I'm as good as new. Honest."

"Well, look. We're just glad that you made it," he said. "Early is just a nice touch. But a good time, too. Not *too* early, you see."

"Nobody wants that," I said.

He laughed generously. Then he unclipped the walkie-talkie from his waist and held it up to talk. "Matt, this is Captain K., over. Code red. Joshua Schulman is here on campus. A tad earlier than expected, but not too early so we should be all set. Let's run seven thirty-two. Over. Can you page Roger and Lorraine? Over." He winked. Maybe it was the relentless sun or the early hour or all the other nameless panicky things going through my head, but once or twice when he shifted or when the sun momentarily ducked behind a passing cloud, I could see that he looked different in the picture posted under "Our Leadership" on the school's website. Older, somehow, though full of life. His skin, while weathered and peeling, seemed vibrant. Also, he only had light stubble in the picture and the stubble hadn't looked red. We were the same height, but he outweighed me by a good forty pounds.

The walkie-talkie hissed. "Copy," a voice on the other end said.

He reclipped the radio to his belt and pushed his square glasses up the bridge of his nose. "It's lucky timing, actually," he said. "I was heading over to finish your file just now. Started working on

it Monday. I don't know if I told you already how glad I am to
have another almost-PhD on staff. It's good for accreditation, for
one. We're up for renewal this year." The walkie-talkie stirred
again, but it was nothing I could make out. He lowered his head
and crossed his arms, as if thinking. "We're slowly moving toward
a model of terminal degrees. I think it's good for an institution, no
matter what population they serve."

He smiled without his teeth. I didn't know what else I could
do but agree.

"Remind me how far along you are in your program. I know
you said on the phone that you were wrapping up the dissertation.
But the other formal requirements are done?"

I laughed stupidly. "Is that what I said on the phone?" It's
funny how that kind of stuff can escape you.

"Loud and clear," he said.

I shrugged. "I mean, I guess it depends how you look at it."

He didn't seem to understand.

"You know, what's a PhD anyway?" I managed.

"A terminal degree," he said, eyes lowered. "What the powers
that be look for when determining an institution's academic character. More and more it's becoming the norm around here. Be
proud, Josh. You worked for it, so you should own it."

I pulled at my shirt because my chest was sweaty. I wanted
to come clean but saw that I couldn't. Not here. Not now. Not
without being sent packing, back onto the long, lonely road towards
New York. And where would I live then? With my father?

I never did well when caught off guard. Kirkland leaned
forward, waiting. This had been my script. This was always my
script. Avoidance, wasn't that what it kept coming back to? I held
my hands up as if forcing a space between my past and present self.
I forced a smile. "I mean, you know. Sometimes I am proud of it,
but sometimes I'm not. It's complicated."

"Tied up with the old beast. I get it. It takes a certain
person, Josh."

"It's just...hard," I said. "It's a real passion project."

Because, you know, dropping out of the program after only writing two-and-a-half inchoate chapters of a dissertation and completing one of three comprehensive exams is a real *passion project*. Still, that's precisely how it started. A whisper. A murmur. In the distance, I could hear what sounded like a trumpet. Kirkland heard it, too. He hummed and swayed in place.

I was in Iowa and maybe Thiago was right: what happens in Iowa...

"Yes, it is hard," he said. "It's substantial work. Overwhelming. I like that: passion project. No, not everyone is capable of that kind of focus, that kind of commitment, persistence, stubbornness. But look who I'm talking to. You already know this. It's a field that tends to weed people out on its own. If it were easy, everyone would be doing it. Writing my dissertation took five years, three longer than it should have. You know why? Three years in, I lost three chapters in a fire. No computers then. No backup devices."

He looked away as if showing me something he couldn't bear to look at himself. "That's awful," I said.

"I know," he said. "Couldn't sleep for weeks. I was devastated. To put it lightly."

"I can imagine."

"But you know what they say," he said. "When the going gets tough, the tough get going. And so, I buckled up and finished." He appeared proud of himself again, his beard glowing bronze beneath the sun. "Just imagine, years of work disappearing to ash." Suddenly I saw my mother's body, being wheeled away, trapped in a casket. Poof. Gone. Kirkland sighed. "Well, what can you do? Anyway, I'd be happy to read what you have and offer some feedback, if you'd like. Wouldn't want you to feel like you're out there alone. That isn't a good place to be."

"I'll keep that in mind. Thanks."

"I'm serious," he said. "Send along the first few chapters. Or heck, the whole thing. I love to see what our people are doing.

You have all our support. And, as you know, I'm especially interested in your project. It's close to my own heart."

"For sure."

"Oh. Another thing I forgot: pay raise for a doctorate," he
said, winking. "Once you're fully matriculated and assuming you
stick around, that is. Just a little extra push."

"That's very considerate of you."

"The least we can do."

I closed my eyes against the sun. Had I not considered how
easy it would be for him to call my former advisers and find out
the truth. *Joshua? Joshua Schulman? Finishing the PhD? Oh, no, no,
Dr. Kirkland. He ran out of here with his tail between his legs. Something
about video games. Here, let me put you in touch with his dissertation
advisor. She'll tell you everything.*

I let out a sharp breath. One more turd in the pile rising like a
mountain beneath Joshua Schulman, the schmuck.

★

The campus sat on sixty acres and consisted of seven buildings
and two sports fields. The building I had parked behind was one
of the two L-shaped dormitories, which they called the Barracks
(Barracks East and Barracks West). The dorms were built around
a courtyard and had winding walkways that crossed each other at
the bottom of a steep hill, on top of which was a metal statue of
a hawk in flight. Other walkways were raised and encircled by
picnic benches and various "learning markers," like stops at an
outdoor gym. The walkways converged at the base of stone steps.
Most of the buildings were made of red brick or "regional" stone,
New-England style. There were lots of tall oak trees with smaller
quads of green grass.

"You ever see grass this green and soft?" Kirkland said. "You
can walk on it barefoot."

I admitted that I hadn't, stopping short of telling him that it looked almost unnatural, manufactured, because I thought maybe that was what he wanted to hear. Though, if you ask me, grass is grass. I had just spent what felt like years staring at miles of green grass zooming past me on the Interstate, none of which looked better or worse than the grass here.

"This is nothing," Kirkland exclaimed, his eyes widening. He grabbed my shoulder and squeezed it tight. "In the fall, the leaves turn colors and form big piles and acorns drop from the trees and the squirrels run around and collect them. You know Constable's 'The Lock?' It's so uncanny that we hung a reproduction of it in the music wing. Even manage to convince a few kids each year that Constable painted it just for us."

"Sounds like those kids could probably use a lesson or two in geography," I said.

Kirkland acted like he didn't hear me, and I regretted saying it. As we walked across the quad to the designated liberal arts classrooms in a building called Academic 1, I remarked how at home I felt. I thanked him again for bringing me here.

"It's nothing at all," he said.

The classrooms in Academic 1 were a mix of classic and modern—all painted in warm and inviting colors and all with computer terminals and Smart boards controlled by remotes that had more buttons than the Atari Jaguar's dinosaur-era controller. Yet they also had creaky wooden doors with rusty hand-crank pencil sharpeners and box fans, pull-down maps on the back wall and ancient wall clocks. Most had tall windows which afforded views of the main quad or tiny glimpses of the cornfield between trees. Others had a white stone finish with framed photos of bikes on manufactured landscapes.

The dining hall was its own building set just off the quad behind Academic 1—one story with shiny, gemlike hardwood floors and ten-person long picnic tables. The place was empty but for a few dining service workers who smiled at us as we walked by. The food was served off one long counter with a sneeze guard and a metal tray rail.

"The staff eat here, too," he said. "They sit over that way. Just added the salad bar not that long ago. Tuna salad, hard-boiled egg, you name it. Chose it off an email survey. A lot of what we serve is farm-to-table. Things grown or raised in the region. The way people out here like it."

Food WASPs like, I thought. "Sounds delicious," I said.

Next was the Rec building, which was sort of a misnomer. It served as a combined gymnasium, library, and study hall. On top of the building was a bell tower open on four sides with a big brass bell in the middle that chimed on the hour. Kirkland referred to it as a gathering space before and after classes. Apparently, students had two mandatory study periods each day.

We headed back to the quad. He folded his arms across his chest. The walkie-talkie jerked to life again.

"What's your status? Over."

He turned away from me and lifted the box to his face. "Heading to the Gunk with Joshua. Over."

"Copy," the voice on the other end said.

He pointed beyond the imposing statue of the metal hawk, which caught sharp rays of the sun. "This way," he said. He walked briskly now—twice as fast as he talked—and led me past the academic buildings to the edge of a football field. We turned left and walked up a hill—a dirt trail surrounded by tall grass. "Now the Gunk isn't a gunk at all," he said. "It's a lake." He wiped his glasses with his shirt and cackled. "The linguistic labels we give things around here will likely interest you."

The wind picked up the higher we got and felt as if it were trying to stop me in my tracks. Even so, I found it to be a much-needed respite from the heat as I tend to sweat twice as much as the average person. Once, at a wedding for one of her cousins, Heloise carried a dish towel in her purse to wipe my face with when no one was looking.

I wiped my face with my shirt, wishing I had that dish towel. Some dirt blew into my eye. "I thought Iowa was supposed to be flat?"

He laughed. "Things aren't always what they seem, Joshua."

When we got to the top, one could see the entirety of a dark blue lake in the shape of a speech bubble, the glare of the rippling sun coming off it. It was the lake I had already seen in so many pictures before getting on the road in the U-Haul, laying naked in front of me as if we were well acquainted. All those nights researching Roll like I had researched my games, like I had researched Mom's illness, like I had researched Yiddish dialectology, like I knew the Pale of Settlement, the mass of land spanning modern-day Ukraine, Belarus, and Lithuania.

The lake was smaller than I had pictured it. Beyond sat a few houses with wooden docks and rolling hills of corn, broken up only by a grove of trees. I hadn't realized it was so close to campus.

"The Gunk," he said. "See why the title's a misnomer?"

"It's as clear as water," I said.

He laughed with all his weight. "The other end is a little state park with a beach and playground. Bought it from the city a few years ago when the economy collapsed. They're really trying to play up the resort town image by catering to folks from Chicago. Just added a lifeguard and everything. Seems wholly unnecessary if you ask me. Traffic has picked up a bit, mostly May through August, but it's still pretty quiet. Livable is the word you always hear from people around here." He fanned himself. "Might see more of those people than usual on a day like this, but don't worry. When winter comes, it's just us locals playing ice hockey on the frozen lake. The league draws a nice crowd each year."

"Is that safe?"

"You've never skated on ice, Josh?"

I shook my head.

"Central Park?"

"No."

"Hm. You know, I took you for someone who's skated before," he said.

I shrugged. "We're learning a lot right now about first impressions."

The trail we were on continued all the way to the lake. We stood where we were and watched the rippling water flow around and over the rocks and snags and lap onto the pebbly shore. I could feel the knots in my body loosening. It felt nice to be talking about something other than video games for once. Not that I didn't wish I were home, blasting alien pixels to my heart's content, pulling myself away to look at the games on my shelf or browse new eBay listings.

That was when it hit me, I guess. I had really done this.

I was in Roll, Iowa.

Kirkland must have noticed something was off. "You seem lost in thought, Josh. Anything I can help you with? Any questions you have?"

I shook my head dumbly. In my mind flashed an image of Mega Man and the Eggplant Wizard fighting with lightsabers at the retro gaming convention. Maybe I didn't have a bright future ahead of me, but at least I wouldn't end up like them.

"That reminds me," Kirkland said. "Students aren't allowed to be out here on their own, only when accompanied by residential staff or for special functions. Inevitably, once or twice a year, a few students will sneak out. Not that I can blame them. We were lackadaisical for a while, but now we have a strict no-tolerance policy. Anything else puts us in a compromised legal position. We've had issues. Understood?"

"Of course."

He turned from the lake and motioned me back down the hill. "I was just thinking how that truck you drove out here is pretty big for one guy," he said. "Though maybe not for a deer." We both laughed. Then I told him it was the size that had been on sale.

"We did tell you the place was furnished, right?" he said. "You aren't stockpiling furniture in there? I know most New Yorkers think that Iowa is just open space but we live in the same little boxes you do. Only difference is our boxes are a bit nicer. I'd hate to see you disappointed with the place."

"Right," I said. "Don't worry. No furniture in there."

"That's good. Mind if I ask what is?"

"The usual. Clothes. Books. Boxes of books." He didn't seem convinced, so I kept going. "I collect them. I'm a book collector." I felt bad lying again, but this one, compared to the last, practically felt diplomatic. Obviously, I couldn't tell him that I had arrived with a truck full of retro video games. How would that have looked? Games here. Games there. And look, don't forget the vanity systems: Atari Jaguar, Virtual Boy, 3DO. Anyway, what were you saying about that PhD?

Kirkland stood safe at the bottom of the hill, straightening his shirt, checking his phone, and I was stuck trying to find a way down, sliding inches at a time, keeping my weight in the back in case of a fall. And now, with the emergence of yet another lie threatening to turn this hole I had already dug for myself into a lake bigger than the Gunk, I felt the true force of the sun against my face and the wind on my back. I slid another foot, then two, then three, closer to flat ground, closer to safety. I thought of my mother dancing in the kitchen: *It's a roll with butter, Jay.* It was one of her favorite sayings. "Once you start, you can't really stop," I said, trying to distract myself. "That's the nature of collecting."

"I get that," Kirkland said, looking at my feet. "So, are these first editions or what?"

"Some of them, sure."

"Very cool. Which one is your favorite? And which is most valuable?"

I paused to think about it just as I was nearing the bottom, but then the wind changed directions and I fell for real. Not on my face, luckily, but on my ass. Kirkland, only a few feet below me, ran over and held out his hand, pulling me up. I wiped my shorts off.

"Well?" he said, smiling.

★

The main administration building sat at the top of the main quad. It was two stories tall, Gothic style, red brick facing with wooden front doors flanked by black wrought iron lanterns. It really was an impressive building, and I wondered why they didn't have more photos of it on the school's website.

Beneath the archway of the administration building was the "Wall of Donors." Kirkland put two hands on his hips and waved me forward. "We have a very active alumni base," he said. I did a brief scan of the names. Luke Haegerman. Paul O'Neil. Kirkland Jennings. As expected, they were mostly Gaelic. Anglo-Saxon. Guttural.

"That's great," I said.

"Indeed." He folded his arms across his chest and led me inside.

"Now, there are a few things you should know about student culture here since it's such an important part of campus life." The hallway was long and wide. Our footsteps created a sort of echo. We passed the foyer of the Ware Auditorium and then turned left. "As you know, we follow the traditional model of New England boarding schools, but with our own Fairbury flair. Maybe you see that reflected in the architecture," he offered. "It's like a little patch of the east coast copy-and-pasted onto the edge of an Iowa cornfield. We like to redefine norms whenever we can. We're very proud of our tradition."

He stopped at the end of the hallway in front of a double set of doors and cleared his throat. "And that tradition isn't just reflected in our academic rigor. Far from it. The students, you see, are very tradition-oriented. It may seem peculiar at first. Unusual. But that's all part of the fun. We really believe in the spirit of the group. In unity."

"How so?" I asked.

"Like this." He knocked twice and pushed the double doors open to reveal a big band room and twenty students facing us. Above them were bright fluorescent lights. Behind them, floor-to-ceiling mirrors in which I could see their backs, their shiny instruments, Kirkland smiling, and myself in a CCNY T-shirt and cargo shorts. Unshaven. Greasy black hair. Thin, lanky. Someone snapped, "One, two, three, four" and the instruments rose to their faces. Drums rolled—ba-bu-bum, ba-bu-bum, ba-bu-bum, followed by French horns and trumpets. Cymbals exploded from the pits. I covered my ears.

Kirkland yelled over the intensifying trumpets. "'It's The End Of The World As We Know It' by R.E.M. The Trilogy of Life."

"The trilogy of what?" I asked.

He pointed to the band, the eyes beneath his glasses giving off a blinking shine. The students were wearing black and white uniforms. On the walls beside them were dozens of banners and trophies. The song ended and they started into another one, swaying as a group, their feet taking in samba steps. He yelled, louder now. "'Dude Looks Like a Lady.' This is an important one. A classic."

A few older staff members spilled into the hallway behind us. One or two were clapping along. Others were filming with their phones.

When the band finished, the students dropped the instruments on their seats and bowed. Kirkland went into a loud, thunderous clap. The staff behind him followed. Even the students, up from their bows, began clapping. I joined Kirkland and the others in clapping my heart away, absolutely baffled.

"Most people don't expect to be greeted with a marching band, huh?" he said.

"Is this how you always greet people?" I said.

"Nope," he said. "You're special. This is special. Welcome, Josh. Welcome to Fairbury."

I shook a few hands, posed for a few photos. "He's finishing his PhD," Kirkland told a few of the photo takers, whose faces were obstructed by the dizzying blur of camera flash.

"Almost done," he added.

It made me feel pretty important. "I guess that's me," I said, waving.

★

At the center of Kirkland's office was a short, fat executive desk, distressed oak with an almost metallic sheen. The top of the desk was a horror show, not unlike how my own desk had looked when I was still in grad school: paper stained yellow beneath the fluorescent light, forming dozens of haphazard piles. The mess put me at ease again. Kirkland fell into the plush computer chair and motioned for me to sit in one of the two armchairs. He gestured to the open shades and asked if it was too bright. I shook my head no. "It'll cool down in a month. That way half the town can get back to saying climate change isn't real." He sighed with exaggeration. On the wall were framed photos of the Academy (including one in black and white of cadets waving an American flag), a diploma from the University of Northern Iowa, and a big white sign that said, "Don't believe everything you THINK." Strangely, it roused me. Beneath it was a photo of Abraham Lincoln with the caption: HONEST + DAPPER.

"You probably know that Lincoln grew up just over the border in Illinois," he said, wiping his glasses with a cloth from his desk drawer and putting them on again. "Easy to be a trendsetter when you have old Abe as a model. There aren't a lot of schools like us in the Midwest, so it makes what we do twice as important. For the kids and for ourselves."

"That's really admirable," I said.

He nodded thoughtfully and leaned forward. "So, how did you like the abbreviated tour? There's a lot more to see but only so much time in a day."

I told him it was great, even better than I had imagined. I admitted that I hadn't been to a boarding school before. "I really think I'm gonna like it here," I said, still trying to convince myself. It was my mother who always said that the more you say something, the truer it gets. Like *I love you*. Or, *that's right, I am getting a PhD*. Heloise would call it denial.

Kirkland leaned back again, satisfied. He said, "Mmhm."

The conversation continued as such for another few minutes. It's hard to remember exactly how it went, line by line. I was tired as hell. At one point, Kirkland squeezed his hands together and said that in all the hoopla he forgot to ask if I had stopped anywhere good on the way out.

"Does the World's Largest Rest Stop count?"

"Sure does. You know you can see the World's Largest Round Barn just about twenty-miles away if you're so inclined."

"How could anyone pass on that?"

Another object in the office that commanded my attention was a long wooden staff perched below the far window. At first, I thought it was an elaborate curtain rod. When Kirkland came back from a short bathroom break, he saw me staring at it.

"Ah, yes," he said, hiking his slacks, shimmying back to his desk. "The Royal Fox Society. Are you interested?"

I told him I didn't understand.

"That beauty has been passed down for years now to the Fountainhead of the Royal Fox Society," he said, tonally flat.

"The what?"

"The Fountainhead," he said, sitting again. "The one with the pen. The one who keeps tradition. The one who documents." He observed me. The office chair squeaked. "Don't worry," he added. "It's a student. These are student groups. Remember what I said about Fairbury tradition? See, the students assign a class hierarchy after the first week of each year, usually based on seniority, though sometimes the parameters they set can be hard to predict. Depends on the group. Then, they elect representatives to different positions. But not like President, Vice President kind of thing. Not at Fairbury. Here we have The Holder of the Duck. The Tideland. The Fate Fairies. The Caloian Rain Ritual. Etc. That one's Romanian. They're all responsible for different things. The parts make a whole."

"How so?"

"The Caloian Rainmakers, for example, run outside when rain is about to fall—as long as it's not during class time, that is—to do a Romanian rain dance, complete with acrobatics, hula hoops, and painted eggs. One year they set dining hall cookies on fire, but we put a stop to that. The campus squirrels sure appreciated that stunt."

"I can't imagine kids lighting cookies on fire."

"Yeah, probably shouldn't talk too much about it. My favorite part of lunch, those cookies. On Tuesdays, they make them extra big. Anyway, most of this happens on the residential and recreational side of things," he said, waving a hand. "There are a few games our community plays as a whole—students and staff included— that do carry over into class time, though. That's where the real fun happens. One game that had been popular for years but was recently banned will be making a comeback this year, so look out for it. I made the decision to revisit that debate myself." I smelled a trace of cinnamon. "You're the first to know about its return, so mums the word. Game's called Splat. The students will certainly want to see you get involved. The staff, too. Being involved is a big part of being here. It's an extended family. No man left behind."

I had no clue what he was getting at, but I said "all right" or "sounds cool" or "bring it on" or some variation thereof. If playing weird games was what it would take to be liked, to play the part, then so be it. Besides, it's not like I didn't know a thing or two about playing games.

He opened a drawer and pulled out a pile of papers bound together by string. He flipped through it. Entire pages had been highlighted, littered with Post-it notes and tagged with flags.

"This is the Fairbury Bible," he said. "Go on. You can touch it. It's what makes Fairbury Fairbury."

He thrust the book toward me, and I took it in my lap. The pages were loose-leaf. Some of the text was typed, some written by hand.

"Rules for Splat are in there," he said.

I turned to a random page with a list of students and their nicknames.

"A few have been wanting to digitize it," he said. "But that debate is for another day. This is the only copy. You can come in and look at it anytime you'd like."

He took it from me and cradled it in his arms before returning it to the desk drawer. He shuffled a few of the papers on top of the desk to reveal a white laptop, which he flipped open.

"So, Josh, not to change the subject here, but let me just triple-check something." He clicked around for a bit, humming. "Okay, so I didn't want to be the bearer of bad news but it appears that the place we have for you isn't move-in ready just yet. It's a nice place. You'll like it. Plenty big enough for one. And it's by the North Bottoms, so an easy bike ride to campus. You have a bike, yes? In that U-Haul? No car, but a bike?"

Did I say I didn't have a car? "I'm actually more of a walker," I said.

"Okay, well lesson number two," he said. Was there a lesson number one? "You'll want a bike."

"So, about the place not being ready yet?" I said. This one really hurt. I was hoping to start unpacking. I was hoping to play the hell out of *Guardian Heroes* on the Saturn, too, but obviously I kept that bit to myself.

"No worries, bud. You'll just have to wait another day. Maybe two. We'll get it done as soon as we can. That's the downside of you coming early. But here's the deal: we have a cleaning crew over there now. There was a little bit of paint bubbling, but nothing serious. They just finished work on the roof and downspouts." This was the only sign of an accent I had heard thus far. "Roof" was pronounced "Ruff." I wanted him to say it again. I wondered how he would say 'route.' "But for now, let's just make sure you have a place to spend the night. I'd let you stay with me, but my in-laws just got into town from Nebraska. You ever been out that way?"

"This is actually the farthest west I've been."

"Right, you're coming from out east. Not much to see in Nebraska. Unfortunately, I think Anne and Roger are the couple who live just above you—it's a two-apartment house. Roger is our assistant football coach, and so both are down in Arkansas for the week sizing up some recruits. That's why we're trying to get some of this work done now. These houses really need it. Most are pretty old. And the Barracks are also being deep cleaned this week before the students get back. Let me just check here. Actually, you know what? I'll call Natalie. She's another one of our writing instructors. She's been here for a long time now. And her husband is one of our own. I'm sure she'd be happy to host you for a night or two."

"That's okay," I said. "Again, I really don't want to be a bother. I'm sure I can find a hotel. Or I can even sleep in the U-Haul if I need to. It's nothing, really. It was surprisingly comfortable. I'll make do with what I have. My mother taught me to be quite resourceful. I'm from New York, remember—everything's cramped out there."

"Nonsense." He pulled a cell phone from his pocket and swiped it on. When he lifted it to his ear, I could hear it ringing. "Natalie. I have that Joshua Schulman here. The new guy from New York. Yeah, finishing up his PhD. He's a bit early and he's looking for a place to stay. I'd host him but I have family in town. Do you have a spare bed? Okay. Okay. You think Brandon would mind? Great. Listen, I've been filling him in about traditions, but I haven't gotten very far. Might need you to do some of the rest. Have some paperwork I need to get through anyway." He gave me a thumbs-up.

After putting the phone down, he had me sign forms—I-9, Technology Agreement, Honor Code. I read the latter closely. *Students and staff alike are expected to behave with honesty and personal integrity, in-person, on-campus and off-campus, including the internet (social media, email, etc).*

I took in the honor code, thinking. As soon as I could, I realized, I'd have to deactivate my Facebook account in order to cover my online tracks. Linked to my Facebook were hundreds of people who knew the truth: that I was a liar, a failure, a dropout. Every post, every update constituted damning evidence.

What did I have in my favor? CCNY's RateMyProfessors profile and Excellence in Teaching page, the online version of my linguistics article with bio—all of which, I remembered with relief, would verify my story.

A robin flew past the window and circled back around. It perched on the windowsill. I thought of the cardinal that had made it into and out of my father's house, how he whispered that it was fate, that it was my mother.

★

It was about lunchtime when Natalie Grey pulled into Fairbury's east lot in her blue Subaru Outback, where Kirkland and I met her. Her first words to me were: "Do you want to leave the U-Haul here or park it on our street? We're in a dead end." That's how she was. Right down to business. She had a brunette pixie cut and red-rimmed glasses. Her dimpled chin formed the point of her narrow jawline. She wore a white cotton sundress and a turquoise necklace, her legs toned and tan. I wanted to ride next to her in the Subaru so my legs could be close to her legs, but I knew I should keep it professional. Also, I couldn't stand the thought of leaving my games for the night. "Might as well take it," I said. "No point leaving it here where it'll just be in the way."

"Nonsense," Kirkland said. "It's in no one's way. You have to come back for your keys tomorrow anyway."

"I can take it," I said. "Thanks, though."

He turned to Natalie and snorted. "You see the poop on the hood there? He obliterated a deer. I guess that's the new thing: they come to Iowa and obliterate deer." I mock-flexed. Natalie yawned. "Don't try that stunt in town, you hear?" Kirkland said. "We'd like to keep you around for a while, if we can."

Over lunch at the half-Subway, half-gas station a block from campus, Natalie finally asked about the PhD. At first, the thought of maintaining the lie for the rest of time seemed exhausting, but I found that it actually came out easier with Natalie. I liked talking about this 'new' me more than the old one. I mostly talked around the dissertation, chalking it up as an "intellectual idea." "But workable," I clarified. "At least, I hope. I mean, it got me this far." She listened. She was interested. I really admired that about her. Like Kirkland, she asked to see some of my work. I told her I'd make her a copy of my article from *The Journal of Language and Linguistics* when I had the chance. "But in all honesty, what does a PhD really matter anyway?" I finally said, sighing. "I know they say it's for the best of the best and all, but really it's just a few extra letters at the end of your name. It doesn't change you in any way. You just…get it done. That's all." Then I joked that the last thing you should ask a PhD candidate is when they're going to be finished.

"Anxiety?" she said.

"Expectation," I said. "Deadline is a hard word. Cross this line, you're dead."

She told me that she was finishing up credits for a second Master's in Educational Administration at Grand Canyon University and was considering enrolling in their PhD program as soon as the Master's was done. I understood now why she was so interested in my experiences at the CUNY Graduate Center. Apparently, there were rumors of an administrative spot opening at Fairbury soon, and she wanted to be ready.

"Where's Grand Canyon?" I asked.

"Online," she said. "You know, the future. Unless you were referring to the National Park?"

"It's a National Park, too?"

We ate. Sometime after I finished, she asked if I wanted the slice of roast turkey I had left on my plate. I said no. She reached over and slid it into her mouth in one motion. "Poor guy didn't stand a chance," I joked.

Then, I asked about the places to check out in town. "Okay, so what do you need to know?" she said, turning to the window, scratching her neck as if flicking a bug. The street outside was quiet, but not empty. The U-Haul was safe across from the drive-thru window. No one seemed to pay it any mind. Not that there were many people around who could. Only twice did I see someone fill up gas. "All right. Don't get your meat at Walmart," she said. "But that's not even worth saying, is it? Casey's is fine, I guess, but what you really want is to go to the butcher on Eighth. It's only open evenings. Weekends are almost too busy to make the trip worth it. The best way to eat at Lili's, the breakfast spot downtown, is to skip the meals and order a la carte. It's much cheaper that way and you get the same amount of food, maybe even more. Oh. The Farmers' Market on Saturdays is a must. Ours isn't as big as some of the others around here, but it's a great place to go for produce. The Dairy Sweet is overrated and overpriced, but worth a visit if you're craving ice cream. Blew away in a tornado two years ago but they had it rebuilt in less than a month. Just be warned that students often take trips there with the residential staff, so you might run into large, unruly groups of them. They give you as many samples as you want. If you want to swim in the lake—as you should at least once while you can—skip the beach. They're charging five dollars now, which is ludicrous. It wasn't like that when I was a kid."

"You grew up around here?"

"Just over the river. Boone. I like it. You know. It's home."

"I get that," I said. "So, where's the closest diner?"

She tousled the top of her hair. "You mean Lili's, the breakfast spot?"

"It's open twenty-four hours?"

"Oh, no. It closes at two."

"Two a.m.?"

"No. Two in the afternoon. There's not much as far as night-life goes, to be honest. You have to make your own fun."

At least I was well-versed in that. "I'm definitely not in New York anymore," I laughed.

"Slow with the uptake, are you?" she said, half-smiling.

I didn't have a response, so maybe I was.

The restaurant door opened, and Natalie waved. Before I knew it, a woman in plaid who smelled so strongly of lavender that I sneezed twice was hovering over the table. Natalie stood and gave her a hug.

"El, this is Josh," she said. "New instructor at Fairbury. I'm showing him around."

"Oh, that's *your* moving truck outside," she said.

"Guilty as charged," I said.

She turned to Natalie. "I thought maybe the Ericks finally kicked the can. Sorry—that wasn't nice, was it? Josh, right? Hi. I'm Eleanor."

"He's from New York," Natalie said.

Eleanor stepped back and raised her eyebrows, impressed or confused. It was hard to tell. I was starting to feel like I could get used to this.

"What brings you to Iowa?" she asked. She had the same long jawline as Natalie except her face was painted with makeup. "Here for the corn?"

I shrugged. "I'm running from my past."

"Ah, one of those," she said, nodding.

We all laughed. The two of them talked some more and then Eleanor went to the counter, where she leaned far over the glass and pointed at the items she wanted.

★

Natalie lived with her husband just off the lake in a dark Cape Cod style house with wooden shingle siding. The living room was painted burgundy and had an old green velvet couch. It smelled like sweet oranges. Unlike Natalie, Brandon Grey wasn't a local. He had attended Fairbury as a student and came back at twenty-two to work there, though now he was editor-in-chief of the local newspaper. He was still on the school's alumni board, which he made sure to tell me as many times as he reasonably could. He had a long lumberjack-style beard and seemed to smile more out of nervousness than joy. He was into old cameras and showed me a small collection of them he kept in the basement, a "half-finished" dungeon-like cellar with spiderwebs, roaches, and wooden planks for shelves, while Natalie got started on dinner—pork chop and mashed potatoes. Framed portrait-style photos hung in the living room and kitchen, a few of them nudes or partial nudes of men and women with their faces obscured. He had taken some of them himself, he said, but most had been found in undeveloped film he picked up at the annual Junk Jaunt.

"I need to help Nat with the food," he said, walking me upstairs. "Did you want a salad? Is ranch okay?" Later, I made a wrong turn looking for the bathroom and ended up in the master bedroom, where there were two small portraits above the dresser. Both were taken from the neck down. One was of a man topless in a pair of skin-tight lumberjack jeans. He had enough chest hair to keep a small family warm through winter. The second was of a woman in lingerie. She was in satin panties which were riding low on her hip. Two dark areolas were visible through the blouse. I recognized the thin gold bangle on Natalie's wrist. If these were on the wall, then what was in the closet? I was still staring when I heard someone clearing his throat behind me. I flipped around. It was Brandon. "Sorry," I said, blushing. "I thought the bathroom was this way." He pointed down the hall and closed the door after me.

Brandon and Natalie told me a bit more about "campus culture" and "Fairbury tradition," though the meat of it didn't come until dinner. As they spoke, I started to see this tradition talk as strange and puzzling. I guess it showed because Natalie stopped herself as she was describing the Procession of Monks— an homage to *Monty Python and the Holy Grail*—and asked what I was thinking.

"Me? Nothing," I said. "Kirkland gave me a heads-up. Said it might seem a little weird at first. And he wasn't wrong."

Then, for the next twenty minutes, Brandon explained that the student traditions as they had been passed down from class to

class had symbolic meaning. It was the way students and staff iden-
tified themselves and it was something to belong to. It put value on
the group instead of just the individual. Finally, I decided to speak
up. "But making room for the individual isn't bad, is it? Independ-
ence. Free will. Progress."

"You're looking at it the wrong way," he said. "Of course, we
believe in free-thinking and progress. That's not what this is about.
Here, think of it like this: how many ethnic groups have assimilated
or are in danger of assimilating. How, then, does the act of assimi-
lation—those situational boundaries it forms—affect their customs,
their traditions? That's when you risk losing language, right? You're
a linguist, Dr. Schulman. I'd think you knew a thing or two about
that." I nodded slowly. It seemed to me he didn't know what he was
talking about. By his metric, mobility eliminated tradition. Yet, his
very argument for shared tradition and collectivism risked the exact
same thing, just coded in language that was acceptable. And speaking
of language, there was something else about the way he addressed
me. I realized that I liked being called *Dr. Schulman* again. It felt just
like it did when I first got into the doctoral program at CUNY,
when I thought the degree would change my life. Make me respectable. And there I was.

I turned to Natalie for direction because I didn't want to argue
just for the hell of it. She twisted and pulled the small gold bangle on
her wrist and I wondered, stupidly, what life would be like as that
bangle, her hands around me, trapped. "Look, Josh," she said, calling
my attention to her face. "I know where you're coming from and
I admit that my feelings about *some* of the traditions are competing
and complex, and Brandon knows that already, but I also learned a
long time ago to trust the process, the *thing*. Because that's what I
used to call it. We're a small school in the Midwest with a unique,
idiosyncratic history. Nowhere else can you find students of this
age so invested in their school's identity, so willing to transmit that
identity from one group to the next, even if—on the surface—such
an identity doesn't serve a practical or educational purpose."

Brandon put an arm around Natalie. "That's it. All schools want what Fairbury has," he said. "You'll see for yourself soon enough. It's why I love it here. It's why we love it here."

I still wasn't convinced. But I could at least respect the fact that all the students took part or were invited to take part. I flashed back to my greeting in the band room, the hallway of staff members clapping in tune. "And all the faculty are into it too?" I asked. "It doesn't get in the way?"

"Oh, no. It does get in the way," Brandon said, laughing. "But you learn to work around it. You have to. There's no choice."

Natalie rolled her eyes. "He's exaggerating. The point is that it's fun if you let it be."

"Hey, I just want to make sure he knows what he's gotten himself into," Brandon said. "He deserves to know."

"Oh, stop," Natalie said. "You make it sound like some kind of horror film. Josh, you'll fit right in. We welcome everyone here."

"As long as you don't do anything stupid," Brandon said.

"I'll keep that in mind," I said.

"Let's change the topic," Natalie said, checking her phone. "It's better to experience this stuff for yourself rather than talk about it anyway. Who all have you met so far?"

"Well, you two. And Dr. Kirkland."

"Captain Kirk," Brandon said. "Sorry—I should have corrected you earlier. I thought about it but didn't."

Natalie took a long sip of her beer, a local coffee porter that had won a Best of the Midwest Small Brews award. I liked the way she drank—eyes half-closed, tongue wiping across her bottom lip. What I didn't like was coffee porters, yet I found this one surprisingly drinkable. She burped.

"Excuse me?"

"Captain Kirk. That's his name. That's what he goes by. Dr. Kirkland, I mean."

"Captain Kirk? Like from *Star Trek*?"

Brandon looked at his watch and yawned. He turned to Natalie. "I mean, the students like him," he said.

And here's where it all went wrong. I haven't stopped thinking about it since. Later that night, Natalie and I were alone in the living room. Brandon, on account of his early mornings with the paper, had already gone to sleep. I was sitting on the green velvet couch. Natalie was on the loveseat by the bookcase. I made a point not to stand over it with a beer scanning all the book spines because I didn't want to be one of those people who judged a person based on their taste in books. Instead, I looked at the Walker Evans-like portraits next to it: morose farmers in overalls on wooden front porches. Natalie's cat tested the space between us. It made me think of my own cat, Marvin, the one Heloise had now. My first mistake? I asked Natalie how long she and Brandon had been married. "Eight years," she said, as if bored by the question. She turned to the darkened hallway. The cat meowed. "Met him his first year here. When he was staff. Before he got the job with the paper. You don't get a ton of new people showing up in a place like Roll, Iowa." She fidgeted with her wedding ring. I had been so busy focusing on the bracelet and turquoise necklace that I hadn't noticed it—a solitaire diamond with a gold band. Simple, modest. "After a certain point they say that you can't meet anyone new in a town like Roll, that what you see is what you get, but that's not true because there he was. When he told me he was from Chicago, I got the impression that he saw this as the kind of place where he could be the big fish. But he really surprised me. You know what I mean? How people can surprise you?"

I took a long sip of my beer. Was it Heloise who surprised me or me who surprised Heloise? Could surprises be bad? Heloise had told me once that she thought I was cool and slick at first. She worried, actually, that I was the type who slept around—impressed girls, fucked them, then disappeared. In truth, I wasn't like that at all. She realized later, much to her dismay, that I was actually a "nervous Nancy."

"It's funny to look back on it now," she said. "But, you know, marriage is one of those things. Constantly learning. Sometimes good, sometimes bad."

I heaved a sigh. "I know," I said. "I've been there."

She cocked her head and looked at my hand. "Oh. Were you married?"

There was no getting out of it now, was there? "You can say that," I said.

Her surprise turned to sadness. "Didn't work out?"

I uncrossed my legs and looked at the vacuum marks on the carpet. I sensed judgment in her voice. Did divorce even exist in the wholesome Midwest or did time move at its own lazy pace and reject change wherever it showed? I, too, was passing judgment.

Natalie was the kind of girl I could fall in love with, in part because she was so different from me. She could challenge me to be better. Not that I would fall in love with her. I couldn't just walk into a new town and make a move on a married woman. In her own house, where her husband was sleeping. I was above that. At least the old me was.

"What happened?" she asked.

And I saw, finally, how this would go. Once I got started with something, I went all the way. It's how it always was. The Holocaust. The Beatles. Retro video games. There was no rest area in the middle. No Midwest in the geography of my own mind. Just a Warp Zone. Point A to Point B. I was helpless. I was shit. I was desperate for another surprise. "She's...gone," I said, gulping.

"Gone?" she asked. "You mean..."

I nodded. "Dead," I said. I was shocked it came out at all, to be honest, and I hated myself for being so rotten. My heart was pounding out of my chest. Natalie put a hand over her mouth. I had to say something else. To take it back. Quickly. Instead, I thought of my mother. I saw her lifeless body being lowered to the wet ground below me. "It was...two years ago. Cancer. Colon cancer."

"Oh my God," Natalie said. "Josh, I'm so sorry. I know it's probably not worth much, but you seem to be doing so well. It really speaks to your strength. And to almost finish a PhD…"

"Yeah," I said, nodding. I took a big gulp of my beer. Then a second. I drank it too fast and went into a choking fit.

Natalie moved from the loveseat to the couch, where I was sitting, one leg crossed over the other, and put a hand on my knee. I finished coughing and stared at the hand. For a second—only a second—I put my hand on hers. Maybe because I thought she had invited me. Her skin was cold.

I pulled my hand away and took another drink. I turned toward the window where the cat was licking itself.

"Josh," she said. "I don't know what to say."

"I know," I said. "It's okay. It just…really sucked." I was tearing up a little. No joke. Was it in memory of my mother? Or was it for Heli, parading around New York with what's-his-name the potter? Or was it for my own sad self—lying, touching Natalie's hand? For the symbolic death, maybe, of that old me?

"What was her name?" Natalie asked. I picked at the label on the beer. I knew I couldn't say Heloise. There was still such a thing as social media. I could deactivate my Facebook all I wanted but that wouldn't mean Heli couldn't be found out there. I panicked.

"Natalie," I said.

"Oh," she said, hand on her heart, as if the mention of her own name was the thing that really got her. "You poor thing," she said, standing up to fetch a tissue.

It rained that night. Before going to sleep, I brought a few of my game boxes in because I was worried about them sitting in the car. Natalie asked what was in the boxes and I said, "Nothing really."

"Then why are you bringing them inside?" she asked.

"It'll just make me feel better," I said. "I don't like them sitting in the van outside for too long."

"And getting stale?" she said. I couldn't tell if she was making fun of me. She draped a white sheet over the old green velvet couch and moved the cat's bed and litter box from the living room to the bedroom. "Otherwise you might wake to him hugging your face," she said. As I slept, I woke instead to the image of Brandon Grey kneeling over one of the boxes, intrigued, lifting a copy of *Duke Nukem 3D* to his lumberjack beard.

IV: THINGS I LEARNED DURING THOSE FIRST FEW DAYS IN ROLL

1) The Internet was slow. And I mean really slow. If Jared were to find a dusty tablet buried in the sand near his kibbutz and flick on the Wi-Fi, I'd bet my right hand he'd have faster internet speed than I did. I tried adjusting browser settings, clearing caches and extensions, and checking for viruses. I tried moving the router across the room, resetting it, and replacing it outright. I made dozens of phone calls to IPs and tech guys, but nothing helped. Because of outdated hookups in my duplex, the only ISP available was from the local Cactus Computer and Internet, which was operated from a garage at the end of a dirt road and offered two browsing speeds ("light browsing" and "lighter browsing"). My games were from the mid-90s and soon my internet was too, and if there's one thing I didn't have nostalgia for, it was Windows 95 and its Pentium 2 processors.

At my new place (more on that later), when webpages did finally load, they almost always loaded improperly. eBay, for example, appeared upside down, all text and no images. And you try ordering an import copy of Atlus's isometric arcade shooter *Princess Daisakusen* on the Sega Saturn complete with spine card and a 1997 fold-out calendar when the "Buy it Now" button appears not as a button but as a string of broken text at the bottom of the page, and when it takes seven-and-a-half minutes to log into your still-overdue PayPal Credit account, because by then, I can almost guarantee someone else will have purchased it.

These were first-world problems, but what you should understand was that I was a man of routine (tradition, you could call it—like the students at Fairbury). The bowl of Honey Nut Cheerios I was eating for breakfast when Dr. Kirkland first emailed his invitation to apply to Fairbury had been my breakfast for twenty-four years. I enjoyed coffee, but since I was sensitive to it, I drank it from K-cups, despite them being bad for the environment (this used to drive Heloise bonkers). God forbid there was a mistake as the coffee was brewing (a spill, major or minor, etc) and I had to dump the cup out into the sink and start over. In the backseat of a car, I sat only on the left. I fell asleep facing the wall (which is always on my right). I wore the same tattered cotton XXL "Bugle Boy" shirt to sleep since high school. Always in my pocket (except when I sleep) was a single dollar earned from my first job at a local bagel shop. It was my father's idea. He really believed in hard work. I used to carry around a small silver/rust-green pen knife once used by my grandfather, with his initials SRS cut into the handle, which he had given to me at my bar mitzvah, but stopped because I couldn't help but consider the many ways someone could rip it from my pocket and use it to stab me. Jared, since his bar mitzvah was first, was gifted a bigger one—a Kutmaster hawkbill with jigged bone. As far as I knew he was still carrying his. When he was alive, my grandfather told us how he had depended on those blades for most of his chores as a kid in his Galician shtetl. He also used them to cut up apples. I used mine to open packages received from eBay or the factory seal around games. The takeaway here is that these things are rarely dynamic. They can't easily be changed. I keep a pyramid of Honey Nut Cheerios boxes in the pantry in the event of nuclear war because I don't want to be forced to face even a single day without my morning bowl.

Roll didn't have a deli or a traditional pizza shop (there was only one pizza in town, and, if you'd believe it, their slogan was "home of cream cheese pizza"), but it did have a small coffee shop half a mile from my house with "high-speed" internet where I often went to complete my eBay searches and occasional cyberstalking (is checking someone's Twitter technically considered cyberstalking? Does it matter if you were once married to said person?). The place was called Twin Oaks. There were two large oak trees painted on opposite walls. They served hot tea and provided headphones. They also closed at 7 p.m., six on Sundays. I got the chance to familiarize myself with some of the locals there. Friendly people overall. At least that was my first impression. They smiled and waved. They said things like "howdy" and "nice day today." They were quiet. In New York, people were loud. They hosted big parties, they had loud sex, they blew horns and rode noisy motorcycles. Even at restaurants, they'd sit in large groups and shout across the table. You couldn't order food without your server asking you to speak up. Sometimes Heli would complain that I wasn't loud enough. That wouldn't be much of a problem here. My upstairs neighbors, too, when they finally came back from Arkansas, were quiet. They introduced themselves with little fanfare. They said they spend quite a bit of time on the road, so I wouldn't see much of them. Shoot, I thought. But even when they were both home, there was no electronic music or late night/ early morning parties. Their footsteps hardly made a sound. Their bed didn't creak. There were no moans. Half the time you wouldn't know they were there. This was an easy adjustment. I simply played my games with the volume on low so as not to bother them. On some days, though, the silence scared the hell out of me.

2) Sitting culture. People in Roll sit. A lot. If my neighbors from either side, Steve and Marley on the right, and Lynn and Claire on the left, weren't sitting on the porch in front of their white bungalows with uneven front steps, they were sitting on lawn chairs in their open, detached garages, balancing a can of soda (pop, as they'd call it) in their palms while watching the grass grow or listening to football on the radio, passing over customary two-finger waves at people like me who were passing by en route to Twin Oaks or Fairbury. You could even find them sitting in lawn chairs at the town lake if you looked hard enough. It wasn't uncommon to see other couples in the parking lot of the town grocery store sitting in pickup trucks with the windows down, sharing a small bag of Cheetos, watching people roll their carts in and out, in and out, like it was some kind of show.

Steve and Marley, my neighbors on the right, were in their 70s. Both were retired. They wore Birkenstocks, silver cross necklaces, and Hawaiian shirts. They were the first to check in on the tornado as I moved in. They came to the door with a small bowl of oatmeal raisin cookies. I didn't like the cookies, but when they stopped by the next day to ask how the cookies were, I told them that they were exquisite. They poked their heads far into the doorway both times, scoping out the mess. "Still getting unpacked?" they said. "Will be for a while," I said. "Any family out here?" they asked. "I've got some video games in the other room. You can call them family, I guess. Ha. Ha." They blinked at me, and I could tell they thought I was a twisted runaway masquerading as an adult. The *Ha Ha* didn't help. "Well, books, too." I said. "Lots and lots of books. None of those are about video games. I'm finishing up a PhD. Ha. Ha." The *Ha Ha* was clearly beyond my control. They continued to stare at me, unblinking. "Do you have a dog?" they asked (dare I say *Nintendogs*? The Chao I had been "raising" in *Sonic Adventure*? My unopened, factory-sealed, and thus indefinitely preserved Tamagotchi? Wasn't *that* responsible of me? I could have cut that thing from where it was encased in its little plastic shell with my silver/rust-green pen knife and it would have been dead in two weeks. But not this guy, not Joshua Schulman. I wanted it to live forever, hermetically sealed). "A cat? *Any* pets?" "I have a computer where I can watch videos of dogs. Cats, too. Ha. Ha." (Seriously. I couldn't stop). "Speaking of," I continued, suddenly noticing how still the air was and how warm the sun felt against my face, "Is the internet slow by you?" "We don't use internet," they said. "But there's a place you can go downtown if that's your thing." "Oh, yeah. Okay. Good. It is my thing, yes. I love the internet." They stopped by again two days later. Steve asked if he could use the bathroom. I said "sure," before realizing that his bathroom was all of twenty feet away. While we waited for him (it literally felt like an hour, and when I checked the bathroom after he left, there was no sign whatsoever it had actually been used), Marley just stood there and smiled, playing with the cross around her neck, asking casual questions about my family, my love life, some of the books that I had brought. "We've lived here for forty-seven years now," she said. "You can tell us anything, you know. Really, anything. Steve used to be a pastor. Open services on Sunday, just up the road. We hope to see you there. We can always use more eligible bachelors." "That's very kind of you," I said. "Thanks." "Love thy neighbor," she said.

Lynn and Claire lived in the house to my left and were a combined eighty years younger than Steve and Marley. They, too, didn't have a connection to the Academy. They came just as I finished stacking my first shelf of Sega Saturn games. We shook hands and said our hellos. "I'm sorry we didn't come to introduce ourselves sooner," Claire said. "We're not bad neighbors. I promise. We play ladder toss every Thursday if you'd like to stop by. You can bring some pop or chips. Whatever you'd like. "Ladder toss?" I said. I couldn't help but picture men twice my size tossing ladders as if they were footballs, catching the legs with a bulging hand. Unbeknownst to me, a spider fell from the ceiling and onto my back. Claire let out a sort of gasp, which I mistook for a sneeze. "Gesundheit," I said. "German, but also a little Yiddish.'" "*Yiddish?*" Claire asked, backing away. "Oh, no, that wasn't—" Lynn, on the other hand, had tiptoed so close to me that I could smell his mouthwash. I feigned indifference and decided to distract myself by wondering out loud what he did for a living. He shushed me. "Don't move," he said. He lifted a hand and I lifted mine, a river of sweat sweeping down my brow. Did he want a handshake? A high five? Claire shouted, "Now!" He slapped the back of my neck and, in one smooth motion, craned my head so that I could see a spider out of the corner of my eye, scurrying down the hallway towards my newly minted game room. "Darn. Almost had him, too," he said. "Do you have a dog? They're pretty good at sniffing them out." "No," I said, shaking my head. "No dog." "Any kids? Other pets? Girlfriend?"

3) When people say, "You don't *talk* like you're from New York," they aren't referring to your lack of raised vowels or front-rising diphthongs; they're insulting you in the form of a compliment by saying that you don't *appear* important enough to be from New York. When people say, "You don't *look* like you're from New York," you know they're insulting you. Passing judgment on your body. The black sandy hair turning grey. The dark eyes. The lanky physique, the underdeveloped muscles, the spot on your arms where you don't have any hair, the patchy fuzz on your neck, the sweat pouring down your face, leaving your skin an oily mess. They're talking about the fact that your eyes are too close together and that your ears are too tall. The fact that you wear T-shirts and jeans when not at work (even if all those T-shirts, in one way or another, have to do with New York: the New York Yankees, the Brooklyn Nets, CCNY, etc). Because, no, they think, *that* isn't New York. None of that is New York. New York is refined. It's where capital power is concentrated. Men there wear Prada suits. This Joshua has crooked front teeth.

4) There were 1,412 people, one lake, three antique shops, two Dollar Generals, four churches, two bars, six traffic lights, two gas stations, and one bank. The town's only grocery store had been sold eight times and changed names twice. There were chalk drawings in the middle of Main Street and signs at nearly every street corner for VFW pancake feeds. A twenty-four-hour Walmart Supercenter sat a few miles beyond the edge of town, closing the space

between Roll and Arnold, the next town over. The campus sat to the west. My place was north, where bungalows with sprawling porches, hipped roofs, and old street trees the size of skyscrapers leaned against endless corn fields. Most houses had some form of décor on their front door— sunflowers, pineapples, Iowa Hawkeyes logos, etc. Mine didn't. The basement, which I shared with my neighbors upstairs reeked of dog piss even though they didn't have a dog. The furniture provided included a full-sized bed that sloped in the middle, an older plaid couch, a cheap faux wood dining room table with two chairs, a dresser that was prone to tipping over, and a pink crib that I can only assume was left by the previous tenants. I disassembled the crib and left it in the closet. The place was fine. Almost too big for one person, but it's hard to complain about something you've been given for free. The windows didn't shut properly and the paint in the living room was peeling. But the air conditioning worked and the bed was cozy. I slept well. Better than I had ever slept in New York.

5)   The closest synagogue? Seventy-five miles away in Dubuque. Closest retro game store? One hundred and twenty miles away in Cedar Falls (a cramped space with a sign that said "we reserve the right to refuse service to ANYONE"). Closest PhD-granting institution? One hundred fifty miles away in Iowa City. Closest shooting range? Thunder Alley. Just down the road. On some nights, when the wind slowed, you could hear the bullets being fired. Pop. Pop. Pop.

V: HOLD YOURSELF STRAIGHT

WHEN I WAS SEVEN, there was a thirty-second TV spot for Teacher Barbie and its mini-classroom set that often played during my after-school Nickelodeon binge (which consisted of *Tiny Toon Adventures* and *Rocko's Modern Life*). The doll wore a flower dress and stood in front of a mini-chalkboard and two small wooden desks. She pressed buttons that made her say "try it again" to the students, or "good job" (speaking of, I'll tell you someone who never said "good job." Not ever. My father). Another caused a school bell to ring.

I wanted that Barbie. I pictured myself writing math problems on the little chalkboard. I saw myself ringing that school bell like I pressed buttons on the toy cash register I had in the basement that said "credit approved" even though it sounded like "credit a food." But add it to my Hanukkah list? No way. I had told my father once that I hoped to read poetry and be a teacher when I grew up and he said usually girls did that.

Still, once or twice I pulled away from the family at Toys "R" Us to sneak into the doll section with its pink tiles and light fixtures, so I could see Teacher Barbie's box for myself. "Classroom filled with magic and sound," it read. It was smaller than I thought it would be, but all that meant was that it would be easier to sneak into a cart and out the door. I thought about it but chickened out.

The set was later recalled because they forgot to give Barbie panties. I imagined sneaking off with the thing after all and my father finding it and lighting it on fire in our backyard, waving the recall notice in the air like a flag. How quickly I would have gone from his disowned gay Barbie-doll thief of a son to sex-obsessed pervert. Would one have been better than the other? Or did he believe all sins were equal in God's eye?

Years later, I taught imaginary lessons to imaginary students in the corner of my bedroom, pacing from the closet to the dresser, pausing every now and then to be sure the students were listening. I wandered into my middle school library and checked out a few teaching journals. One was about the stock market, another was about diversity and inclusion. When the weekend came, I gathered a few of the younger neighbors on our porch and lectured them about the stock market, working directly out of the journals. Teaching was in my blood, even though it wasn't. My father was an accountant before he rediscovered religion and became the financial manager of the local synagogue. My mother made her living as a tailor, but she had a gift for numbers too. My brother Jared went to school for accounting and ultimately earned his MBA with high honors. So where then did this urge to teach come from? Moral indignation? A quest for empowerment and liberation? Or was it because I was only ever good at one thing: being different?

I was thrown into the classroom for the first time at twenty-two as a first-year in Brooklyn College's MA program. Despite his refusal to accept the practicality of my liberal arts degree, my father was excited to tell his friends that his son was now a college professor. In fact, he started calling me *professor*, though the sarcastic tone he used often made it feel smug and contemptuous. When I confronted him about it, he said I was too sensitive. "If you really want to be a professor, then you need to learn how to talk to people," he said. "You think everyone you meet is going to like you all the time? Is going to speak exactly the way you want them to? Is going to say nothing but good, friendly things about you?"

I groaned. "That's not what I'm saying, dad."

"I mean, if you want to be a *good* professor, then fine. But a *great* professor, for that you need to listen to both sides, to everyone. What if these kids came to you with problems and questions, is that the way you would talk to them? If you did, they'd fire you so fast you wouldn't even know what hit you. Trust me, I'm doing you a favor."

There isn't much to say about teaching as a practice because if you've done it before then you already know what it's like. Some days, it's as simple as having a well-rehearsed song-and-dance routine and trying with all you've got to remember the names of students who seem to pass in and out the classroom like shadows. On others, it's like making precision jumps in a cinematic plat-former like *Prince of Persia*, leaping across pits of death as hundreds of thousands of pixelated falcons lunge after you. You walk off with a pile of papers and grade them until your hand goes numb. Then, on no sleep, you hand those papers back, laden with thoughtful, constructive comments, only to watch as students glance briefly at their grade and drop your work and theirs in the garbage can on the way out the door.

Heloise visited my Community Writing class at CCNY during my second year in CUNY's PhD program. I had structured the class around three units of equal length: writing *from* community, writing *about* community, and writing *for* community. She didn't tell me she was coming that day, though she had been threatening to sneak into one of my classes for months. I had just started playing Neil Young's "Southern Man" for an experimental lesson on music as a political and rhetorical medium. I turned off the lights and heard the door in back creak open, assuming it was a student of mine excusing herself for the bathroom. When I flipped the lights back on, my eyes tracked to Heloise, sitting next to that semester's token frat boy. She was in disguise: notebook open, bag at her feet. She winked at me. I was so flustered that I had to sit down on the radiator and regain my breath.

That instant—her sitting in a too-small seat in a red cotton sundress, legs crossed, pushing a pair of reading glasses up the bridge of her nose—was when I first realized I was in love with her, though it would be another few days before I finally said it out loud, over bubble tea and scones in Washington Heights.

"You're blowing their impressionable little minds," she told me when class was over, gesturing with closed fists. "Poof."

"Poof," I said, imitating her.

She hit my shoulder playfully. "*You*," she said. "You were good."

"Me? No."

She rolled her eyes. "I really wish I could have had a teacher like you. All my teachers were old and boring. You would have been just my type."

"I guess we can talk it over during office hours," I said. "My office is tucked away pretty good. And my office mate is at a conference in Pittsburgh. How convenient."

She lowered her eyes. "Are you saying you'll offer me extra credit, Joshua?"

"Come upstairs and we'll see how it goes," I said.

I wish I could stay in that moment forever. I can still picture her following me up the stairs, then sitting at the edge of my desk—her red cotton sundress pulled up to her waist, legs spread on the back of the chair, me with a hand against her mouth. Then, a knock on the door and a soft giggle from her lips.

"Hiding in plain sight," I whispered, pausing.

"You're naughty," she said.

Later, when the coast was clear, I said, "We don't talk much during sex, do we?"

She stroked the stubble on my cheek. "Because I'm too busy *feeling* you."

"And what's that like?"

"Like my cup is being filled up. Like you're filling my cup."

"With old rotting milk? Sewage?"

She shook her head.

"Then what?"

She looked like she was really thinking about it. "A hot foamy latte," she said. "A dirty martini."

"Well said," I said. "Descriptive."

"Does that mean I get an A?"

"A+," I said.

With the right group of students and the right amount of prep, I felt confident that I would come to see the classroom at Fairbury as the kind of sanctuary it had once been for me, where I morphed like a toy Transformer into my better self. Stats increased. Level-up. Why else do you think I took the job? I could have scoured the want ads in New York and found something tepid if all I was really after was some money. But I wanted more than that, even if I hadn't been willing to look for it myself.

On my first few nights in Roll, after the last of my games had been organized and stowed, after the discs and cartridges had been checked and tested, after a few games, like *Three Dirty Dwarves*, a hand-drawn D&D-influenced beat-em-up, and *Fighters Megamix*, a 3D arcade fighter, had been played until my hands were numb, I stood in my teaching outfits in front of the bathroom mirror. As I often did during my hyperfixation with the Holocaust, I imagined selection at Auschwitz or Bergen-Belson or Treblinka. To the left. No, to the right. *You?* Do you have any redeemable skills? I don't think so. I didn't look like the men I had seen thus far around town with their hollow cheekbones, boots, and denim. They all stood a certain way, too. Hands in their pockets, tall and straight. Not me. I slouched like a bone was missing in my back. A Jew from New York. The physical image of my father's father. After retirement, he had invested in a laundromat on Brighton Beach Avenue where we sometimes went as kids. He'd give my cousins and me five dollars in change from the machines with which I'd promptly cross the street to the Ukrainian bodega and buy a gaming magazine. Once, when I returned with it, he tore it from my hands, held it high in the air and said to my father, "This is what your son thinks

of money. This is what money is worth to him." He died at seven-
ty-four of kidney disease.

I checked for grey hair. It was like a math equation. How
many single greys does it take to make you officially grey? At
least I still had my hair. I couldn't say the same for someone like
Kirkland. I parted it to the left and then to the right. I would have
done knee slides across the wooden living room floor if I knew it
wouldn't disfigure me. Maybe I'd get a new haircut or try bleach-
ing it. Maybe I'd go shopping for new clothes. The point is with
each day that passed unchecked, I began to see myself emerging on
the other side of that window like the cardinal who had escaped
from my father's house. If I could clear *Strikers 1945* and *Gunbird*
in one credit, which is exactly what I did after hours of practice
and unpacking, then I could be set free, set apart.

I wish this could have become that very story—one of me
rising again like my ancestors or that desperate little cardinal instead
of what it actually is: a story in which I see just a broken reflection in a foggy mirror, eclipsed by a shadow I can never escape, a
merry-go-round spinning round and round.

Maybe life is just an illusion. A gathering of rocks like a gathering of stories. But how then can we tell the front from the back and
the back from the front? How can we learn to clear our lives with
just one credit—which is all any of us get—like I cleared *Gunbird*
with one credit, avoiding death on every screen? The problem is
you need years of living to clear a single life. Because only then can
you learn where the next wave of pirates are, the bullet patterns,
the artificially changing environment. The rest of the time you're
just flying blind.

I'd walk from the mirror in anguish, still glad to be thinking like
this. Academically, I mean. Maybe a paper or two would follow.
Maybe I really would end up with a PhD. Maybe, after all this,
CUNY would take me back. Or maybe that just fed my delusion.

★

I avoided Natalie after the night I spent at her place. I was already stressed about the PhD thing, but now I had to contend with this new, still hypnotic set of lies, to know that the person she saw when she saw me wasn't really me. There was also, of course, the issue of self-control. At the mandatory all-staff meeting, during which I met most of my colleagues and was given an eight-pound folder of curriculum materials and pedagogical advice, I saw her as soon as I walked in and sat as far away as I could. At one point, we met eyes. She wore a black-and-white fleece. A pair of white rimless glasses had replaced the red-rimmed ones. She wore that same turquoise necklace, that same gold bangle. She gave me a full and warm smile. I smiled back.

The next weekend, two days before classes began, the school hosted a power-up covered lunch party on the sunny grass overlooking the Gunk, just to the west of the football field. Natalie, plate of food in hand, found me as I arrived and peeked into my grocery bag.

"Did you bring us New York bagels?" she asked.

"The next best thing," I said. I pulled out a bag of chips. "Sour Cream and Onion."

"You really went all in," she said.

It was a joke, but I felt embarrassed. And that was before I got a good look at the spread. I had decided against getting a second bag of chips and regretted it. Last time I was at a department bring-a-plate, I brought two bags of chips, only one of which had even been opened. Worse yet, I watched frozen with anger as someone walked off with the unopened bag when the event ended. Never again, I vowed.

Natalie said, "You don't cook, do you?"

"I do," I said. "I'm not a New York cliché. I don't live on take-out. As good and as fast and as convenient as it is. I also don't frequent these kinds of events, which is why I didn't expect deconstructed enchiladas."

"You're barely scratching the surface, dude."

"What do you mean?" When she brought her plate up to my eyes, I nearly gasped. "Wait. Is that flank steak?"

"Meg Lemming's dish. Open-faced steak sandwiches dressed with arugula and horseradish aioli."

"What?"

"Wait until you see the Thai chili peanut Brussels sprouts. Locally grown."

"Thai chili peanut Brussels are locally grown?"

She laughed and offered me a sprout.

As I ate it, she pointed at Kirkland. He was wearing an untucked dress shirt without a tie even though he had the top button buttoned. A few I recognized from earlier in the week formed a half-circle around him. "Captain K. Brings them every year. We mean business here, Josh. It's back to cafeteria food in a few days. You've got to enjoy it while you can."

I spent a good chunk of the event introducing myself to some of the people I hadn't met yet while my bag of chips sat untouched at the end of the table. Even though I came to eat my weight in sockeye salmon pasta salad, eventually I stacked a few rainbow cookies on a paper plate and brought them to the shade of a cottonwood tree, where I stood and watched a group of instructors toss a Frisbee. One could see a few umbrellas scattered around the lake. Or down the hill to the parking lot, where cars absorbing the rays of the sun deposited the first of the student arrivals, the early birds, who were struggling to push giant wheelie carts of luggage to the Barracks. Music wailed in the distance, momentarily getting louder before being drowned out by a jackhammer. I couldn't tell if it was coming from campus or from the other end of the lake.

It was another hot one. I slipped on my sunglasses and undid the top button of my navy-blue button-up. I pretended to have important business to attend to on my phone.

Earlier, when examining the crockpots of pulled chicken dishes and Tupperware of purple marshmallow fluff, I found myself next to a guy named Glen Gill, who had been walking around with a bright orange backpack over one shoulder. He was in his 60s, teaching History. He had grown up on a farm outside of Topeka, Kansas. "You ever been to Topeka? Best tacos on Earth," he said. He took heaping spoonfuls of everything and joked about how the spread gets worse every year. Then, after finding out I was here to teach writing, he asked if I had ever read Philip Roth. I thought for sure he was being ironic. He wasn't. "Hold on," he said, dropping the backpack from his shoulder, digging around in it. He pulled out a file folder and a notebook and stacked them at his feet. Next came a copy of Roth's *The Plot Against America.*

We talked for a few minutes about Roth. Then, unsurprisingly, he squinted and said, "Wait, are you Jewish?"

"I'm from New York. Everyone in New York is Jewish."

"That's a factual embellishment," he said, tossing the backpack over his shoulder again. "It's like one in ten. And that's a generous estimate."

"Are you sure about that?"

"Positive," he said. "One in ten in New York. One in a hundred everywhere else. Listen—I love Judaism. It's my favorite religion. By far. Sorry. A Jew in Roll. You'll have to excuse me. This is really exciting. Like finding a unicorn in the wild."

"Wait. You're serious?"

"No, I'm not. I mean, yes. I am. Yes. I love the Jews." His face lit up. His eyes got bulgy and his shoulders tightened.

"Like what kind of Jews?"

"All Jews."

"What do you love about them?"

"Everything. Their passion. Their survival instinct."

"But you're not Jewish?"

"No. Oh God, no. But I wish," he said.

He went on for a while more about Judaism and Jewishness. The Holy Spirit. The Talmud. Maimonides. The Schulchan Aruch.

"I'm blogging about Jewish sitcoms right now, show-by-show.

Critical theory stuff. Like *Seinfeld*—it's not a show about Jews in the city who get themselves into trouble, you know the way most people see it, but rather the violent force of law. Real heavy-hitting stuff. Like Exodus. What do you make of Exodus, Josh? The Book of Exodus, I mean."

"It's the force that brought me here."

"Heads," someone shouted. I dropped to the ground, still balancing my pile of rainbow cookies. When I looked up, Phil Sgourakis, who went by the nickname Pants, hovered over me waving a Frisbee.

He tossed the scratched and battered disc back to the group. There were a few giggles.

"Dude," he said, wiping sweat from his forehead. I stood. "Close call. Who are you hiding from out here?"

I had already met most of them individually, usually in an unremarkable exchange of names and ranks. But I soon observed that this group didn't operate individually. They were defined in relation to each other, forming a sometimes loud, sometimes pensive, always clumsy pack of misfits. These were the people who truly believed in the Fairbury mission, the brand, who would have someone like Brandon Grey in their ranks. Not that everyone else on staff didn't believe in the Fairbury mission. But this group really owned it, and it was most obvious when glancing at their names, that lovely linguistic currency. There was Molly Newton, the History teacher who went by the name Jane for irony. She was the unofficial leader of the group. Ozu, who taught Paleontology and who carried around a too-small Indiana Jones hat as if it were a talisman. Hunter Reed, who wore only a hunter-green sweater vest (even in the summer sun), meaning that his given name (hunter = green) informed itself. Bimby, who taught Computer Science and wore stretchy logo shirts under an open button-up because he was above the school's dress code. Pomm and Timmer, who taught Physics and Chemistry (Pomm for Physics and Timmer for Chemistry) and wore around her neck a dozen or so lime green lanyards. Their function and purpose unknown.

Pants was my favorite. We had met at the very beginning of the first faculty meeting. He was half a head taller than me. Bald with a neat goatee. His voice was thick and grumpy, even though he glowed with life. This was reflected in how involved he was, a walking/talking CV: leader of the Society of Secret Engineers, a voice during faculty development groups, a constant, smiling face in the hallways of Academic 1, a regular at the Rec. He looked older than he was, maybe because of his knee-high white socks and beat-up Nikes. But he talked like he was younger. He taught Logic and Number Theory, stuff I couldn't tell you about if you offered to pay me in import shooters.

His mother was Dominican and his father Greek. His mother had emigrated to the U.S. during the Dominican Civil War, which ignited after Kennedy was shot in Dallas, only a few miles from Waxahachie, Texas, where his father lived.

On the surface, his ambitions seemed similar to Natalie's, but his path to get there was different. He was younger, newer at the school (seven years to Natalie's thirteen). He wasn't enrolled in educational administration credits online. He didn't mingle like good buddies with the other admins. He was just tossing a Frisbee, confident in his status as *one of the guys*, talking with fever about the upcoming year.

He had crusties on the side of his nose and a metal T-shirt with the neck white and sweaty. He smelled like dirty laundry but seemed nice enough, so I sat next to him. I was still avoiding Natalie at the time. He extended a hand and shook mine so hard I thought one of the bones had cracked.

"Welcome to the Hotel California," he said. His voice carried across the room, which made me uneasy. I was aware then that others were listening.

I licked sweat from my lips. He was waiting for me to respond but I wasn't sure with what.

He huffed. "Check in, never leave."

"That's a lot," I said, naively.

He let go of the Frisbee and we stood in silence for a bit, watching the others. Whereas at first they were tossing the disc to the person next to them, now they made the space between them wider and tossed it *across* the circle, sometimes to two people at once. The air smelled like warm dirt—earthy and mellow. I snuck another look at Natalie. Meg was the one talking now, gesturing with both hands. Natalie had her back to me. I thought about going over to join, telling Meg how much I enjoyed her steak sandwiches.

Pants pointed to the Frisbee circle and said, "You wanna get in this?"

"Not my game," I said, meeting eyes with Ozu, who was standing at the far end of the circle. "I'm a streetball and handball kind of guy. That's life in Brooklyn for ya. Can't even drink the water."

Pants frowned and looked hard at my face. "But the water in New York is some of the best there is. Isn't that why y'all are always bragging about why the pizza is so good? Because the water is filled with fluoride and magnesium or something like that. Makes for a better baking profile?"

"It's just a saying," I said, trying not to sound defensive. "Don't drink the water. I mean, I didn't drink it much, but I just don't drink a lot of water."

Another lie. I drink plenty of water. I literally had a bottle of water at my feet which I told myself not to look at for fear of Pants calling me on it.

He turned to watch the Frisbee. I could tell he thought I was crazy. I was sure that most people did. But maybe it would be a good look for me: the erratic, neurotic New Yorker. Maybe it would help establish some distance between me and others so that they would take anything I said with a grain of salt.

"It's still early," he said, shrugging. "Come on. Jump in. We can always use another pair of hands. Just not another pair of pants." He paused so I could chuckle. "We're getting in some early practice for the student/staff game. We win every quarter. Mostly because of Jane. She played professionally."

"*Professionally?* Frisbee?"

Almost on cue, Jane took a big step back and launched the

Frisbee high into the air. I shaded my eyes to watch. It hung there loud and proud like the Hindenburg before collapsing into her hands, yo-yo like.

"Shit," I said.

"She's on point, man."

She did it again, like she knew we were talking about her.

"Yup. She's flexin'," Pants said.

Ozu, who had shifted spots with Pomm and Timmer, waved Pants back into the circle.

"Last chance," he said.

"I'm okay," I said.

And the one I didn't like? Hunter Reed.

Hunter Reed was the only one on staff with a moustache, but that wasn't why I didn't like him. Like anyone half decent, I disliked him as a person first and his moustache as an object attached to that person second. It was full and bushy. The Walt Whitman beard of moustaches. He was teaching a new course, as he told me quite proudly and almost immediately, in Utopic and Dystopic fiction. Apparently, he had slaved over the reading list for the better part of the summer. "They start with Tomas More then Plato," he sighed, staring off into the distance like the reading list was coming to him in a vision as a confirmation of his genius. He was from Columbus and was married to a woman named Milena, one of the school librarians. She was taller than him, even when she wore flats. She had a mousy brown haircut with bangs. The kind of person who didn't look tall until she stood. When I met them earlier in the lunch party, I thought I'd be clever and said: "Hunter, I have friends who teach at Hunter," forcing a weak handshake. "CUNY."

"Look at that," he said, yawning, turning to Milena. "They named a school after me."

"They should pay you royalties," she said.

Then, he lit a cigarette and told me that he was working on his dissertation at Indiana U. on von Goethe's *Faust*. I told him I was finishing up a dissertation myself on Yiddish dialectology.

"Have you read much von Goethe?" he said.

"Not my thing."

He blew a big cloud of smoke into the air. "Too dense?"

"No," I said.

"Then what?"

I hated being challenged like this. It was just like how my father functioned. Pull you into his wheelhouse and grill you. Then make you out to be uninformed, dumb. Obviously, you could effectively interrogate someone about an author on whom you were writing a dissertation. Did you see me asking him to tell me about Yiddish dialectology?

"I'm not writing a dissertation on von Goethe," I said.

I could see that my answer bothered him. "But you have opinions of your own, don't you?"

"Of course."

"Then what are they?"

I let out a sharp breath. Maybe this would be a good exercise if I were going to commit to this PhD thing (lines drawn in the sand, lit on fire). I was out of practice, after all, having purged my ability to talk like a true academic. But of course I took the low road. "Wasn't von Goethe an anti-Semite?"

"An anti-Semite?" he scoffed. "How?"

And of course it backfired. "I don't know," I said. "I thought this was common knowledge."

"Bud, if you can't tell me how then you don't get to make a claim like that. For one, Faust is all biblical parallel. It's inspired by the Talmud. Goethe had an *affinity* for Jews. Not a lot of Germans back then did, as I'm sure you know." He talked and talked. Milena put a hand on her hip and nodded furiously. "So, what are *you* into then?" he finally asked, chuckling. Right here Glen Gill walked by, holding up his copy of Roth's *The Plot Against America*, giving me a thumbs-up. I nodded at him and felt like an idiot for it. "Philip Roth?" Hunter said.

"No," I said, my face burning. I checked to make sure Gill was out of earshot. "Roth offends me, too. Jews can be problematic. We aren't all saints."

"Sounds like a lot of things offend you," Milena said.

"I think you should give *Faust* another read," Hunter said. "But carefully this time. We'll talk, man. You know where to find me." Did I? He started walking off but stopped. I prepped myself for another *Faust* lecture. "Oh, also, I like getting some of the writing classes together for a combined reading at the end of each quarter, that way we can see what everyone's working on. Usually do it in Eppley. The auditorium. I imagine your classes will participate?"

"I don't see why not," I said.

He gave me a thumbs-up, and then they were gone.

★

Sometimes I don't know what I'm doing. I worry I'm just drying myself to get wet again. Painting eggs and shimmering past mirrors, candle burning out. I could walk and walk and walk from one end of town to the other, I could skip or run across campus, past the lake, past the Grey's Cape Cod style house next to other Cape Cod style houses, up and down North Main and South Main, until I finally ended up safe at the other end of that paint-chipped hallway, to my newly minted game room, my happy place, transported to the person I was at the start of this, at the beginning of it all, to the kid I was then—on the wall: Sonic the Hedgehog poster, framed comic books.

In the final days before school began, I moved from my play-through of every ferocious Japanese arcade shooter I owned to slower, longer JRPGs like *Shining Force* and *Albert Odyssey*. Games that had been relegated to the middle of my queue because of their length. I'd sit in my beanbag chair for hours at a time, listening to the rain if it was raining, immersed in stories of someone else's redemption. I should have been lesson planning. It felt like I was floating. It had been a while since I had to question my self-indulgence. After reaching an adequate save point, I'd power the system down for the night and think: What's Missing? Obviously, I could stand in front of the shelves and bins of games with a beer and scan the same empty spaces. *Battlesport. Panzer Dragoon Saga. Daytona USA Championship CCE Net Link Edition.* But what else? Not since New York had I managed to fill the important holes in my collection. And though I had made it a point to introduce myself to the mailman, the games I needed weren't packages at my doorstep, taped and bubble-wrapped.

Game nights with Thiago and Jordan. That was what was missing.

Looking for a friend, I popped into Trivia Night on Thursday to see if I might find someone on the faculty who could fill the spot left by Thiago and Jordan. But no one from school was there. Just a slim and tired bartender who told me to grab a seat and a few guys in cowboy hats and jeans who were sitting at the bar, watching me as if I were an alien. I asked about Trivia Night and she said I had missed it. It started at five. It was eight. I ordered a Boulevard and scrolled through pictures of Heloise on my phone. I wanted to touch her skin. I wanted to hear her pronounce *shiksa*. I wanted to see her figure in the doorway, turning all the men's heads and saying, "Are you done with that beer yet? I need you to put me to bed."

"*To* bed or *all the way* to bed?"

"You taste like honey, honey."

But now she was dead. Symbolically, at least. If not literally. I had to believe it to maintain it. At least with Natalie. I couldn't just push her away. And what would Heloise say about all this? Nothing, I guess. Because her voice was missing, too.

I typed and erased a text to Heloise. I didn't always have control over these things, you see. "All settled in Iowa. Lots has happened so far. Met a new group of friends. Just got my course roster. Only twelve students per class! New girl, too. More on that soon. So—how's life in New York?"

I liked it. It felt just desperate enough.

She "viewed" the message three hours before she responded to it (the morning of the first day of school nonetheless). Her response: "Hi Josh. Glad to hear it. Good luck out there."

She wasn't dead, after all. Soon it was me who felt dead. Alive, I mean. I'm not usually this lucky, am I?

★

On the first day of class, the students filled the room before I could figure out how to operate the projector. One blonde head after another. Some were tall, others short. They arrived eager, their faces glowing, the Fairbury Academy seal embroidered on the chest next to a silver nameplate and identifying lanyard. Because of the uniform, loose blue button-up over navy blue slacks, they looked alike from the neck down. They became floating Fairbury heads.

These heads found their seats and then located friends with finger guns and fist bumps. One, when passing by my desk, asked how to pronounce my last name. Another asked if I had a nemesis. "Yes, this projector," I said, ready to destroy it and its overly complicated remote with a clenched fist, pressing this button and that button, waiting, tapping my feet, all the while letting them talk of baseball games and weddings. Of Great Lakes and *Game of Thrones*. It seemed at least half of them spent part of the summer at some island resort. Some chatted from where it was most convenient, others screamed from across the room.

Then, finally, the projector sprang to life.

Intro to Writing was a class for first and second years, part of the school's CORE curriculum, meaning my students were somewhere between thirteen and fourteen and, unlike elective courses like Hunter Reed's Utopic and Dystopic Literature, didn't choose to enroll.

Eventually all but a few eyes finished their scan of their room, locking briefly with friends a final time, before settling on

me, the fraud, here because of an article I had written years ago
when I might as well have been someone else.

I gave a friendly wave and wrote my name on the board,
punctuated for coolness, for Fairbury effect. "That's almost Dr. J,"
I said. I explained the aims and scopes of the course and then some
of my academic background. "Does anyone know what linguistics
is?" I asked. Someone did. "What about Yiddish?" Someone did.
"Great," I said. "Sounds like we're all on the same page." Next, I
used an impassioned monologue to demonstrate why our work in
the course was important, how it could result in translatable skills.
I set a worksheet down on the glowing projector, about the many
myths of writing. I had just started introducing it when a voice
from behind me interrupted. "Dr. J."

"Almost Dr. J," I corrected.

"You know you've got half a roll of toilet paper on your foot."

"I do? But I didn't even use the bathroom." I spun to the
board and kicked my feet against the wall. Nothing was there.

Laughter erupted.

"Ha, ha," I said, composing myself. "Very funny. Do you do
that to everyone or am I special?"

"Not everyone has toilet paper on their foot," one of them said.

"Oh, right. I should have figured."

"Do you actually *speak* Yiddish?"

"A bit, yes."

"Can you say *toilet paper* in Yiddish?"

"No."

"What about *class dismissed*?"

"No."

"Do you know the meaning of life?"

"Do *you* know the meaning of life?"

"Forty-two."

"Okay then. How silly of me to miss that."

"What brought you here from New York?"

"Who said I was from New York?"

"You did."

"I did?"

"Have you ever seen Donald Trump?"

"Once, at the Plaza Hotel. I was lost. I think Macaulay Culkin was there."

"Seriously?"

"Hard to say."

"Are you in the Witness Protection Program?"

"Who asked that? Good eyes. I am, yes. Gambino crime family. Italian mafia. Bensonhurst. I *saw* something. Didn't *do* something. Saw it. I can't tell you my real name. This Almost Dr. J is just a cover."

"Wait—are you serious?"

I ducked my head. "Unfortunately, yes. This is where they sent me, of all places. Roll, Iowa. Can you believe it? I can't."

"What in the heck."

"You're lying."

I shook my head.

"But wait, if you're in the Witness Protection Program aren't you like, not supposed to tell anyone?"

"Says who?"

"And how could you get a PhD?"

"You can't. That's why it's a cover."

"But what if one of us reveals your alibi?"

"I'm not worried. I don't think anyone here is connected to the Gambino crime family. Has anyone even been to Bensonhurst?"

"Where?"

"New York? Brooklyn? That's what I thought. Now, this was fun. It was. Really, it was. And I'm sure we'll get the chance to do it again, but we should really move on. We have a lot to cover today."

"But it's the *first* day. Usually we just chat."

"Oh, yeah? Do you play hopscotch, too?"

"They save that for the second day."

"No, the third. Remember? We take naps on the second day."

"Okay, well. This is what *we're* doing today," I said.

"But why?"

"Because we all need to start somewhere," I said. "We can't just sit here and chat. Okay? Moving on…"

And so, I turned back to the white screen and did just that. I hadn't done much of it in the months since my mother got sick. And now that the noise had died down, the first twelve of my students in those tiny wooden desks were taking notes and raising hands to answer my questions and nodding as if what I had to say was important, as if it could help them in some way, as if I had passed their little test. It was reassuring to see how quickly they could pivot from rowdy joking to tenacious learning. It meant I could really have fun with them.

On the second day, I paired everyone up and had them interview their partners to gather info so they could formally introduce them to the rest of the class. The only catch, I said. They had to be absolutely silent.

"Define silence," they asked.

"No noise."

"So, we can write to our partners?" they said.

I thought about it and said no.

"Can we draw?" they asked. "Mime? Text?"

I said no.

"Then, what—?" they said, objecting. "I don't get it."

"Hey," I said. "Like sixty percent of our communication is nonverbal, right? So what's the problem? Chop chop, okay. I want you to find out as much as you can about your partner. And I want absolute silence. Go on. Begin now."

For the next few minutes, I paced around the room. A few were mouthing commands. Others were miming anyway, despite being told not to do so. Then, after letting the group struggle for a few minutes, I asked how it was going.

"Stupid," one said.

"Is this a New York thing?" a second said.

I lifted my hand requesting silence again. "Does anyone else find it curious," I asked, "How in a class where language—where *words* are so important—that I'd start our second day by stripping them from you? Is there a lesson to be learned here, perhaps?"

"That you're a masochist? A sadist?"

"Besides what it potentially says about *me*," I said.

There were a few hands.

"That communication exists in different spheres?"

"That's definitely true," I said. "Anyone else?"

"That words don't tell the whole story."

"That's good," I said. "I like that. Language is power, right? Words are important. Words can change the world. That's why we're here. But sometimes what we learn most about *people* doesn't come in the form of language at all. You know, it's like peeling back layers of an onion. We protect ourselves and don't always tell the whole truth about ourselves, at least not via language. But we keep the truth in other ways. Do you know how to read it? And do you know how to transmit it?"

I liked talking myself through it even if it didn't entirely make sense. From the looks of the class, it seemed that I was getting close to saying something significant but didn't quite get there. Luckily, no one seemed to mind.

"I'm going to let you talk to your partners," I said. "I'm giving you back your language. Then we'll introduce each other and maybe even talk a bit more about why we did this. On the count of three: one, two, three."

The room exploded with conversation, the dusty textbooks trembling on the wooden shelves in back.

Smiling, I crossed my arms. I was the captain of my own vessel. Move over, Captain Kirk, Hunter Reed, and make way for some new blood: Almost Dr. J. I was here. I was there. I was on my way back. Full speed ahead. Exiled no more.

★

It was expected that staff eat lunch together—a fact that Kirkland had neglected to mention during his comprehensive tour. All it did was further solidify the divide between groups, the believers and the non-believers, the young and the old.

On day two, I was late arriving to the dining hall after my pleasantly successful silent interview activity, so the only line short enough for my sensibilities was pizza. I grabbed three slices of greasy pepperoni, filled up a glass with water, and walked over to the faculty seating area, which was in the very back of the building and consisted of various circular tables, whereas the student section— separated by a small partition—consisted of long wooden tables.

In the middle was the biggest staff table in the room—occupied by Pants, Hunter Reed, Jane, Ozu, Pomm and Timmer, and others, a Frisbee serving as a party favor in the middle of them all—with only a tight spot or two open in between already crowded people. I decided to sit alone against the far wall, where a few of the older instructors like Glen Gill tended to lay low. I waited for Natalie Grey. It had been long enough, I decided. I'd ask her to sit with me. See how she was. Maybe, if the timing were right, I'd back-pedal on the dead wife thing. It had been eating at me in a way the almost-PhD thing wasn't. I just wanted to move forward. See what was there. Even if it meant being friends. I had really enjoyed my time with Natalie, and I was still mad at myself for digging this percolation pond between us. I cut the pizza and watched the kids from over the partitions, trying to identify the few that were mine, when Pants tapped me on the shoulder and waved me over to the big table. "Why are you eating alone?" he said. Then, "Woah, hold up. Are you cutting your pizza with a fork and knife? Aren't you from New York?"

"It's not real pizza," I said. I held up my glass of water. "The water, remember?"

He laughed. "Look. Your secret is safe with me. Now come on, man. Sit with us. There's plenty of room." I glanced over and acted surprised.

I found an open spot next to Hunter Reed (lucky me) and squeezed myself in. He was eating a salad and reading from an old, earmarked von Goethe book called *Italian Journey*. He was wearing the same hunter-green sweater vest he had worn during the potluck and on the first day of class. I wondered if his real name was actually Hunter. Milena was in the seat next to him, eating from a plate of steamed vegetables, one group of vegetables at a time—the broccoli then the carrots then the peas.

"How's it going?" I asked Hunter, putting my tray down, thinking, while I was feeling good, that I'd try to smooth things over with him. "Reading von Goethe, I see. At least you're consistent."

He laughed, but not in a friendly way. "I'm writing a dissertation," he said. "Dissertating. You of all people should know the focus it takes."

I sighed theatrically. "Don't remind me," I said. "Still fixing a few things here and there. So glad to be almost done."

He put the book down and we met eyes. I hadn't noticed before that his eyes were green, too. "Hey. You're in A1 35, right?"

"Yeah. Thirty-five," I said. "Why?"

"That's what I thought," he said. "I'm the room next to yours."

"Lucky you."

"Yeah, lucky me. Your class this morning was so loud that the floor in my room was shaking. One of my students thought we were having an earthquake."

"I don't know what to tell you," I said. "That's how I roll. In Roll." He didn't laugh. It wasn't one of my better jokes. "I don't believe in a quiet classroom. My students aren't just gonna sit around and write in silence. Not under my watch."

"This is how we do things here," he said.

I heaved a sigh.

"What were they doing anyway?" Ozu asked me. He was sitting directly across from me, wearing his signature Indiana Jones hat. He had been grading a pile of "pre-assessments," ferociously circling the student's grade on top.

With the straw, I twirled the ice in my glass. Now that Ozu had joined the conversation, I had to take a different approach. I'm sure many of the other instructors didn't yet know what to make of me. I had to be slick and cool, but I didn't want to come off as aggressive. "It was just an icebreaker," I explained. "Silent interviews."

"*Silent* interviews," Hunter repeated, eyes wide.

Jane giggled from the other end of the table. Everyone else grew quiet.

"Speaking of icebreakers, what did you all do this year?" Pants asked, maybe to come to my rescue. "I'm always open to new methods."

Ozu perked up. "One word: Bingo. I printed off bingo cards with a different milestone in each square, and obviously the goal was to find people in the room who reached said milestone. I even included one or two squares that only applied to yours truly, so they had to find and talk to me, too. Because what can I say? I like being included." He sank into a big belly laugh.

"Which two do you include for yourself?" Jane asked.

"I'm curious, too," Milena said.

"Dug for fossils in the outback. Can recite twelve digits of Pi."

"Wait. They can't recite twelve digits of Pi?" Pants said, blowing out heavily through his mouth. "I'd wager that most of them can go well beyond *twelve* digits. At least I hope so."

"Not this year," Ozu said.

"Sad," Bimby said.

"Remember that time a student recited, what, eighty-two digits of Pi for the talent show?" Jane said, perking up.

"And the one who did it backwards." Pants said.

"Remember that student who memorized the full ceremonial name of the capital of Thailand?" Ozu asked.

"Yes," Pants yelled. "That was awesome."

"I made their seating chart a logic problem this year," Bimby said. He was sitting on Pants's left. His T-shirt, another seemingly constant look, said "Idaho" today.

"Oh, that's fun," Ozu said.

"I think they liked it. Also," Bimby added, turning to Jane. "I have my first quote of the year, if you want to start that annual quote doc soon." He cleared his throat. He recited a joke a student told him about *The Lord of the Rings* and popcorn that I didn't understand, though everyone else did. Ozu belly-laughed again. A few others followed. I felt a hand at my shoulder. Natalie Grey.

"I have one," Pants said. "We were doing basic algorithms and one of mine yelled, "Dude, this is not a satellite of entangled hair barrettes. This is basic HTML. Command. Prompt." He practically screamed it, his voice thick like mud. Ozu nearly choked on his apple.

Natalie tapped my shoulder. "Hey, quick question," she said. "For my capstone, I'm writing a paper about teaching philosophies, and I need to interview a few educators. Are you interested in participating?"

"Hey, Natalie," I said, putting my fork down, turning my head to block out the noise and make sure I was hearing her right. "Come again?"

"Can I interview you for my capstone?"

The thought of being interviewed formally about my almost-PhD made me uneasy. "So we're not looking at wide distribution or anything?"

"Depends how good your answers are. We can do it at my place. Brandon wanted to have you over again. He felt bad about crashing so early."

"Oh, no. I didn't mind," I said, suddenly sensing an opportunity. "Actually, what about my place? It'll take some of the pressure off."

"Intimidated by an interview, Josh?"

"Should I be?"

"Maybe just a little," she said. "How's Friday? Your place."

"It's a date."

She walked to a small table where a tray was waiting for her.
I thought about joining her but before I could make my move,
Meg Lemming with dark bags beneath her eyes put a clipboard
and tray down in the spot across from her, let out a soft whistle,
and started venting.

★

We were required to have one hour of hall duty each day. My
spot was at a desk just outside my classroom. All I had to do was
make sure students didn't leave the building during class, that those
who opted to spend their study hall in my classroom were working
quietly, and that someone who shouldn't be in the building didn't
force their way in, not that me alone at a wooden desk would
be any match for someone breaking into the building. What hall
duty really meant was time to check eBay or Sega Saturn forums
or Reddit to browse retro game reviews. Something that baffled
me during these duties (besides how hard it suddenly was to come
across good deals) was how well it seemed teachers like Hunter
Reed connected with the students. My hour was right after lunch,
and so I'd set up shop early enough to see his small group, shoul-
ders-linked, migrate to his classroom for the next period. Hunter
would be there in the doorway with his arms folded, finishing up
a dessert, chatting with the students with enviable ease. It's like
they were *drawn* to his arrogance. Soon, I noticed it everywhere.
He was surrounded by these kids like he had been surrounded
by teachers at the faculty meeting. He'd crack jokes that resulted
in almost synchronized laughter—toilet jokes, theory jokes, jokes
that relied on the dumb ignorance of a live studio audience. Pants,
too, had at least one kid who seemed to shadow him everywhere
he went. As I'd lock up my classroom at the end of the day, I'd
see Pants and a student or two emerge from the computer lab
carrying wooden supplies and wheeling carts of textbooks. As the
days passed, I found that my own students would sometimes wave

to me beyond the sacred walls of the classroom, but most stayed glued to their smartphones or chatted only with friends.

On Wednesday, as I was ready to head home, I saw a kid from my first class sitting cross-legged on the grass of the quad. He was reading from a mass market paperback with yellowing pages.

I veered his direction and stood over him. He wore mesh gym shorts. He had a pair of twin moles on his neck and a birthmark on his cheek. A Harry Potter tattoo, his partner had said when introducing him after silent interviews. I leaned down to see the title of the book he was reading. *White Fire*. I remembered when I was drawn to reading like that. I was aloof, too. I used to leave books behind at restaurants and on trains. They were my escape long before video games were my escape.

"Heya, Tyler," I said. I remembered now that he was from Wisconsin, near Lake Superior. He was one of my smallest students, which made him look a year or two younger than he actually was.

He shielded his eyes and looked up. "Hello, almost Dr. J," he said.

"*White Fire*? Is that sci-fi?"

"Fantasy."

"Cool. You read that stuff often?" He looked confused. I wasn't really sure what I was asking either.

"I try to read a book a week," he said.

"That's cool," I said. "Really impressive."

"Yeah."

"Have you ever tried writing?"

"Here and there, I guess," he said, squinting.

I told him about a writing prompt one of my college instructors had used about inciting an intergalactic war and how I set my response at a hockey game.

He closed the book on his finger and glanced up at a nearby tree. I looked off in the distance and watched a few students playing Frisbee, trying to see if I recognized any more of mine. Beyond the metal statue of a hawk in flight, Pomm and Timmer and Meg

Lemming came into view, heading this way. At the very least, they'd see me here and take mental notes. That Joshua Schulman, look at how he's trying.

★

On Thursday, fueled by some high-quality nighttime gaming and nervous yet delightful anticipation about my impending "interview" with Natalie Grey, I loosened up a bit and told my three classes more about myself and tried to find out more about them. I asked what kind of music they were into (some claimed pop country like Luke Bryan and Dierks Bentley. Others claimed indie bands like Twenty-One Pilots and Wavves) and what their hobbies of choice were. The first few answers all had to do with their phones. Snapchat. Instagram. TikTok. Other apps that sounded alike but were apparently different. They were things I didn't know much about, being a generation too late. One of them suggested I cash in my millennial card. "Don't judge a book by its cover," I joked. Still, others mentioned things like Model UN or origami or football or basketball.

"Any gamers here?" I asked. They had probably expected me to say "readers."

There were a few skeptical nods.

"What do you play?"

They said mostly PS4 and Xbox One.

"Anyone play retro stuff?" I asked.

"Like *Halo*?" one of them asked. "PS2? They just remastered *Devil May Cry*."

"Not *quite*," I said, rubbing my chin. "The physicality of it all is what makes it special. Blowing into the cartridges to get them to run. Full-color instruction manuals. Fold-out maps in strategy guides. Eighty-nine character passwords. That kind of thing. Don't worry—we'll get there. There's something you still don't know about me: I love a good gaming conversation. Surprising, huh?"

I had been asked to work out of two Academy-assigned texts: *The Language of Literature* and *The Field Guide to Writing*. The first book was impressively boring but guided by a YouTube documentary I had favorited, and the fact that none of the kids pursued me after my plea to talk games, I realized that I could show them I was serious by spending a bit of time breaking down the infamous console wars rhetorically. That is, Sega Genesis vs. Super Nintendo. Sonic vs. Mario. Move over, Mr. Reed. Who wouldn't love a teacher who taught a lesson about video games? It sure as hell beat silent writing.

So, on that last Friday, I wrapped up a quick reflection on MLK's "Letter from Birmingham Jail" and flipped emphatically through the extra-large textbook. "Anyone else think this book is boring?" I asked. I was faced with blank stares. "I'm serious," I said. There were a few shy nods. Others sat up, sensing that something interesting was about to happen. I pushed it aside, gently, thinking that students might appreciate this moment of offhanded defiance. Somehow, though, it slid with force off the desk and hit the floor with a thud. "Oops," I said amid a few giggles, bending down to pick it up. "Ready to talk about the sixteen-bit wars then?"

More blank stares.

"Is that a yes? A no? Come on, guys. Talk to me here."

"The what wars?" someone finally asked.

I feigned shock. "What happened to all my gamers? I told you I wanted to talk games."

Then, I powered up the projector and started playing YouTube videos of commercials such as "Genesis Does What Nintendon't," and walked the class through a detailed spec list for both systems. The thing about the matchup, of course, was that the Super Nintendo had better specs than the Sega Genesis, which isn't surprising because it was released two years later. But there was a single category in which the Genesis had the edge: processor speed. So, what did Sega do with this info? They invented the term "blast processing" and used it in all their commercials to make the case that the Sega Genesis was the "cooler" console (the '90s was an era of 'tude, I explained, thinking of my brother at Toys "R" Us, clutching that *Sonic CD* box.). In one such commercial, the two systems are lined up next to each other while a voiceover says, "The Sega Genesis has **blast processing**. The Super Nintendo doesn't. So what is *blast processing*?" Next, we see a dizzying montage of "fast" Genesis games like *Sonic the Hedgehog* and *Ecco the Dolphin* alongside "fast cars." Then the commercial asks, "And, uh, what happens when you don't have *blast processing*?" It cuts to a beat-up white van sputtering exhaust with an old Philips TV taped to the trunk playing *Super Mario Kart* on the Super Nintendo.

The talk went on as such and, I thought, was really building up steam until we were interrupted by a bell. I looked at the clock and then at my watch. It was thirty minutes early.

"Nine forty-two," one of them said, pointing at the loudspeaker. "Pink Gorilla."

"Pink-what?"

Then the commanding voice of Dr. Kirkland filled the room. There was some reverb at first which caused the students to scream and clutch their ears. "Oops. Sorry. Sorry about that," he said, clearing his throat. "Students, staff, *welcome*. Whether this is your tenth year or your first, welcome to our Fairbury world, our Fairbury life. It is with Fairbury fortune that we meet here, as many thousands before us have. And with such history on our side, I would like to officially welcome you to Pink Gorilla 1.1 on this lovely First Friday of the academic year. Temperature: Eighty-four degrees. Sunny. The hills are most certainly alive with the sound of...*fruit*."

The sound was coming from the quad, too. I walked over and shut the window. I looked to my students for guidance.

"What's Pink Gorilla?"

"First Friday of the month," they said. "Nine forty-two."

"Why nine forty-two?"

Before they could explain, the announcement continued. "Dr. Kirkland here, henceforth known as Captain Kirk, proven leader

of this well-oiled vessel. A few announcements to help make the
academic year a good, productive one. As is Pink Gorilla tradition, our first monthly talent show will be happening tomorrow
afternoon in the Ware Student Room in the Rec. Please sign up
with Residential Staff in the South Barracks before 4 p.m. today if
you're interested in showcasing your talents. Because of anticipated
rain, the first dance, also on Saturday, with the Rosa Academy will
be moved from the quad to the big gym. As usual, student positions will be announced by The Fountainhead at the afterdance.
This is not to be missed. Rainmakers be ready. Finally, remember
that we gather here, first and foremost…to learn, so I wish you all
an invigorating, challenging, and rewarding academic year. Maybe
you've heard already, but for the third consecutive year, 100%
of our outgoing Fairbury Faithful have been placed at four-year
colleges and universities. A majority of them with scholarships and
fellowships and many to the school of their choice. This is really
exceptional. Fourteen students enrolled at Ivies, which is a new
record. And our inaugural class is one of the strongest yet. We're
really glad to have you all here. Finally, you may notice a few new
faces around the halls. Be sure to wave to them and say hi. These
are people you'll want to know. First is Stephanie Bell, one of the
new nurses. She's joining us from just over the rickety bridge in
Blue River. Next are new members of the dining staff, John and
Marcy. Both are committed to keeping your growing bodies fed
with locally sourced meats, dairy, and veggies. Please do them a
favor and remember to clean up after yourself when in the dining
hall. We've already had a report or two of students leaving trash
at their tables. Also, don't use your fingers. This isn't the Middle
Ages. Utensils exist, folks. If these behaviors continue, certain
privileges, such as the dining alcove, may be revoked. Last, but
certainly not least, is our new English Instructor Joshua Schulman,
who joins us all the way from New York City. Joshua is just about
finished with his PhD in linguistics from the City University of
New York. Studying Yiddish. Interested in all sorts of Jewish

literature. Games, too, I hear. Soon, we'll have another doctor in our midst. I've been hearing that he goes by *Almost* Doctor J. The J is for Joshua, I presume. Be sure to pick his brain about anything and everything. Don't let him get off easy. Show him what we're made of. Until next month, cadets. Stay safe and learn well. This is Captain Kirk, signing out."

"He didn't mention the Witness Protection Program," a student said.

"You didn't tell us you were Jewish," another said.

"You didn't catch it the first time?" a third said. "*Yiddish?*"

"The nose?" said a fourth.

"But no hat," said a fifth.

"Not all Jews wear hats, stupid," the fourth added. "I have a friend back home who's Jewish."

"Your hair is kinda light," another said.

"It's like he can *see* you now," said the third. "Like he knows you're teaching us about video games."

"That's ridiculous," I said. "It's rhetoric anyway. Not video games."

A few giggled, unconvinced.

"Anyway," I said. "Now you tell me: why is that announcement at nine forty-two? And why is it called Pink Gorilla?"

"Forty-two is the meaning of life," someone said. "Remember. Also, nine. September."

"I don't get it."

"From *The Hitchhiker's Guide to the Galaxy*. The meaning of life: forty-two."

"So why is it called Pink Gorilla?"

They shrugged.

"No one knows? I don't believe that. Not a single one of you? It isn't in the Fairbury Bible?"

"Not everything needs to be explained," they said.

"But when there is meaning it shouldn't be withheld."

"You withheld our language on Tuesday."

"But that was to prove a point. Is there a point to this or is it all just a game?"

"You haven't seen anything yet," they said.

★

After the last of my classes for the week, I sat at my desk and started typing and erasing text messages to Natalie. The plan, as I had known it, was to meet at six, just in time for me to order us a pizza pie from the town's only pizza place. When that was done, I loaded eBay from my phone. I had been closely monitoring the status of two games in particular, but wasn't quite ready to pull the trigger on either. The first was an import copy of *3 Wonders* (a Capcom arcade game released only on the Sega Saturn as part of the coveted *Arcade Gears* series). The seller wanted $150 for it, which was more than I was willing to pay. There wasn't a Best Offer button, but I had sent him a private message a few days earlier asking if he'd accept a lower price. This was a tactic that often worked for me. The most recent listing with a US Seller, I told him, sold for just over $100. He still hadn't responded, so I checked the listing to see if there were any updates and sent him another message. "I'm a serious buyer," I wrote. "I'm willing to pay asap, but I won't go above 120. Let me know." The second was an auction for *Earthworm Jim: Special Edition* on the Sega CD. I had the game (picked it up from a Sega CD lot in Hackensack alongside *Shining Force CD* and *Lunar*), so I wasn't interested in bidding on it. But, to my surprise, the current bid was almost two hundred dollars more than its current value. Every time I looked, the price rose. I didn't often ruminate on the price of games I already had in the collection, but sometimes I liked to think about how much they were all worth. These games were becoming rare, and unless the bubble suddenly burst, they added up to a small fortune.

I clicked around other listings waiting for a response from the first seller. If I didn't hear from him by the time I walked home,

I decided, I'd spend my money elsewhere. There were plenty of other holes in the collection that needed to be filled. And, after a long but productive first week, this was a vice I was happy to feed.

The door was open, so I didn't see Captain Kirk until he was behind me, leaning down to look at my phone.

"So?" he said, hand on my shoulder. "Almost Dr. J. Now that it's over, how was the first week?"

I put away my phone. "Oh. Ahoy, Captain. Didn't see you walk in."

"I'm trained in the art of stealth."

Clutching his walkie-talkie in one hand, he struck a ninja pose, his hands perpendicular and his knees bent. He was fishing for a laugh, so I threw him one.

"Nah, too much trouble," he said, delighted. "Not to be trusted." He hiked his slacks and turned to examine the board, where I still had my notes on rhetoric from the previous day alongside my manic Nintendo vs. Sega scribbles. He read aloud. "Purpose, Audience, Genre. The Rhetorical Triangle. A trilateral relationship."

I slid over with an eraser. "Kairos, elements of setting." I pointed out. "You know, speaks to the *timeliness* of an argument. An ad featuring NSYNC would be more effective in 2002 than in 2018, for example. A triangle within that triangle."

I erased what I could.

He smoothed his red beard. "So where does the Sega and Nintendo stuff fit in?"

"The what?"

"The console wars. The sixteen-bit battle."

"Oh, right." I cleared my throat. It was sore and dry from teaching all week. "Kairos," I said, pointing again. "Rhetoric. Marketing."

Smiling, he blinked slowly. "An awareness of audience."

"Right. Exactly. They—Sega, I mean—really appealed to the zeitgeist of the '90s. What with blast processing and all. A made-up term. A neologism, if you will."

"No, I mean you, Josh. Talk about appealing to your audience. I bet they loved it." He gestured at the empty desks. He raised his red eyebrows far above his glasses, which were sliding low on his nose.

"It went pretty well," I said. "At least I hope it did."

"This looks like it says 'Koala,'" he said, gesturing to the fourteenth instance of 'Kairos' on the board. "Might want to work on your handwriting."

He stepped closer to me. I fixed the collar on my shirt. It was moist with sweat. He smiled again. His teeth were sharp and straight. His gaze narrowed until his eyes turned dark and his cheeks sunk.

"Josh, I didn't realize about your wife," he said.

"Pardon?"

He sighed gently and closed the door.

I looked down at the floor. I let in a deep breath. Natalie.

"It's okay," he said, leaning closer. He put a hand on my shoulder. When I looked up at it, he took it away. "I don't usually talk about it, but I lost my wife, too."

"Oh?"

"She taught here for twelve years. Thanksgiving '11. She was visiting her folks in Washington and was T-boned by a semi coming out of the airport."

"That's awful," I said.

"I'll never get over it," he said.

"Me neither," I said.

He sighed. "I miss her embrace most of all," he said. "But you know what, you find ways to cope. I'm sure you understand."

"I do," I said.

We stood there in silence. "Josh, are you sure there isn't anything I can do to make your transition here easier?"

"Nothing I can think of," I said. "You've done plenty. Really."

"Are you sure? I mean it. Anything."

"Anything?" I couldn't believe Natalie would violate my confidence like that. I felt hurt, betrayed. But what about the fact that it had all been a lie?

"Anything," Kirkland said, as if he could hear me.

"Like a...framed reproduction of Picasso's *Guernica*?" I joked, my head spinning.

He laughed so hard he needed to hike his pants up again. "I'll see what I can do."

★

Natalie rang the doorbell five after six. I had spent the two hours after school shifting between tidying up and trying to figure out if I'd confront her about what Kirkland had said.

She was carrying an Elizabeth II of Austria tote. She wore jeans and a white linen blouse. The lenses of her red-rimmed glasses were smudged, as if intentionally disguising her eyes. I noticed that something else about her face looked different, like she had been out in the sun. Then I realized she was wearing a touch of makeup. Some eyeshadow and blush.

"So, this is the place," I said, welcoming her in. "There's a good view of corn from the other room."

She dropped her bag onto the couch. "I know. I've been here before."

"You have?"

"Dude, this place has been Fairbury-owned for years. I helped the last guy move in."

"What happened to him?"

"He left. Roll wasn't for him."

"Something bad?"

"Depends who you ask. It's kinda depressing, actually. Sorry I brought it up." She went into the kitchen.

"I've got pizza coming in a few," I said.

"Good. Because I'm hungry." She opened the fridge. The gold bangle slid down her wrist. "I thought you said you cook."

"I do," I said.

She pointed into the fridge. "I see cereal and milk."

"So?"

"Walk me through a usual week," she said.

"What do you mean?"

"What's on the menu?"

"Oh, just a few things here and there. Depends on the mood. Pasta. Eggs."

"What was the last meal you made?"

"Penne alla Vodka."

"I don't believe you."

"Well, it's true." Actually, it wasn't. The last meal I had made was a salami sandwich with cheese.

"Show me a picture of it."

"Why would I have a picture of it?"

"Because you seem like the kind of guy who takes pictures of his food."

"That's not true." Actually, it was.

She walked over to the sink and ran her glasses under the water, drying them off with a flick of the wrist. "Sure. So, what in this place isn't a work-in-progress?"

"That's a good question," I said.

Eventually, she wandered back into the hallway and stopped in front of the game room. I had the door closed tight. I stepped in front of her.

"Work-in-progress," I said. "Bedroom's down that way. Bathroom's next to that."

"But why is this door closed? The bedroom door isn't."

I blushed. "No reason."

"Can I see it then?"

"Maybe later," I said.

"So that's a no? Okay. I guess we'll just get right down to business. Fair enough because I have a ton of questions prepared."

I wasn't sure yet if I could trust Natalie. After all, she had told Kirkland about my undead wife. Was I supposed to just pretend that didn't happen? But I also didn't want to get "down to business."

The interview lasted about thirty minutes. She asked the typical questions about pedagogy and practice. Nothing groundbreaking. I probably talked more than I should have, as usual. When we were done, Natalie mentioned that the finished product—which she'd share with me if I wanted her to see it—would be part of her PhD application.

"So you're applying after all?" I asked.

"I figured, why not? You're only here once. What it means is we'll probably have a lot to talk about in the coming months."

"It takes a lot out of you," I said.

"So does teaching," she said.

"Good point."

"But gives a lot back too."

What I wanted to say was, don't do it. It's no good. A PhD won't help you like you think it will. You think it will improve your life and make you respectable, but it won't. It won't change anything. Except for the time wasted.

Instead I just smiled a big smile and said, "See that. You've got it. I don't know what it is, but you've got it."

We got to talking a little bit about PhD-related things, questions that I answered honestly. She asked about my application process, how long it took to hear back, what the competition was like in classes, the workload, general tips, etc. She also asked about my life in New York. She had always wanted to go—but who didn't want to go to New York, she joked—mostly to see the usual attractions: Times Square, Broadway, and the Brooklyn Bridge. Yet she also wanted to see the Guggenheim and check out the Garment District. I had never been to the Garment District, so I talked a bit about Jewish delis.

"Seriously, look at this pastrami," I said, showing her a picture from my phone.

"Pictures of food," she said. "See."

"Eh. One meal."

"Do you have any pictures of your wife?" she asked.

"I'd rather not," I said.

Things were going pretty well, but I couldn't help thinking that the only reason she wanted to build a relationship with me was because of these experiences I had that she didn't, so she could occasionally interview me about them, because, you know, I was like an exotic animal in a zoo. The Bronx Zoo, obviously.

No, I wasn't planning on bringing her into the game room. That's what I had decided. But then, when the interview was done and when we had talked at length about PhD applications, Natalie pulled out her phone to say that she should leave soon. It was starting to get dark. Suddenly, the thought of being alone in this place was too much for me to bear. So, I figured, I had two options to buy me a little more time with her: ask her then and there about my exchange with Captain Kirk or bring her into the game room.

I waited until she finished her drink. A local beer I had picked up from the grocery store. I took the bottle and walked it to the sink. In the living room, I leaned against the doorframe and pointed towards the hallway. "Before you go, did you want to peek behind door number three?"

"Now you're speaking my language," she said.

I took her around the corner and down the hallway. I could hear my neighbors whereas usually they were quiet. I thought out loud. "Okay. Anything you should know beforehand?"

"Stop stalling," she said.

I counted to three and opened the door. "Ta-da."

Natalie leaned in. "Books?" she said.

"Not quite."

She walked forward, taking it all in. When she realized what she was seeing, she let out a shriek. Then she giggled. "Seriously? Are you serious?"

I exhaled. "Do you hate it?"

She walked to the Saturn shelf, pulling a game or two from its stand. "This must have cost a fortune."

I shrugged. "I search for good deals. You'd be surprised what people don't know they have."

"*I'm still settling in,*" she mocked. "Pardon the mess." I laughed. Mostly out of relief. She was flipping through some of the old magazines now. *Nintendo Power. Electronic Gaming Monthly.* I led her back to the Saturn shelf.

"This sub-collection is almost complete," I said. "Sega Saturn. Hugely underrated system. Just missing one or two titles. A game called *Battlesport* is the one that I'm really holding out for. It's eluded me like the Rosetta Stone. It's a futuristic arena-based sport thing. Ultra-rare."

"*Battlesport,*" she repeated. "How long did it take you to find all this?"

"Only about a year. A little more. There are two types of collectors. Some are slow. They pick things up here and there. Others, like me, are pretty fast. I just kind of went all in. What helps is that I had a bunch of these as a kid. Grabbed them from my parents' house."

"All while getting a PhD?"

"Everyone needs a hobby," I said. "It's sure better than drugs."

"Oh my God. Do you know what I just thought of? Maybe you have it. For Nintendo. *Space Station Silicon Valley?*"

"The N64?"

"Yeah," she said. "I think so. With the little dogs?"

"How do you know about that game?" I asked, walking over to my N64 bin, the one Heli helped me organize. I flipped through the cartridges and pulled it out. "That's a pretty obscure little gem."

She rolled it around her fingers. "So many memories, man. I used to play this with my brother. Saturday nights."

"Wait. How old are you exactly?"

"Rude," she said. "Thirty-five."

"Nostalgia is a dangerous beast," I said.

"No kidding."

"I've been thinking of writing an article about it, actually."

"Seriously? Like how?"

We talked and talked. Finally, I stopped myself mid-sentence and motioned to the TV where my consoles were set up and ready. The controllers on the floor in front of them, waiting to be held. "Do you wanna play?"

★

The dance filled the Rec Center with a feverish pulse. I got there at ten after nine, after an hour of course prep and two hours of gaming, and headed straight for the edge of the track where Pants, Jane, Hunter Reed, Milena, Ozu, and a few others were standing in a half-circle. I had the sudden impulse to leave before anyone noticed me, but again it was Pants, the tallest of the group, who poked his head up and waved at me to join them. This time, I squeezed between him and Jane. Spirits were high. Maybe because it was Saturday and we had all survived our first week. Ozu leaned over and shook my hand. "Good to see you here, *Almost* Dr. J," he said, tipping his hat. "And Shalom."

"Oh, right. Pink Gorilla," I said.

"Where there's no happening, there's no forgetting," he said.

"Is that Neruda?"

He pointed to the sky. "No. Oblivion."

I looked at Jane and shrugged, thinking that maybe we could share a moment for the first time. She turned away.

Apparently, I was the only one who didn't get the memo to dress casually. All but a few of the students had traded in their traditional school uniforms for button-ups and slacks, but also polos and shorts; while the girls from Rosa Academy, who seemed infinitely older than our students, wore dresses and makeup. Rosa Academy, I learned later, was a therapy school thirty minutes from Chicago. They had their own staff circle, pushed against the far bleachers, mostly in jeans and plaid. It all felt straight out of a sitcom. Ozu was wearing a shirt with a dinosaur on it that said "In Training" over cargo shorts. Pants had on an off-white T-shirt to match his knee-high white socks. Bimby wore a red shirt that said

"Massachusetts." Only Hunter Reed had long pants—skinny black jeans with his usual sweater vest and flannel.

"Joshua Schulman," Pants said, folding his arms. "How familiar are you with the work of John Hughes? We're talking *Sixteen Candles*?"

"A bit," I said.

"You seem like a guy who can appreciate the trials and tribulations of adolescent archetypes. We think this kid here is dancing like Geek in *Candles*, just waiting to sprain his leg. See the resemblance?"

"He definitely splits open his pants," Jane said. "It's right after he does a split. Classic '80s trope."

"Classic whenever trope," I said.

It was one of my students. He was hopping and sliding like no one was watching, though eight of us were.

"He's really killing it out there," Bimby said. "Oh, wait. Here comes a friend."

"And it's over," Pants said, frowning. "Might as well talk about Greek mythology. Or just *Wonder Woman*. Or *Apocalypse Now*, which is essentially a journey through the subversive underworld."

"Down the River Styx," Jane chimed in, segueing into an impromptu lecture. I hated how frequently these conversations made me feel invisible, which is almost as bad as stupid. Like I had to prove myself. Like I couldn't be me. I had to be Almost-PhD me.

"Goethe, of course, revived Greek drama and attempted to mimic Greek poetry," Hunter said.

"That's right," I said. "Can confirm."

It's hard to describe one of these dances except to say that it's hard to describe. The residential staff and Dorm Chairs (the oldest students on campus who were officially called Old Men but sometimes referred to as Death Doors) were the ones running the show, frantically organizing and executing the change of guard when a new song got underway. A DJ booth—consisting of one of the two RDs (Residence Director) and a laptop—sat just beneath the basketball hoop. Other Dorm Chairs were stationed in the middle of dance circles or guarding the two back doors or taking slow laps around the dance floor motivating students to join in. Captain Kirk was working the room, shuffling back and forth between different stations, occasionally stopping to chat with a student or staff member. He looked over my way once or twice and waved. I waved back, but so did Hunter Reed.

I couldn't figure out why the instructors were there at all since all we did for the first hour was stand and watch the kids dance, which only got stranger when I saw a kid thrusting a fist-full of glowsticks. But no one else seemed bothered by it. Even when an entire group, literally a few feet from us, started twerking, the instructors and Dorm Chairs stood idle. Bimby joined in before they were done, with Pants and the others clapping and cheering him on.

There was no sign of Natalie and I wasn't in the mood for any of this. Plus, the gym was hot and sticky with hormones and I was sweating uncontrollably in my nice shirt. I was getting ready for a quiet exit when the Trilogy of Life started with the flustery drumbeat at the beginning of "It's the End of the World as We Know it."

Pants grabbed my shoulder. "Here we go. This is why we're here."

These were the nine "immortal" songs, which, in groups of three, collectively formed the Trilogy of Life. They had to be played in order at the end of every dance. This was especially important at the first dance, Pants explained, because the first years in attendance, like myself, hadn't been introduced to them yet.

What's another few songs? I thought, shaking my arms to air myself out. *I'm here already, aren't I?*

The next song began with a roaring drum and half the gym lifted their fists into the air and shook their chests like Tarzan. A loud cheer erupted. A disco light—which I hadn't noticed before—turned green.

"'James Brown is Dead,'" Pants said, turning to me. "Keep an eye on the Caloian Rainmakers. They're gonna twirl like pixie dust."

"Wow," I said. Soon, the circle of instructors lined up, crossed their arms, and watched the students carefully, no longer interested in simple conversation with each other. A few of the older white men on staff showed up during the next song, Lionel Ritchie's "Easy." It was a fine playlist but I couldn't figure out how the songs were connected. Glen Gill had forced his way in between Hunter Reed and Milena and was filming with his cell phone, shuffling his feet as if dancing to klezmer.

For the next song, "In Your Eyes" by Peter Gabriel, everyone started twirling green and blue and pink glow sticks until all one could see were green and blue and pink strobes of light circling the gym floor like icy contrails. This was a song I had played for Liz Hoffman after we broke up, and the first notes took me back to her dingy suite at SUNY Albany, when it felt like the world around me had stopped, turned to concrete.

A student shaking the glowsticks with both hands like maracas walked right up to Hunter. He was a small dude, though a field of wild hair sprouted above his lip. Some of the students were like that—on the awkward cusp of adulthood. "Mr. Reed, what is your pseudonym?" the kid said.

"It'll disrupt society," Hunter said, fidgeting with his own moustache.

"Do you think The Fisher Kingdom Snowblood Outsiders can function as a monarchy?" the kid said.

"Only time will tell." Hunter spoke matter-of-factly and turned to Milena. "We made our own utopia, but unfortunately it's turning dystopic already. Gave the monarchs too much power. A million years of history and we learned nothing. Shame."

"Long live the king!" the kid shouted, thrusting his glowstick into the air. "Snowblood! Boogers!"

During "Dude Looks Like a Lady," the kids did the Cotton-Eyed Joe. During "Down Under," they swam like jellyfish on the gym floor.

It wasn't until "Time Warp" that Natalie Grey appeared at the end of our faculty line, along with Brandon.

I straightened the bottom of my shirt and walked over.

"You're late," I said. Brandon stepped forward to shake my hand. "We've been here for more than an hour. Dancing our hearts out." I wiped my hand on my pants. "Sorry, I'm sweaty."

"No, no, no," Natalie said. "*This* is the only part you need to see. Everything else is borderline insufferable. Didn't they tell you?"

"No," I said. "But neither did you."

Brandon put a hand on my shoulder. It was something a lot of people seemed to do around here. "Maybe you're just talking to the wrong folks," he said. "By the way, I hear you've got quite the game collection at home."

"It's just a hobby," I said.

He smiled at Natalie, more with his cheeks than his teeth.

"I should have you over some time," I said. "Do *you* game?"

He frowned. "I don't. Busy with other things. Work, deadlines, the wife. But I'd love to come see it, sure."

"You're welcome anytime," I said.

He just nodded and patted my back twice. Then he pulled his hand away and wrapped it around Natalie.

We turned and watched the rest of the Time Warp. A large yell lifted from the crowd. In the middle of the dance floor, Dr. Kirkland waved the Royal Fox Society staff. The students chanted drunkenly. "Cap-tain Kirk. Cap-tain Kirk. Cap-tain Kirk." Natalie and Brandon seemed to think this was completely normal. Just a regular Saturday night in Roll.

I slid over to Natalie. "I guess you weren't kidding then when you said that this is what people do here on the weekends."

"It's the wildest club in town," she said.

"The only club," Brandon corrected. He faced me again. "Have you ever seen anything like it, Josh?"

"Mardi Gras?" I said.

Natalie laughed.

"What?"

"You've been to Mardi Gras?"

"Okay, maybe not. But you know, I've seen it. In pictures."

Brandon grunted, lowering his eyes. "Some of these songs haven't changed in two dozen years."

I did the math. "But aren't some of them newer than that? "In Your Eyes" is what? 1986? 1987?"

Brandon sighed. "And how many years ago was that?"

"Oh. Yeah. I guess so."

"Anyway, it's tradition," Brandon said.

"Sorry. Sometimes I forget that you were a student here." What I wanted to say was, *Doesn't that mean you've never left?*

He crossed his arms and straightened his back until he was taller than me. "More than a student, man."

"What do you mean?"

He looked off as if the memories were flashing before his eyes. "He was Captain Kirk before Captain Kirk," Natalie explained.

"Wait. Really?" I said.

"I cannot tell a lie," he said.

"So what did they call you?"

"Captain Brandon."

When the song ended, during the slight hush, I pulled Natalie aside.

"I hope this doesn't come out wrong, but can you not tell anyone about my ex-wife? I mean, I get why you told Kirkland the other day. I do. And I know I didn't say not to. I just, I don't like to talk about it, and I don't want other people knowing. It's a sensitive subject. I realize I should have said something about it yesterday while you were over, but I didn't want to ruin the fun. Same with the games. I'm just really private about that kind of stuff. It's who I am. It's my way of coping."

She put a palm on her chest. She wore a green "Denver" T-shirt over yoga pants. I looked at her ring, snug on her left hand. Brandon was watching us. "I didn't tell anyone about your wife," she said. "Why would I do that?"

"You didn't?"

"I *did* tell Brandon about the games, yeah—but only because he wanted to know why I came home so late. I said we were gaming. *Space Station Silicon Valley.* It was fun. I still feel a little hungover from it. But he's my husband. He doesn't care. He's a collector, too. You saw all those cameras. Those photos he displays on every wall."

Did I ever. "But back to my wife," I said. "Captain Kirk."

"Kirk?" she said, surprised. Her voice softened. "Oh. He told you?"

"Told me what?"

"That he lost his wife, too."

I pointed to my chest. "But also that he was sorry because I lost mine."

She shrugged. "He hired you, didn't he? On his own really. But you can do that kind of thing when you're head of the show."

"What do you mean?"

"Said we were in a pinch and that you'd bring more diversity, but I was like...he's *white*, so..."

I didn't say anything. The students, all at once, jumped. "Hah," they screamed.

"I'm confused."

"The point is," she said. "If anyone here knows about your wife, it's probably him. He has your file."

"But I never said anything about it," I said. "To anyone."

"Maybe he looked it up. Did a background check and saw you were married. You can find anything you want these days. But you can trust me, Josh. I promise. You can trust me, okay? My word is good as gold. I'm serious."

"Okay. It's just—"

"A small town," she said. "Oh, I know. Welcome to Roll. People talk. People here love to talk. Number two hobby behind walking. You get used to it pretty quick. That's what my father taught me."

I didn't know what to think. I wanted to believe her, and maybe I did. In her eyes I saw something genuine. A pain when she talked about her father, like a ghost passing through me. But then how else would Kirkland have known? It was a lie. A lie shared only with one.

There was only one way to test it. Tell another one and see where it ended up. But was this the time and place?

"I read your article, by the way," she said.

"Oh?"

"I liked it," she said. "I really did."

"I'm glad," I said. "Yeah, good." I thought of saying that it had been nominated for an award, that it was retweeted by Mayor De Blasio, that it was adapted into an off-Broadway show, but none of it felt right. I didn't want this to get in between one of the only friendships I had here. It wasn't worth it.

The first notes of "Bohemian Rhapsody" started, the most important song of all I had been told, and the entire gym screamed and formed two circles. The line of instructors forged their way into the middle circle, along with a couple of students. Natalie took my hand and brought me in. "Come on," she said. She sounded so much like Heloise it made me want to cry. Sure enough, we ended up next to Captain Kirk. Arms were wrapped around shoulders. His hand gripped mine tight. One by one, groups of students ran into the center of the circle. Some were wearing capes. Others, shiny crowns. During the a capella bit, Kirk took his hand from my shoulder and led me into center of the circle, where he, Pants, and Ozu skipped around me as people cheered. The song ended and the music stopped. A big balloon with the air let out. A drowning chorus of headaches and whispers when the dance was over.

Pants asked for my impression of it all. Captain Kirk in his sweaty stupor gave me a half-hug before walking off. Natalie was swept away by a group of students. The Rosa Academy Staff took a headcount of their kids. The Dorm Chairs tried to get everyone else under control, leading them in lines out the door. I watched, then, not paying attention to anything in particular, when in those lines of marching students, I saw something I recognized.

Something I couldn't believe. The Eggplant Wizard. The big purple cape. A long stick with eggplant intact.

"What?" I said.

"Huh?" Pants said.

"Do you see that?" I said, pointing.

Pants looked. "See what?" he said.

Then, the lights went out. Everyone screamed. They came on again and the Wizard was gone.

"That eggplant?" I said. "Just there. Before the lights went out."

Pants scratched his face. "Eggplant? What are you getting at?"

"I gotta go," I said to Pants and ran off. He called out something about the afterdance, but I was already outside, following the crowd of hundreds of students where they were being deposited into their dorms, group by group. I couldn't find him again, so I sat on the grass in the quad and shook it off as the third of my Midwestern illusions. Dead deer knocking on my car window. Brandon Grey ripping open my box of games. Now, the Eggplant Wizard, staff and all. My imagination was really getting the best of me. With it, I had even created a new me.

When I got home, I played *Kid Icarus* on the regular Nintendo for the first time. It took me two hours and a few passwords before I encountered the Eggplant Wizard in all his glorious pixels. He was small on the screen, as most 8-bit villains were. All you had to do was touch him and you were turned into an eggplant, cursed. The only antidote was an expensive potion, often miles and miles away.

Beware the eggplant curse, the game said. Beware the eggplant curse.

You know what happens next? I spiraled. YouTube. Wikipedia. Google. In bed, I replayed those final minutes at the dance over and over. I made a list of things it could have been and of things it couldn't. If I did this long enough, I could trick myself into thinking I saw a whale or a unicorn. It was a dangerous skill, I suppose. Consequences of a damaged brain. But what I couldn't shake, believe it or not, were those final notes of "Bohemian Rhapsody," Freddie

Mercury bringing it home, and a student population of more than 600 singing along with him. I looked for a connection. I tried to draw conclusions. I missed my dead wife, so I decided to call her.

I should have known that she wouldn't answer me.

★

On Monday, I sat with my binder of lessons on my desk and tried getting into the right headspace for the second week. On Saturday, when I couldn't get through to Heloise, I talked instead to Thiago. He said that besides the eggplant-thing (which he shrugged off rather quickly as my "usual mind games"), it sounded like I had hit the jackpot, but that, you know, I should be careful getting too close to a married woman. "It's not like that," I said. "We're just friends." Then I told him about how I told people I was an almost PhD, which was the real reason I had called, but he just said, "Well, technically you are."

"Good point," I said.

I elaborated further about the extent of it, in case I wasn't being clear, and he said "no, you didn't."

Ashamed, I said, "You're right. I'm kidding. The kids want me to get a PhD, though."

"Who knows," he said. "Maybe you will."

"Maybe," I said. "I don't know. Do I really want to put myself through that hell again?"

"No," he said. "You don't. Trust me."

The students marched in as usual and we began. It had been cloudy and on the brink of rain since the dance. The Caloian Rain-makers were outside early that morning doing their rain dance, but it didn't work.

Midway through taking attendance and reading an article aloud, I noticed something on the back wall, just below the old pull-down wall maps and above one of the two hand crank pencil sharpeners. It wasn't like me to miss a sign so obvious.

I walked over to it and everyone turned.

"Dude," the students said.

"Sweet."

"*Guernica*. Nice."

Yes, it was a reproduction of *Guernica*. Hanging off the back wall of my classroom. A Post-it note on the top corner was signed CK.

"What's it say?" a student asked.

I read it aloud. "Hope you enjoyed the dance."

"Captain Kirk is the best," someone said.

"Long live Captain K."

"CK for President!"

"But why *Guernica*?"

"I've never heard of it."

"*Guernica*," another said, looking at his phone. "Says here it was vandalized by an anti-war activist once and used in a German war campaign."

"It looks like a four-year-old could have painted it, to be honest."

The student reading from his phone held it up. "Hey! That's exactly what the Nazis said. It was part of a degenerate art exhibit in Berlin."

Amidst boos and hisses, I took it down and leaned it against the window, just beneath the box fan. It was cheap and light. It felt like I could snap it in half without even trying. I thought about it. The louder the students booed, the more I wanted to.

VI. SPLAT

TWO WEEKS PASSED AND like that it was the end of September. With it, one could feel the last sputter of summer as it faded bleakly into cool prairie days and long, windy nights. But also, an email to faculty and staff from Captain Kirk on behalf of the "Splat Kings," dated September 27th. The Big One, the subject line read. The name of the game, the memo explained, was Splat. Splat had been publicly announced at a faculty meeting three days earlier, during which Thomas Rivers—of the Science wing, as old as two Magnavox Odysseys (his body arched over a stick whenever he walked, without which he'd probably be the tallest instructor on staff in addition to the oldest)—beseeched us to reconsider the "exigence" for such an abrupt re-trial of Splat. "It seems to me," Rivers said, struggling to stand, his deep, throaty voice making him sound like a well-trained political candidate. "That we would have learned our lesson the first time. He who doesn't learn from history is doomed to repeat it. Is that not what they say?" A few of the others rolled their eyes, high on spirit, as I imagined the students themselves would have done had they been there. It was easy to forget amidst the day-to-day of lesson-planning and grading that this was a youth-driven enterprise and that the loudest voices of all were the kids themselves. "What lesson is that?" one of them said. Though this one was forty years old and went by the name Jane. She sat two rows behind Rivers with a

Frisbee in her lap, arms folded over her chest. She leaned back and her chair let out a piercing squeak. Rivers remained on his hobbled feet. "That a few students got carried away?" she laughed. "God forbid. Ban football then. Ban tennis. Why do we let young boys swing baseball bats? Why do we let them access the internet? More people get hurt walking down the stairs than they do playing Splat."

"I'm talking psychologically," Rivers quipped. "Training an entire school of boys in the art of stalking. What could go wrong? In a day of heightened emotional tension, you're playing with fire and you know it."

"Do I, though?" Jane said. There were a few muffled laughs. "Sorry that I like seeing the kids have fun."

Kirk, with the leisurely help of Meg Lemming and one of the other unit chairs, eventually got things under control. I pretended to take notes, as I did during most of these meetings, when really, I was checking eBay and browsing the occasional photo of New York. "We're obviously aware of the current social and political landscape and I assure you that we're going to be extra careful this time," he said. "If anything is amiss—anything at all—we'll pull the plug. Immediately. This conversation isn't over, okay?"

The lore and relative ambiguity of *what happened* "the first time" followed me for a few hours, until I ended up alone in the windowless Academic 1 copy room with Natalie Grey, one of the only people I had a speaking relationship with who was there *the year Splat died*. I hadn't realized until I saw her running a mountain of photocopies that Captain Brandon might have been head of school then. I leaned against the wall, waiting for her to finish, and decided to ask about what she knew. She told me it involved a group of parents, but couldn't say more than that, nor did she want to. "But what got them worked up in the first place?" I asked, as she stapled her photocopies, a nonfiction piece on bullying complete with color cartoons. A group of students were playing Frisbee by the window. I was pretty sure I heard Jane out there with them. I lowered my voice. "Or did they just not like the game?"

"You'd think they would fix the staple function on this thing," she said. She straightened her papers on the face of the wooden desk. I slid over to give her more space.

Natalie admitted that she was all for bringing back Splat. I told her that it didn't matter to me either way. "I'm just wondering if there was something bigger there because people seem pretty affected by it," I said.

She stiffened. She held the pile of papers to her chest. The last page appeared to have been copied upside-down. "The kids almost killed someone," she said. "But they didn't. It was an accident. They took things too far. We can't talk about this. We're not allowed to." With that, she was gone.

I didn't realize until I got back to my classroom that my own copies had faded ink and were unusable.

In the official email sent on behalf of the "Splat Kings," Kirk referenced a few of the concerns that emerged from the meeting. "To reiterate," he wrote, "I personally made the decision to reexplore the Splat debate this summer after a long and thorough process aided by a few alumni/donors that we just wrapped up recently. The student response is still very strong, and we'll have a few new policies in effect. We agree that now is the time to reclaim this immutable part of our school's storied tradition."

The second part of the email included a bit of that history, taken from the Fairbury Bible. Apparently the game rules appeared mysteriously on a sheet of paper under the bleachers of the old football stadium some thirty years ago, after a triple-overtime win against a prestigious prep school in Illinois that, along with most of the other private academies in that "belt," no longer exists (coded in that message was that we outlasted all of them). They were written in silver and gold and were only visible in the school's darkroom. Back then, the school had one of the largest photography studios in the Midwest. Now, that studio was part of the library. Students in the old Society of Secret Engineers (the same group of neo-anarchists that was subsequently disbanded some

twenty years later before reemerging under Pants's guidance as
a physics club) acquired the artifact as Fairbury was transition-
ing from a military academy (rumors circulated that the game was
actually part of a military training program). At lunch, Jane and
Pants talked about the failed campaign a few years earlier to bring
back Splat after it had been banned (#FreeSplat, #SpitforSplat,
#DontSpitonSplat). That was Pants' first year at the school. "I, for
one, have heard enough Splat stories to last me two lifetimes," he
said. "One day, a small plane flew out of the clouds and did circles
over Admin bearing a banner with the FreeSplat hashtag. I guess
one of the rich students from Chicago convinced his parents to get
it for his birthday or something. There were students who told me
they literally *came here* to play Splat. Enrollment dropped for a year
or two after that, didn't it?" Jane nodded. Ozu, who compiled a
document each year detailing the often inconsequential changes
in the staff handbook, said that numbers dropped as much as 5%,
though upper admin played it off as a result of the recession. The
game fell into obscurity soon thereafter, yet another tradition lost.

The rules themselves were simple once you got a handle on
them. Creepy. But sometimes the best games are—creepy, I mean,
though simple too. It's obvious after a quick scan why one might
see the game as politically and socially dangerous. Basically, partic-
ipants were given a bendy straw, which they had to carry with one
hand at all times and spaces outside of safe zones (the bathrooms,
the dorm rooms, and the classroom during class) and a "target,"
which in the students' case was another student and in the teachers'
case another teacher. The objective was to stalk your target, ideally
without them noticing you (in case there was any ambiguity about
what the term stalking meant) in order to catch him/her without
their straw displayed. Then, assuming you were quick enough,
you hit them with your own straw and yelled "Splat." The person
Splatted was out and their stalker earned a point and inherited their
victim's target. All the while, of course, you had to outlast your
own stalker. The last one standing or the person with the most

points won. There were a number of guidelines about the straw itself, such as the fact that it could not, under any circumstance, be carried in your mouth or used in place of a real straw. It was unclear to me if such rules had been carried over from previous iterations of the game or if they were part of Kirk's new "safer Splat" initiative.

At the top of the bracket were two Splat Kings (usually the Kings were students, but this year they were Kirk and someone from the alumni board, unnamed to prevent bias) who would preside over the game and the two Splat crowns, whatever that meant. They'd be the ones to settle issues and keep track of the scoreboard. Their decisions would be final. For the Splat Best, the email warned, the game could last well over a month.

The more I read about it, the more I thought it sounded like more work than it was worth, but I'd play, because Natalie was into it. And also because I had nothing better to do. Anyway, I was still making a name for myself. Maybe I'd even win, which would surely impress her. The kids, too.

The day after we got the email, Pomm and Timmer showed up to our usual lunch table with an air glider that had been signed with a Magic Marker by a dozen students. "Shield the UFO," one of them wrote. "P.S. 2000x," wrote another. It was for an activity for the basics of aerodynamics. Pomm and Timmer often carried around interesting things like that. No wonder her students loved her. "This lives in my classroom now," she said. "Made it on Sunday."

Pants reached out to touch it. "Gnarly."

"You know what we should do now, right?" Ozu said, watching as Pants stroked the wings with his thick, hairy hands. He held the glider to his face.

"A homing device?" Pants said.

Ozu lifted the glider and examined its undercarriage. "You guys ever see *Our Man Flint*? Ready for some diabolical spy training?"

"More MacGyver than Flint," Jane said. "No offense, Pomm. It's still pretty sick."

"You mean Timmer," Pants corrected.

"This took a little of both," Pomm and Timmer said. "Might have been too many cooks in the kitchen."

"But can we all for a moment imagine straws raining down from the sky from this thing?" Pants said. "How freaking epic would that be?"

Everyone laughed, even if no one knew what the hell was going on. At least I was getting used to it.

Just like that, the campus was awash with people stirred up about Splat. Everywhere you went students were talking about it, some already carrying their straws, forming "illegal" alliances with other players. A big Splat leader's board was posted in the quad just outside the Rec. In blue chalk students wrote on the now leaf-filled walkway leading up to the dining hall: "3 Days until Splat." "2 Days until Splat." "Sign up NOW." "LAST Call for Splat." "#Shh." "#TheFirstRuleofSplatIs…"

One of the office secretaries watched over the official sign-up sheet. Someone thought it would be a good idea that she stepped away from processing paychecks for a week and oversaw Splat sign ups instead. I signed up on the last day of the signup window, for no other reason than I was lazy (also, I was busy grading my first official batch of student papers—a rhetorical analysis of an adver-tisement—which took longer than usual because I was also busy participating in gaming discussions on Reddit in which I learned how to mod a few of my consoles to play emulators and ROMs so as not to risk wearing down some of my most valuable discs and cartridges. Even with the utmost focus, I found that I could only make it through a paper or two before going back to playing/downloading/searching). I took especially close note of Tyler's assignment, the student of mine from Wisconsin who had been reading on the quad. He wrote about a popular Tide commercial and how it appealed to feelings of emptiness and grief. It was a great paper with a strong thesis, but the way he defined emptiness as "inside us at all times of day" made me worry about him.

"Tyler, can I talk to you for a minute?" I said, after handing back the paper that morning. "You're not in trouble. Don't worry."

The other students ducked out of the room and Tyler went back to the desk. I walked over to join him.

"Did you sign up for Splat yet?" I asked.

"Not yet," he said.

"Are you going to?"

"I haven't decided," he said.

He was holding the paper with both hands. I gestured to it. "I really liked this," I said. "It's really well written. Sorry if some of my notes are a little hard to read. The harder I try to work on my handwriting, the worse it gets. Some paradox, huh? I can't win."

"Thanks," he said, chuckling. "And that's okay. My handwriting isn't so great either."

I wasn't sure what I wanted to ask. Maybe I was looking for something in his face that would tell me what I needed to ask. This was all relatively new ground for me.

"How's class going so far?" I finally said.

"I like it," he said.

"What else are you taking?"

He thought about it, shuffling the paper from both hands to one so he could count on his fingers. "French. History. Poli Sci."

"I just want you to know that I'm here if you ever want to chat, okay? About anything."

He seemed confused, but then he didn't. "Okay," he said.

A few days later, he selected my room as the site of his study hall, which really made me feel good.

On the Splat sign-up table, there was a pen and two blue balloons on a silver string. When I walked over, the office secretary produced a marble notebook that said STAFF and turned to a clean page. I signed my name under Stephanie Bell, a school nurse who was also new that year.

I was sent off with a wave, a toothbrush, and yet another copy of the official rule sheet. Among the rules, one was highlighted: Do not

speak of or about Splat to anyone who isn't playing Splat, including family. Social media posts about Splat will get you banned from
Splat indefinitely. There is no guarantee that Splat will be played
until Splat ends as ending Splat is at the discretion of the Splat Kings.

I held up the toothbrush. "I thought we were using straws?"

"We are."

"So? Is this like a red herring?"

"It's a toothbrush," she said. "For your teeth."

"Right."

It was a Monty Python skit without the punchline.

Later that day, after the last of my classes had been sent off and
my classroom locked, I ran into Captain Kirk. He waved me over
as soon as I stepped outside. It was unseasonably cold and the trees
around campus were already turning brown. I was eager to make
it home and pick up my current gaming playlist where I had left it,
but I pretended that I was happy to see him.

"Just the man I was looking for," he said. He wore a red
FILA hat, which matched his beard, and a down jacket. He wasn't
wearing his glasses.

From the pocket of his coat, he produced a bendy straw.
"Look who finally signed up for Splat. Started thinking I'd have to
do it for you."

I reached for the straw because I thought it was mine.

He shook his head and cradled it against his chest. "Yours is
coming," he said. "Patience."

Realizing I might not get out of this quickly, I lowered my
backpack to my feet and crossed my arms across my chest to keep
myself warm. The weather app on my phone had said high seventies
today, so I didn't bother to bring a jacket. It wasn't anywhere close
to seventy. A group of students congregated beneath Academic 1's
exterior staircase in some late-afternoon ritual, their heads down,
silent. They didn't seem to mind the weather. It was they who
Kirk had been out here watching.

"What took you so long to sign up?" Kirk said.

I shrugged stupidly. "Thirty seconds to midnight. Keeps the heart in good health. At least that's what my mom used to say."

"Not my heart," he said, mock fainting. He motioned to the door. "Remember, we brought the game back for you, Josh."

He held his chest out and rolled his shoulders. I checked his face for signs of a lie. "Pardon?"

He put a hand on my shoulder. "God, you're gullible. I'm kidding, bud."

"I know," I said. "I was playing along. Come on. I'm not dumb."

"I know you're not," he said. "PhD, right? Say, in more serious news: what's the story with..." I leaned forward because I thought he was waiting for me to finish the sentence. He scanned the students who were huddled beneath the staircase. Then he produced a piece of paper from his jacket and handed it over. It read: TYLER J. "Your student," he continued softly. "Confidentiality. The counseling office left a note on my desk. You were the one who wrote the Rorschach Report, right? It's just so hard to make out your handwriting sometimes. It's very scribbly. Very poor handwriting."

"Still working on it," I said. The Rorschach Report was something we were instructed to complete if we noticed something amiss. Tyler hadn't just worried me with his rhetorical analysis. Earlier in the week, he had also been teased and called "gay." It was during lunch. He was standing in front of Pants and me on the food line, sliding a few slices of the disgusting hot-dog pizza onto his plate when two other kids popped out of thin air and said, "Wieners on top of cheese. The perfect choice for Prissy Tyler. Hey, Tony, you know who the real wiener is here, right? Prissy Tyler. I hear his wiener is tiny, too."

"That's called being *gay*," the other one said, walking off. "I hope he enjoys mouthing those things." Pants heard it, too. I told him Tyler was one of mine, and he said I needed to write a Rorschach Report or he would.

"How has he been in class?" Kirk asked.

"Fine. His writing is great," I said. "Just graded his first paper. To be candid, it was one of the best I read. Good thesis. Clean prose. Well supported. The subject worried me a bit, though."

"Oh?"

I explained. Kirkland cleared his throat.

"What about socially?"

"He's a little distant," I said. "But that's just his personality, I think. He's quiet. He's a reader."

"So, withdrawn?"

"You can say that, yeah."

He scratched his red beard and straightened his hat. "It isn't only your class," he said. "So, don't worry. You aren't doing anything wrong. From the sound of things, he's been withdrawn in most of his classes. And recreationally, too. I should check to see if he signed up for Splat."

"I asked him that today. He said he wasn't sure yet."

"I'll have to check then," Kirkland said.

"You think maybe it's best if he didn't?"

"Absolutely not. I think not signing up would only make him feel more isolated. Better to be involved than excluded."

"I guess."

He blew out his pale cheeks and shuffled his feet. The walkie-talkie on his waist made a piercing sound. "I'm afraid he might just be homesick. Laura or Mark from counseling will speak with him later this week. My gut is telling me there's something there that neither of us can see. Locked away deep within him." He said it almost theatrically, exuberantly. His voice lowered again. "I don't know if you know this, but he's one of our equal opportunity students. Between you and me, Almost Dr. J, we've had issues with students like that before. It might just be that this isn't the right place for him. I don't know."

"He enjoys class," I said. "And he's doing well. He's a voracious reader. Probably reads more than I do. Always asking for things to read. He's genuine. A good kid. A really refreshing presence." I took a breath to steady myself. "Sorry, Captain K, but we are talking about the victim here, aren't we? Shouldn't we be doing what we can to defend him and not chalk it up to a bad fit?"

He looked hard at me. "I think you're missing my point, Josh. Look, I like him, too. But there are things that go on behind the scenes that you aren't privy to, given your position. Trust the process, okay?" He paused as two students came running by, one chasing the other. "Excuse me," Kirk yelled. "Walk, please." He faced me again. His beard caught some sunlight and I remembered how cold I was standing there. "Okay?"

"Okay," I said.

"Anyway, to a lighter subject, since we're talking about "reading" and all, you do know that I'm still waiting to read your dissertation chapters. Please tell me you aren't afraid of these old, critical hands."

"No, no," I said. "I'm not."

"Sure hope not," he said, laughing. "I take it that it's coming along? That you're back on schedule now that you've had a chance to settle in?"

"Little by little," I said.

"Is something slowing you down?"

I shrugged and motioned with my head toward my classroom: room 35. Framed reproduction of *Guernica* occupying space on the back wall, an extra face, a mirror. The computer terminal. The smart board. The rusty hand-crank pencil sharpener and the creaky wooden door. The four rows of desks, recently arranged in a square, all of which were loaded with notebooks and stray papers. At home, a list of games on my queue. Truth was, I did attempt, once or twice, to get back into some academic work, fueled by an image of Natalie Grey asking about my PhD. But no sooner did I try than did I find myself back in the game room. Or on Reddit. Or looking up family photos. Which family? Both of them. Mom, Dad, Jared, and me. Heloise, Me, and Marvin the cat. Her parents, even. Her Mom's lovely French accent. "Teaching. Grading. Everything."

"It gets easier," he said. I was a little annoyed that he could say that to me about my fake PhD but not to a student like Tyler.

"It's fine," I said. "I'm just easily distracted. That's the New Yorker in me."

It was really getting cold now. I still had to walk the mile home. I visualized the beanbag chair waiting for me in the game room. It made all the work worth it. Kirkland looked down at me, smiling in a way that made me doubt myself, that made me feel small.

"I should probably get a move on before it gets any colder," I said. I blew out a puff of air and watched my breath wade into the sky. I pointed to the flap of his jacket. "Came unprepared. Still have to walk."

"You never did get that bike, did you?"

"Not yet," I said.

He shook his head. Then he held up the straw again so that it caught the same sun ray that his beard had. "Just a heads up, and you ought to know this: people will be bringing their A-game this year. There's a lot to prove. Lot on the line. Now go home and practice, okay? Warm up."

"What choice do I have?" I said.

I started walking off. He started too but stopped. I wanted to keep going, to pretend I hadn't noticed him waiting there, but virtue tricked me into looking over my shoulder and we met eyes again. He seemed to do this often—just when you thought things were over, he pulled you back in. He smiled bravely, scratching behind his ear.

"Say, silly me. I almost forgot to ask amidst all the commotion, but you're in touch with people in New York, right?"

Was I? That was a complicated question. He stepped closer. I looked down at my shoes and picked at the little bristles of hair on my face. I hadn't shaved in about a week. Soon, Kirkland and I would look like twins.

"Why do you ask?"

"We have an endowed speaker series here, maybe you've heard about it already? We set it up almost like TED Talks. You think you'd be able to invite one of your colleagues to come speak? We haven't had a Humanities person for a few years now. It would be interesting to hear from an author."

"Like on Skype?"

He laughed it off. "No, no, they come out here, body and all. I know. Hard to imagine these days, huh? But listen, we'll cover everything. I understand that some New Yorkers might need added incentive to show up at a boarding school in a humble little town like Roll. Hey, I've been there. Syracuse, remember?" He winked. "So just tell us what they need. After you talk to them, of course. Figured your influence would really help."

"Yeah," I said.

"It was Meg Lemming's idea to ask you," he explained. "I can get you a list of potential targets if you want. That way you have a sense of what we're looking for."

I nodded. "That would be helpful."

"Great. I'll email it. We're looking at mid- to late October. No, that's not right. November, but we're flexible. We can even do early Spring if that's better for your people. The series has a big profile around here. We had John Lafountaine come last year. From the Cold Spring Harbor Laboratory. And Doris Mann from NASA the year before that. Gets a ton of local coverage. Brings back a lot of alumni, too. Usually there are two talks—one for the public and one for the students. Smaller workshops are possible, too. Like I said, we're pretty flexible."

"I'll make some phone calls, but I can't guarantee anything," I said. "A lot of the people I know are busy this time of year. And you know New Yorkers. Not always easy to get them off that island."

"I'm available if they need to talk with me, okay? We'll stop at nothing."

I forced a laugh and gave him a thumbs up. He leaned forward and pretended to start a thumb war. Then he laughed, too, generously this time, and hit my upper back.

"You know what I've been thinking a lot about?" he said.

I shook my head no.

"That I like having you around. You've got a good spirit. You and me, we're more alike than you think."

Was he talking about his dead wife? I didn't know what to say to that. I suddenly felt a pit in the bottom of my gut.

"We'll be in touch," I said, making a phone with my hand. Then I wrapped my arms around my chest to show I was cold.

"Go on," he said, gesturing beyond the quad, beyond the school's tall metal gate, the Fairbury insignia frozen on top. "Get out of here." I walked off, slowly, so as not to seem rude.

I didn't look over my shoulders.

★

At home, instead of working through my gaming queue like I had planned, I paced the living room feeling sorry for myself, waiting for this email from Kirkland. Because if this experiment didn't work, then what?

All I wanted was peace of mind. Why was it so hard to be liked and happy at the same time? Wasn't there a place you could sweep petty lies? Scribble them in Yiddish, leave them for the pigeons in the park. *You look pale, Schulman.* And you look…invisible.

I was sick of swimming in my own head, so I put on a coat and started for town. When I first moved from Long Island to Brooklyn, I used to sit by Queensbridge Park, facing Roosevelt Island, and watch the boats in the river. I'd use a finger to trace the cantilevers of the 59th Street Bridge. I'd hum Simon & Garfunkel's "The 59th Street Bridge Song." I would try to find where, exactly, the tunnels buried deep in the bedrock were. I looked for signs on the surface of the water—like rift, imbalance, suspended sediment.

There, I'd say to myself, the egrets, the black-crowned heron, that must be the Midtown Tunnel. Then, I'd see it like it was all around me. A stone cylinder penetrating the water. A sewer. A warp pipe.

Heloise and I would spend nights wandering the foggy streets of Bensonhurst. Every trip was different. Sometimes we stopped for pizza. Other times we didn't stop at all.

In Roll, I ended up at the edge of downtown and ducked into the family-owned convenience store for some warmth. While there, I thumbed through a few of the magazines. Then I made my way to the Halloween candy.

"How's your night going?" the man behind the counter asked when I dropped a few candy bars on the table. Natalie had told me that her mother worked here just before she had gotten pregnant with her. The place, she said, hadn't changed. It was like a fly suspended in amber. I had been inside three times. This guy was working the counter each time.

"Just fine," I said.

"That's good," he said. "Grabbing some candy? I love these. That'll be four-oh-three. You need a sack?"

I got the "unofficial official" list from Kirkland via email later that night. He had put a lot of thought into it, even including some potential talk topics based on the research and scholarly interests of the people named ("Modernist Fairy Tales," "Transnational Periodicals," "Pop Culture Medievalism"). There were a few I had had good professional relationships with before everything went to shit.

Of the eleven names on Kirkland's list, the only one that I didn't immediately disregard after my thorough mental evaluation was the standoffish misanthrope Dr. R.R. Huffman, an aging new-critic and self-declared "world's leading scholar on Robert Penn Warren's *All the King's Men*." He didn't use computers and once drew a swastika on the board during a Teaching of Literature class, even taking a giant step back to admire his work, saying, "This. What is this silly, misunderstood symbol? Why does it get so much hate? How did it become so out of style?" Later, when erasing it, he said, "I always make sure to erase these nice and good so nobody sees them." It was entirely possible that he wouldn't recognize me at all, since I had a semester-long seminar with him and he didn't once refer to me by name. I imagined Dr. Huffman and Kirkland and Natalie Grey and Hunter Reed and Jane and Pants and me in the school's dining hall, passing around a bowl of mashed potatoes.

I called Thiago, but he didn't answer. While waiting for him to call back, I realized that I could invite him as the speaker. I'd obviously have to push his value as a PhD candidate and an up-and-coming scholar who was primed to make it big. And apologize to Kirkland for disregarding his list, but it seemed like a small price to pay given the consequences.

Thiago called me back an hour later. Just after eleven.

"Yo," he said. "I was getting sushi with Z. Reverse happy hour." Z was his forever girlfriend. It was short for Zadie. She was a first-grade teacher at PS 150 in Sunnyside, Queens.

I told him about the speaker series. I checked the windows to make sure no one was standing outside, listening. I took a big shot of air and lowered my voice to a whisper so my neighbors wouldn't hear me. "I told them I was still in the program," I said. "At CUNY. The PhD."

"Wait, hold up. You were serious about that?" His tone surprised me, like he found it more funny than reprehensible.

"I panicked. I don't know. Because I'm stupid. You know how I get."

"Shit. Dude. That's not smart."

"I know."

"This speaker thing is suspect, man. They want a speaker from New York to come to middle-of-nowhere Iowa? Sounds fishy. It feels like he might be testing you, checking you out."

My forehead was warm. "Well, look. You're right. That's why I called. He said it's a big deal, but I haven't heard about it from anyone else. But it's not like I've been here long enough to know every little thing they do here either. So maybe it really is a big thing? Who knows? It is on the school's page. But if he really knows I was lying then why would he keep me here, right? Why not just show me the door? It's easier. It's cleaner."

"Waiting for you to break? It's more fun that way. What else is going on in Iowa?" There was a pause while he spoke Spanish away from the phone. "Look," he continued. "This one is hard to read. Maybe they really don't care. You're not applying for tenure. You're not at an R1, some world-class university. It's just a boarding school. A PhD isn't a requirement or anything for the job, right? It was just a bad judgment call on your part. Dumb move. Maybe all he wants is for you to come clean. To get spooked a little. Or could be religious allegory."

I had warped to the game room now, looking at my Sega CD shelf with heavy eyes. There was a thrumming against the window which caused me to jump. It was raining again.

"I'm fucked," I said. "Just say it. I need to know, man."

His voice grew soft and remote. Cold even, as if I had managed to suck the life right out of him. The rain seemed to slow before picking up again. I checked to make sure the other window in the room was shut as far as it could go. "No one is suspicious, okay, man? Take a deep breath. You're fine."

I did. One. Two. "Right," I said. "They would have sent me home already. This Kirkland guy is weird and all but he's super genuine. Like really genuine. He even said he and I are alike. That he likes having me here." I remembered the *second* lie, and it made me feel sick again. It was all catching up with me. "What am I supposed to say if it comes up?"

"Say it stresses you out. They'll understand."

"I guess," I said. "Say, I'm gonna call in a favor, okay? If it really does come down to it, then you'll be my speaker. It'll look great on a CV. You can talk about anything. Demagoguery and Democracy. Pedagogy. Fiction. Edwidge Danticat. I don't care. Just make it relevant for teens, if you can. You know, keep it YA."

"Me? Talking YA? You know I don't do that. What about Jordan? He can do his fly fishing bit."

"Dude."

"I'll think about it, okay? Remember, I'm brown. I can't get away with this...*deception* as easy as you can. They'll hang me to a tree. You, they'll slap on the wrist. If *anything*. Serve you cold potatoes for a month. Ban you from the dessert bar. *Especially* if you show remorse."

"I know, I know."

We said our goodbyes and the call ended. I sat in my beanbag chair and counted to one hundred, struggling to hear myself over the erratic pounding of the rain.

I checked my phone. If I made it to bed right away, I'd only get about six hours of sleep. Much less than I typically needed on a school day. But I couldn't do it. There was too much thinking left. I could think about my father. My mother. Heloise. Kirkland. Natalie Grey. Hunter Reed. All of it, I realized, would only make things worse. Or, as I ultimately did—as I had been planning to do all along—I could stay right where I was and play games.

I loaded a Japanese bullet hell shooter and got to work.

★

On September 30th, I was grading papers in my classroom, still trying not to think about Kirkland's lecture list, when two students walked in, their shoulders linked. Neither of them were mine, but I recognized one of them—one of the few black kids in school— from Pants's afternoon class. Their eyes were hidden by plastic round sunglasses and their hair by blue beanies. One was holding a beige messenger bag, the other an envelope. Neither had their school lanyards.

I sat up. "Can I help you?"

They didn't answer. They shuffled over to the desk. I noticed an intentional smudge of blue paint on both of their chins, like war paint.

"What's with the outfit?" I asked.

The one on the right handed me the envelope without speaking. My name was on it, big and messy. Almost Dr. J. Then out of the messenger bag, the other produced a clipboard and pen. The envelope said: "certificate of receipt."

"What is this? Is this for Splat?"

I started opening the envelope, but they put up a hand to stop me.

"Your target," read the back of the envelope. "Your straw. Confidential. No one may see these contents but the Splat Kings. Sharing contents amounts to immediate disqualification."

"Captain Kirk?" I asked.

The framed reproduction of *Guernica* shimmered from the back wall. I signed the form and placed the envelope at the edge of my desk. I listened as they marched next door to Hunter Reed's room. "Awesome," I heard him say. "So ready. Let's do this."

I took out the stack of papers and unfolded them. I felt around for the bendy straw. It was small in my hands, almost slippery. Could I really carry this thing around all day? For what? Bragging rights? I started reading. Introductions. Rules. Safe spaces. Finally, I found a page that said only: "Your Target: Natalie Grey. English/ Language Arts." Great. Just what I needed. An excuse to "stalk" Natalie Grey. Did that mean I was her target, too?

"No," Pants said, when I asked him later. "For the umpteenth time, your target only has you as a target if you're the last man standing. Didn't you read the rules? Have you been out to lunch all week?" We were both at lunch, yes, which is exactly what I told him, laughing in the hopes that he would too.

He didn't. "I've been busy," I said, composing myself. "Doing a lot of grading."

"Ah. So the nature of the work finally catches up to you," he said. "You're no longer above us non-PhD prep school mortals."

"No, no. I still am," I joked. It was only he and I at the table. I wasn't usually there so early as I preferred to wait for the rush of kids to be done with the lunch line. One thing I liked about Pants

was that it was easy to joke with him. Another was that he was easy
to find as he was the kind of person who seemed to be everywhere,
at everything. It was good to know someone like that. Take lunch
for instance. If it was even remotely close to lunch hour, he'd
be there at the lunch table, working on a plate. Already he was
holding his straw even though the game technically didn't start
for another day. With the straw in his left hand, he used a knife
with the right to cut into a big chuck steak. He swapped the knife
for a fork and ripped off a big piece of the meat. It was red and
bloody, which almost made me vomit. "The key is to train your
active limb," he said, holding up the straw. Swallowing, he flipped
the straw into the air and caught it. He reached for the saltshaker
and shook it violently over the steak. "Now there's something
they neglect to mention. How easy it is for your wrists to lock-up,
because you never know when your stalker is near. Then, bam.
Splat. You're out."

I leaned back and watched a group of students hustle into the
cafeteria in small groups, some running straight for the ice cream
cones. Others to the tables. Hunter Reed appeared behind them.
A student was shadowing him, doing most of the talking. The
student ran off to grab a tray and Hunter walked over to us and
put his bag and books down to save his usual spot at the table, two
away from Pants. There were some white flakes on his moustache.
He said, "Now—we eat" and rubbed his hands together before
disappearing again.

"See, what I really need to do is remind myself that it's just
a game," I told Pants. "I don't know how thrilled I am to have
someone follow me around all day. It could turn me into a nervous
wreck real quick. Even worse because I might not know who it is."
I started working on my own lunch—turkey with mashed potatoes
and green beans, once piping hot, now cool—and realized, after I
had picked apart the turkey to see how it had been cooked, that it
was the most honest thing I had ever said to Pants.

"Yeah, that's kinda the point," Pants said. "But you get used to it."

"Exposure therapy," I said.

"Huh?"

"Oh, nothing."

He stuffed his mouth with meat then seemed to swallow it whole. "I, for one, don't mind being followed. It's part of the challenge. We use the transit method to discover exoplanets and we literally have a model for space-time. I think somewhere there exists a model for Splat. We just haven't cracked it yet. I don't know why. We aren't talking about Inkala's Sudoku here."

Jane put her stuff down next to Hunter's and disappeared just as he returned with a tray of food. I nodded and took a bite of my green beans.

"You two aren't talking about Splat, are you?" Hunter said.

Pants tensed. "Of course not," he said.

"But if we were?" I asked. "The game hasn't started yet. I could chat about Splat if I want to."

"Talking about Splat is a surefire way to get Splatted," Hunter said, getting his body settled onto the bench. "It's also against the rules."

Pants nodded in tacit agreement. I couldn't help but roll my eyes. "Thanks for clarifying."

Hunter lowered his gaze at me. "'There is nothing either good or bad, but thinking makes it so.'" Hamlet. It was as if he didn't think I knew the same texts he did.

I couldn't hold it in anymore. I slow-clapped. I tried recalling a line or two of something but could only think of a few songs. "'You don't need a weatherman to know which way the wind blows,'" I said. "Dylan."

Pants was uncomfortable and wasn't afraid to show it. But then Hunter scrunched his nose like he was about to sneeze, and I broke out laughing. I'm sure I looked like a psychopath sitting there but I didn't care. I was letting my feelings out, I guess. A green bean shot straight out of my mouth. Hunter watched it with disgust, which made me laugh even harder.

Jane sat down, confused, and Hunter turned to face me. I pointed at the green bean and said, "Hunter green."

"Am I supposed to feel threatened by your circle-time charade?" he said.

"Did you get that from your German buddy von Goethe? Just one step removed from the Nazis."

The table was suddenly silent. Maybe I took it too far.

Hunter crossed his legs and smiled. "Josh, why is there so much bitterness in your heart?"

"That's not true," I managed.

Jane was looking down at her food, eyebrows raised. I tried getting Pants's attention, but he wouldn't look at me.

Ozu dropped his stuff next to Pants. "You guys see they put out churros? Next to the pizza."

"Finally," Pants said, jumping from his seat.

★

I finished eating well before my second class began, in part to get the hell out of the dining hall and in part so I could carry two churros on a bed of napkins up to Natalie's classroom, room 213 of Academic 1. I didn't often go upstairs, mostly because the main staircase and elevator were glass-enclosed and outside the building, meaning they didn't get any air conditioning and were unbearably hot and stuffy no matter the weather outside. Natalie was always late to lunch. Sometimes she didn't show up at all.

I found her classroom door ajar and her sitting at her desk, the eyes beneath her red-rimmed glasses lit up from a computer screen. I knocked twice before pushing open the door and walking in. Yes, I thought. Fuck Hunter Reed and his high-brow presumptuousness. Maybe people like him were the real reason I had left academia. Maybe my depression did me a favor? Otherwise I might have spent the rest of my life surrounded by Hunter Reeds. Anyway, it didn't matter because at least this game of Splat would be a breeze. I knew my target's schedule as well as anyone could. Not yet day one but there we were. I imagined myself on the winner's podium, smiling down at Hunter Reed and his sweater vest.

"Any requests?" Kirk would ask. "Yes," I'd say. "The moustache. Bring it here." Then a group of students would drag Hunter forward and I'd pull at that thing like hell. Or maybe I'd call over Natalie, with a wave, a wink. "Some alone time, please," I'd say. "We have some games to play. Retro."

"Special delivery," I said. "Churros today. They're going fast. Get them while they're hot. Is it okay if I close the door?"

She turned away from the computer and smoothed out her skirt.

It was the first time I really got a good look at her classroom. I had passed by once or twice and had stood plenty of times in the doorway.

Bulletin boards with folders and notecards lined the walls facing the desks, which had been moved into a semicircle. On the top corner by the door was a daily schedule. 1:20: Free write. 1:30: Writing Analytically: The Road Map. Her desktop was a Mac whereas I had Windows. The room was lined with sketches that appeared to be drawn by her students. Four or five per student, in small clusters on the wall, some simple portraits, others in which they were skiing or lying in bed or floating on water. Some were on loose-leaf paper, the perforated edge still intact, others on large or small graph paper.

"Self-portraits," Natalie said. "Once a week I ask them to draw themselves. This new thing I'm trying. It's like a twentieth-century selfie."

"That's cool," I said.

"They seem to like it," she said. "I'm still figuring it out. I think eventually they'll create symbols that represent their values or beliefs. For now, it's just a teaching method. A form of expression to improve their self-awareness. We'll see how it plays out."

"They're quite good," I said. "I can't draw to save my life."

"But see, it's not about being good," she said. "It's just representation. Here, this one is mine."

·

She beckoned me with the wave of a finger—and smiled first at me, then at the churros. I walked them over and put them on the desk. "Oh. They are hot," she said.

"Maybe I should just bring my lunch up here from now on," I said.

She gestured to the table as if saying, "Go ahead."

From the drawer, she pulled out loose-leaf paper.

"Here I am," she said.

In the picture, Natalie was staring straight ahead, not smiling. Her pixie cut fell over her eyebrows, covering them. Her ears—lines like letters—each formed half a heart. Her eyes were big and brown. She wasn't wearing glasses.

"Wow. It's beautiful," I said.

"I don't see myself in glasses. We don't do this with mirrors."

And now I could see the power of the activity. It made me realize that I didn't see her like she saw herself. Which meant others didn't see me the way I saw myself. And how did I see myself? Broken. In pieces. Unworthy.

We looked at each other, blinking.

Suddenly, against my best judgement, I wanted to kiss her. I decided that I would do whatever it took to see that other side of Natalie and to show her that other side of me. The ambivalence I had been harboring for weeks on account of my conversation with Kirkland about Heloise and her being married to Brandon and rejecting my requests to go game hunting suddenly seemed like green bean casserole. *Hunter* green bean casserole. There was still something no one could take away from us, and it wasn't the dozens of conversations about PhDs and teaching we seemed to have each week. It wasn't even that she was the only one here who had been in my game room. That we had played games together. It was that we really, truly connected. In the way that you sometimes can't place, don't need to place. Maybe she felt it, too.

She was searching her desk for a fork.

"Oh. I brought one," I said, pulling one from my pocket. "They're clean. I promise."

She held out a hand and said, "Very good. Pass it over, please."

I did. Then I heaved a breath and leaned against the chalkboard.

She ate, and I scanned her desk for a bendy straw. Just a pile of folders, pens in a wooden cup, and a few textbooks. She dabbed her face after each bite.

"So—how often does the schedule change?" I asked, pointing to the board.

"As often as the days do," she said.

"Touché."

Her phone buzzed. She tilted it up then put it down.

"Grad school stuff?" I asked.

"Fuck. Yes. A few people didn't do their shit so now we have to post on the discussion board five days a week instead of three. It's obnoxiously redundant. Read an article, respond to it. Read an article, respond. You know the routine."

I sighed. "It's cool. I understand."

She used the edge of the fork to cut another piece of the churro. It was soft like sponge cake. "Did you ever take classes online?"

I shook my head. "No."

"Would you?"

"I don't know. I like the flexibility of it, but I think it would feel too impersonal for me. They offered to let me teach online once but I turned it down because it was prepopulated with a schedule and assignments, so I would have just felt like a glorified grader."

She sat up. I had the feeling, yet again, that whatever I was after was unobtainable. That this would never work because I had lied too many times, that none of it would be authentic.

"They definitely put crack in this," she said. "Someone should call the health board. It's dangerous. Want a bite?"

"I'm good," I said. "But thanks."

She danced the fork in front of me. "Are you sure? Can you really resist the temptation of warm churros?"

"Okay. One bite."

"So," I said, chewing. "What does the computer bot want you to write about this week?"

She patted her lips with the napkin again. "Um. The ACRL's Visual Literacy competency standards. Administrative jargon, mostly. Learning outcomes for curriculum needs. That kind of thing."

"Sounds enthralling."

"I'm having so much fun," she said. "Seriously."

"If you want even more fun you should take a class on Speech-Language Pathology."

"What. Like communication disorders?"

"Yeah. I mean, it's important work but when it gets theoretical it loses its...luster." I was talking about Hunter Reed.

Natalie didn't seem to notice. She asked if I had plans for the weekend.

"I don't think so. Why, what's up?"

"There's a hike at Cedar Ridges State Park I've been wanting to try. Thought I'd go on Saturday. Skip the dance this time. The second one isn't as important as the first. It's, like, a two-hour drive? Figured you'd might want to see the real Iowa before the weather gets bad."

"I don't know much about hiking."

"Can you walk?"

"Yeah."

"Then you're good. It's a short one. About ten miles or so."

"Ten miles is *short*?"

"It'll go fast," she said.

I thought about it for all of two seconds. "I'm in."

"Nice," she said. "Wear boots. It can get muddy."

"What if I don't have boots?"

"Buy them," she said.

We looked at each other for a moment. She pushed her glasses up the bridge of her nose. I folded my arms.

"Is it just you and me?" I asked.

"If that's okay."

"Yeah. I mean, of course. What about Brandon?"

"Forget Brandon," she said.

Yes, I thought. Forget Brandon. So much potential in those two words.

There was a knock at the door. It swung open and hit the wall with a crash.

"Ahoy, you two."

Captain Kirk. He was standing in the empty hallway, wearing a wool coat with two big buttons and front pockets from which he pulled an empty lunch bag. He crumbled it and shot it at the garbage can. He missed, but stayed beside the door with both arms raised, seeming to try and will the bag into the can.

"Use the force, Kirk," I said.

He snickered and went to put the bag in the trash. "Fancy seeing you up here, Josh."

"He brought me churros," Natalie said.

"Sneaking churros out of the dining hall," Kirk said. "I wish someone would risk detention like that for me."

"Guilty as charged."

"I'll write the Rorschach Report," Natalie joked.

Kirk stepped forward.

"Almost Dr. J, since you're here, thought you should know that I found a speaker for the series after all. An old buddy of mine in Ithaca. Lance Vespa. Didn't think it would work for him, but something opened up, like magic."

I felt sudden, immense relief. Once again, my fears had proven unfounded. He hadn't been on to me. It wasn't a test. "That's great," I said. "I just started making phone calls, but schedules are so tight this time of year."

"I might still have you give it an honest shot with your people next time," he said. "So keep those contacts fluid."

Kirk's walkie-talkie sprang to life. He stroked his beard. It seemed to be burning off a golden light.

"Well, I better run," I said. "Those kiddos will be here before you know it. Enjoy lunch, you two."

"Later, bud," Kirk said. He turned to Natalie. "Hey, did you tell him about the hike?"

I stopped.

"He's in," she said.

I looked at Kirkland then Natalie. "Oh, are you coming too?"

He snickered. "Me? No, no. But you—we're gonna make an honest man out of you. I told her about you on that hill."

I blushed. Kirk imitated me sliding down.

"I do have a few things to learn," I said.

"A few things?" he laughed.

I left the door open on my way out, but as I inched my way down the hall, I heard it slam shut.

★

It was only ten minutes into Splat when I realized that my own stalker was the philo-Semite Glen Gill. He was waiting outside my classroom the next morning holding his Splat straw low at his waist, nervously explaining that he had an interview with Philip Roth to show me. "I think he really appeals to Jewishness as a metaphor for humanity's suffering here," he said. "My wife was surprised by it. I believe it's pretty controversial. But let me see, let me find it." With the Splat straw shaking in one hand, he pulled a stack of papers from his backpack with the other. "It's in here," he said, handing it over, sniffing. His voice was faint and rusty and he kept making noises with his nose as if he had a cold. Sweat was dripping down his forehead and onto the collar of his white shirt. "I'm curious what you think of the two major points he poses when answering that last question. Personally, I was more shocked by the first half of his response and delighted by the second, but what do I know? I'm no Jew. Nor am I a writing instructor." I grabbed the stack of papers and sidestepped to the

hallway table, where my monitoring duties were performed—
straw included—so I could give it all a closer look. I had been
carrying the bendy straw for all of six minutes. Then, feeling Gill's
tenseness as he began his slow lunge forward, I stopped myself.

"Whoops. Almost let go of my bendy straw," I said.

He stepped back. "Oh. Did the game even start?"

"Today, yes."

He scratched the bald spot on his head and fixed his collar.
"It's okay to loosen up every now and then. It's just you and me
here. You don't want to let it control your life."

"Yeah, good point," I said.

I walked to the other end of the table and put the straw down.

"That's better," I said, cracking my knuckles. "Who really
wants to be bothered carrying that thing around all day?"

He leapt forward, his own straw clenched in an extended fist,
but—having already measured the space between us—I had no
trouble snatching my straw and jumping out of his reach. "Spla—"
he started to yell, thinking I was his dog's dinner.

"Ha. Nice try, Gill."

He straightened his pleated slacks. "It was *I* who was testing *you*,"
he said, sniffing again, He scrunched his nose as if he had smelled
something putrid. "Just a little day one practice. We all do it."

Being someone's target was easy enough. Gill was small, but
he wasn't smooth enough to disappear in a crowd. The worst
was lunch. Every time I stood, he stood, wrapping me into some
conversation about my Bar Mitzvah or kosher laws and pastrami.
Once in the hallway, when I was busy disciplining a student, Gill
squeezed my shoulder.

"Everything okay here, Mr. Schulman?"

"I've got it, Glen," I said. "Thanks." He stepped aside and
watched, smiling. I couldn't even go to the bathroom in peace.
Gill would take the urinal next to me, nodding at the wall. Bathrooms, of course, were safe zones, but it was yet another place
where Glen tried to wear me down.

"Nice circumcision," I heard him say once. "Your mohel did a fabulous job. Send him my kudos."

"Excuse me?" I said.

"Nothing," he said, walking off.

Routines changed. People seemed to appear in strange places. Pants was no longer a fixture in the cafeteria. He would linger by the stairs in Academic 1, stubbornly, trying to act casual by pulling me into conversations and then looking at anyone but me as we spoke.

"Earth to Pants," I finally told him. "He isn't here."

"Who?" he said.

"Your target. He took his class to lunch early."

"You don't know who my target is," he said.

"Poli Sci?"

"Well, then," Pants said, straightening his jeans.

As if peeing next to Glen Gill wasn't bad enough, twice, when exiting the bathroom, I was nearly tackled by Jane. Once, she smacked my shoulder with her straw and yelled *Splat*. "Oh. Sorry," she said. "Anyone else in there?"

"I don't know," I said.

"You don't know?"

"Sorry." I didn't feel like it was my job to rat out others. Except maybe Hunter Reed. Even Natalie, my own target, seemed to seek a balance between protection and prescience. Luckily for me, we ate together a few times that week, which wasn't something we had done before Splat. After the day was over, we'd sometimes meet in the hallway, chatting about anything and everything that didn't start with Spl and end with at. She never once let go of her straw, otherwise I really would have thought about going in for the kill. I don't think she suspected that I had landed her as my target. My plan was just to wait. I knew that at some point she'd get comfortable enough to put the straw down. And that was when I'd make my move. Of course, I had another move to think about too, which was really tripping me up. I knew it was wrong, that it could really get me trouble, but I also knew that wouldn't be enough to stop me.

The game progressed like this for the rest of the week. Once or twice a student got Splatted. He was upset, mad even, but that was that. There were occasional tears, like when a student en route to lunch realized he had left his straw in the classroom. It gave him two options: hide in the bathroom and skip lunch or get Splatted. I know this because I literally found two students in the span of a week hiding in the bathroom. For the most part, the student bracket was quieter than I expected it to be, save the addition of a few hundred straws around campus and a few creative ways of carrying them. One student even dramatically cut his straw down the middle in the hallway outside my classroom and yelled "suicide." "I was getting bored," he said, taking the Splat and slithering away. The staff seemed really on edge. I admit that I was starting to feel it, too. Sometimes, at home, or while teaching, I'd break out in my signature sweat when I realized I wasn't holding my straw. I'd hear Glen Gill sniffing behind me. It appeared in some of my dreams, where little bits of light would hold themselves in front of me like snowflakes. The mountains with the trails spiraling into the river. The current too strong to fight and the sun so bright that even looking at the grass caused a deep whiteness to overpower me. One night, it was Glen Gill in a yarmulke, standing at Coney Island, on the shore. Calling me not by my name, but by "Ivan." Waving to me. Blowing kisses. Saying, "Guess I won't be seeing you tomorrow, Ivan." Saying, "Don't forget to brush your teeth, Ivan." Then he was at the top of the Wonder Wheel, holding a pickle in each hand, biting into them so that sonic booms rolled through the water, taking me further and further away, until I wasn't on the shore, but in the water, where the lights from the boardwalk were dancing in the distance like thousands of cameras flashing at the same time, and where the water was so cold that it should have woken me up. But, of course, it didn't. Getting out of these dreams wasn't easy like that.

As Splats happened, one could feel the stakes rise. Then word spread that the winner of each bracket (student and staff) would receive a mystery prize and that the first "purge" (King Splats from Kirkland himself) would happen at any moment. By the eighth day of October, the word was this: Knock out your target or risk being eliminated yourself. The clock was ticking.

But that Natalie Grey, she wasn't budging.

★

We were paid monthly. It came to about a thousand dollars a week, which was almost all pocketed since my only living expenses were primarily food and electricity and the occasional rental car. With my first paycheck in early September, I paid off a chunk of my aging PayPal Credit debt and only spent moderately on new games. When the second check cleared, I took it straight to eBay. But alas, there on Friday evening in the back booth of Twin Oaks, eBay's infinite kingdom was desolate. A few items here and there were worthy of a closer look, even a bookmarking, a "watch" perhaps, but nothing was making me excited enough to pull the trigger.

I grabbed a refill of hot water for my tea and browsed a few of the "sold" listings to see what I had missed during my days away, when I was too busy playing a different game. Of course, there were a few solid scores throughout—the luck of the draw—and some pretty, near-mint rarities, but those were long gone. I sipped, and I searched. If there was something worth getting, I knew I'd find it.

Just as I was about to make yet another unwise impulse purchase so that I didn't walk off empty-handed (this time on a copy of *TNT Motorsports*), I decided to give the local Craigslist a skim. Xbox 360. Skylanders. Earphones. Gaming Rocker. Then a post—picture excluded—caught my eye. *Old games from estate sale. Sega. For collectors ONLY.* It was two days old. I clicked and read. "Hello. I have a small haul from estate sale. Old Sega video games. Still in box with booklet. Clean discs. High value. Message for details if interested. Going fast." I did. The person responded within minutes saying that some of it already sold in other places, but that he was glad to hear from me because there was a game or two he had just listed on eBay. "These are real rarities," he wrote. "I can cut you a deal since you're a local. Hopefully it's of interest to you :)." It was strange enough to be given a link to eBay from Craigslist (heck, it might have even been a violation of the Craigslist policy), but no matter. People who didn't know any better did strange things in these spaces, like spell Sony "Soney," ask $50 for an old Atari cartridge worth no more than a few dimes, or title a listing for a filthy Atari 2600, "computer entertainment system," which, to be fair, was precisely what it said on the front of the thing. But this was all hot air, wasn't it? The link took me to a listing for the ever-elusive *Battlesport* for the Sega Saturn, a port of the 3DO original. One of the last remaining holes in my North American Sega collection and really one of the only games I was consciously looking for at the Philadelphia Retro Games Convention (to no avail, alas). Without a doubt, one of the rarest North American releases. How had I missed this the first dozen times I had browsed eBay? I saw it now. Because the title wasn't "*Battlesport* Sega Saturn," which was the only way someone like me would really be able to find it, but "CD video game. RARE." I blinked twice to make sure my eyes weren't deceiving me because it felt like discovering a new word, a new language, like a game that no one else had ever played, one that was available only to me.

The item's location was listed as Des Moines. It struck me as especially fortuitous, there in my first few successful days of Splat, immediately after the direct deposit of paycheck number two, and just before my planned hike to Cedar Ridges State Park with Natalie, to finally discover a listing for *Battlesport*, a game that was, oddly enough, about being in an enclosed arena trying to "tag" your opponents. I couldn't wait to tell her about it. Immediately, I messaged the seller. "Hi! Yes, I am interested. Does the manual include the registration card? It should be on the inside flap." "Yes, it does," he wrote back. "Everything is mint. Glad you're interested!" I zoomed in on the pictures again. It was complete-in-box, just a few scratches on the case. I couldn't believe my luck. The price was higher than I was willing to pay. At least out of the gate. But, like all good things, there was a Best Offer button. I cross-referenced the last few "sold" listings (all of which were months or years old) to see what I could suggest as a fair offer. There were two ways to do this: before the seller has time to figure out what he really has (though the frequent mention of "RARE" and the high "Buy-it-now" price signaled that maybe this one already knew) and how much he could get for it with a little patience and/or adjustment of the listing itself; or after it had been sitting unsold for weeks or months, when he's finally tired of waiting and desperate to take whatever the hell he could get. I took my chances and sent a lowball offer, adding a note indicating that I was the "buyer from Craigslist" to appeal to that Midwestern niceness. "A collector," as he had wanted. "Thanks again!" Then, I sent him another email. "Sent an offer!" I could have bypassed eBay altogether to make the same offer via email, but I didn't for two reasons. 1) I was accumulating major reward points on eBay and 2) I was protected by eBay's Money Back guarantee in the case of a defect or issue. This was especially important when considering we were talking about a game worth hundreds of dollars. I wasn't about to wire that kind of money to a stranger for a game that might never arrive. Or, conversely, hand it over in a parking lot only to discover a few hours later that the disc didn't work.

When nothing happened after a few minutes, I ordered a hot chocolate without whipped cream, absentmindedly forgetting that, amidst all the excitement, I hadn't made a dent in my most recent tea refill. I watched the preteen behind the counter fix it with whipped cream, looking at me cross-eyed as if I had suddenly revealed my true identity as a visitor from a faraway planet. She looked no older than my students. I wondered if she knew any of them. Surely some of them snuck off campus to take part in the local scene. I scooped the whipped cream out onto the table and sat sipping, but it was too hot. I couldn't focus. Pomm and

Timmer walked by the window. I pretended not to see her. My phone buzzed. "Offer accepted-pay now." And I literally jumped, hitting my head on the dangling light above me. My body was shaking as I finished the transaction. Then, I waited and waited until, only a few hours later, I received my favorite notification of all: Item Shipped. In my email, another message: "Thanks, friend. Glad I could be of assistance to you. Happy we crossed paths."

I played a lot of Saturn that night, swapping discs in and out, occasionally listening to music. I moved a few games around to leave a space for the new addition. I posted about it on my retro gaming forums. "I don't know what system to collect next," I wrote. "Lol. I can't believe it. I found the Rosetta Stone." The only games left—*Panzer Dragoon Saga* and *Daytona USA CCA*—weren't rare, alas, just expensive. I'd save up for them in turn and that would be that.

It made me sentimental. Roll had given me a lot thus far. But this felt like the greatest gift of all.

There was change in the air and a beer in my hand. Lucid, sweet. I swapped discs. While waiting for the new game to load, I heard a voice calling my name, though I managed to convince myself that I had just imagined it. I checked the window. The door. Nothing. No one. The next game loaded. Then another.

I texted Natalie. "Really excited about tomorrow," I wrote. "Already stretching."

"Good," she wrote back. I was disappointed at first. Then she sent a wink face and added: "You better be loose."

"Oh, I meant my hands," I wrote back with a wink of my own. "Gaming."

My bendy straw was on the empty chair next to me.

VII. THE FOOL ON THE HILL

IN NEW YORK, COLORS are muted. You can't tell green from brown unless you pull up a chair and stare at it. Foliage-this and foliage-that. But in Iowa, a single color like brown can appear, for example, coated in an amber red or a warm sunny yellow, all of it forming a golden blur as it passed by the windows of Natalie's car. Maybe it was the good luck I had been having, but everything around us seemed to pulse with life. Even when we pulled off the interstate and the world went still again—but for a herd of cows grazing in a dry field—it felt as if we were driving through a painting. Like an art attack, reverse Stendhal syndrome.

We pulled into the park, skipping admission at the gate on account of Natalie's "Park Pass," and drove around a thin, stately road cluttered with wooden swing sets and cabins. She knew where we were going, turning the car this way and that, following signs that seemed to point nowhere ("Woods Trailhead." "Moreway Trailhead." "Falls Trailhead." "Cedar Ridge Trailhead.") until my ears popped and we reached a few cluttered parking spaces near a trailhead with no label and a building that said, "Youth Nature Center."

"Last chance for a bathroom," she said.

"Isn't peeing in the woods the whole point of hiking?" I asked.

She laughed and got her gear together by the trunk of the car while I laced my new boots. When she first pulled up outside my place, she gave me a full up-and-down and told me I'd be hot as hell if I hiked in jeans.

"Is that a bad thing? I don't remember the last time I was called hot as hell."

"You won't be feeling so gung-ho about it once we get going."

"But it's cold," I said.

"Oh, Josh," she said.

The trail was narrow and coated in fallen leaves. I let her lead, watching her momentarily disappear around a sharp turn, the smell of sunscreen hanging in the cool air behind her. "You're not really that slow, are you?" she said, when I rounded the corner myself. Then, "Oh my God. Are you sweating already? What did I try telling you?"

"I'm always sweating."

"Not like that," she said.

It was easier than I thought it would be. Then again, going up was always the easiest. Getting down was the problem. Natalie and I chatted along the way, exchanging easy jokes, talking about *Battlesport*, about the art of collecting, about Fairbury. As we walked, we passed a handful of others, some of whom had gear and hiking sticks, others who had young kids and dogs. One woman was even wearing a pup pack with a big, fluffy black dog fastened inside, tongue whipping against his vampire teeth.

We moved out of the way so they could pass.

When they were gone, Natalie and I exchanged looks. "That's why I'm a cat person," she said.

Eventually the trail evened out, revealing a view of the valley below. I talked her into stopping on a big rock for a quick snack and a pat-the-sweat-from-my-face break.

"You wanna stop already?" she said. Then, "All right. If you insist."

We ate the peanut butter sandwiches that Natalie had packed while swatting away bugs. Every few bites, I lifted the bread to inspect the contents.

"Is the peanut butter still there?" Natalie asked, watching me.

"Just making sure I'm not eating the colony."

"You know, a little extra protein wouldn't kill you."

"No," I said. "I think it would. And before you ask, yes, I melt in the rain too. Into a big puddle. It's a sad show."

"You are an interesting one, Josh."

"Better than being uninteresting," I said.

She let out a weak laugh and rolled her eyes. We went back to eating the sandwiches.

"The view was a lot greener the last time Brandon and I were here."

There was another pause as we both looked out at the valley, the tops of trees, a long, winding road like the ribbon of a present, and acres of brown fields interrupted only by the interstate, which was visible just above the horizon. The cars and trucks rolled east and west silently. Natalie rubbed her hands on her thighs and pinched a bug between her fingers, flicking it off into the distance. What a waste of protein, I thought.

She leaned forward to touch her toes. "He wasn't too thrilled with us coming out here."

I heard leaves and sticks crunching. A young couple passed by us. They waved with two fingers and then disappeared again. "Oh?"

"I was like: Josh is a nice guy. And we've got to get a few pictures for Kirkland. Gotta introduce him to great outdoors."

"And here we are," I said.

"And here we are."

Our eyes met and a wave of affection struck me. I wanted to grab her hand, to spin her around cinematically and rub our cheeks together. But I looked away. Was it guilt? Fear? I decided I'd let her make the first move instead, if there was even a first move to make. I had no idea what I was doing.

She stood and took a step closer. "I've been wanting to ask," she said. "About your wife. Natalie. If that's okay, I mean. I don't want to be a downer, but we haven't had much chance to talk about it. I get that it's hard to talk about. I can't even begin to understand what that must have been like." It wasn't the move I was hoping.

With my free hand, I grabbed a stick from the ground and traced the dirt. "Sure," I said. "Natalie. What do you want to know exactly?"

"Anything. Everything. Like, what did she look like?"

"A person. A girl."

"No, Josh. What color were her eyes?"

I looked at her standing there, the same watery expression in her eyes that Heloise had when I last told her I loved her. But those eyes were closing, these were open. "Green."

"Dark green?"

"Yeah."

"Her hair?"

"Brown."

"Did she take your last name?"

"She did," I said, even though she didn't.

"Natalie Schulman," she said, as if trying it on. "What was her favorite song?"

"I'm not sure that she had a favorite song. She liked Jack Johnson. But she'd listen to anything but country."

"Where did you meet?"

"An art show in the city."

"That's sweet. What did you like most about her?"

I really had to think about it. "Everything?"

"You don't want to talk about it. It's fine. You could just say so."

"I'm sorry."

"Don't be."

"Do I think about her?" I said. "I think about her every day." And even that felt like a lie. "But life goes on. It has to."

"And now here you are," she said, winking.

And something about the way she said it this time hurt me. She smiled. I smiled back. Then, she bent down to fix her boots, to make sure the bottom of her leggings were tucked into her socks. She put her hands on her waist. Then on my shoulder. There it is, I thought, steadying my breath. I leaned in, ever so carefully.

"See all those fields," she said, changing the topic. "Now that's a good word to describe life in Iowa. Take it from someone who lives here."

"I live here, too," I reminded her.

"Someone who was born here," she said.

She paused to think it through. She pulled her hand away. "I actually had a student describe it like this once. You get your first job detasseling corn in fields. You go to your first concert—and first date—in a field. You play sports on a field, drink your first beer on a field, and then, just when you think it's done, that it's left you, nearly everyone comes back after graduation from wherever and works in a field."

"But you don't work in a field."

"I wish I did sometimes. Look how nice it is out here. I can suck that fresh air from a straw. Splat."

We both laughed.

"Take you on a roll in the hay," I said.

"Good way to get covered in ticks."

"Maybe today? I'm coming your way. Take you on a roll in the hay."

She started skipping, singing it. The wind joined her, blowing through the trees and rustling the dying leaves. "Roll in the hay. Roll in the hay. Take you on a roll in the hay, Almost Dr. J."

She stopped and motioned for me to join, and I jumped to my feet. With my chest feeling like it was about to split open, I finally reached for her hand.

She raised her eyebrows. I sucked in a whiff of her sunscreen. Maybe it was an aphrodisiac?

"Can I do this?" I asked.

"Yes," she said, looking at my hand. Her hand wasn't sweaty like mine. She really was a lot stronger than she looked. She could easily beat me up. It turned me on.

She leapt onto a rock and looked down at me like she wanted to say something but couldn't. She reached for the phone from her mesh bag and snapped a picture of me. She showed me the pic. The screen was so small that I could barely see myself. But then I realized that it was I who looked small, standing beside this endless valley; fake, like a person I didn't know. She pinched the screen until my body took up the entire frame.

Also, I looked happy.

We held hands again later, but only briefly as we neared the end of the trail. Neither of us talked about it. Our conversation, still, was guided by the usual things. We shared a laugh here and there. At one point, she hid around a corner and jumped out to scare me. If you asked her about us holding hands, she might have told you that it was an accident, a show of support.

But it wasn't. I know it wasn't. She clasped my hand even tighter the second time.

★

On the drive back to Roll, thousands of moths careened into the windshield and were wiped into goo, just like on my first drive into town. The Third Plague.

"I keep thinking about all these dead moths and I feel awful," she said.

"I don't think of you any differently," I said. "Even if you have killed forty-five thousand and a half moths."

"A half?"

"You didn't see the one cradling the windshield back there?" She grimaced.

We pulled into town around 7 p.m.

"Just in time for the dance," she said.

"Oh, joy," I said. "The party continues."

She looked off into the distance. "Or, you know, we can skip it and play a few games? You still owe me a round of Tetris." It took everything within me not to cry.

"Now you're speaking my language," I said.

VIII: JOSHUA WALKS ON WATER

THE PACKAGE FROM EBAY arrived on Monday. It was sitting beneath a basket on the porch. I was especially worried about packages left unattended for hours at a time, exposed to the elements and/or an easy grab for passing thieves so I sprinted from the cool tiles of Academic 1 at the first sound of the final bell, Splat straw in hand, down Main Street, and over the small bridge. Sweating, I waved to my neighbors Steve and Anne who were sitting, as usual, in their garage drinking from bottles of water and listening to Christian radio. They didn't wave back. They had stopped trying to talk to me weeks ago. When I climbed the porch, I snatched the thing from the basket and brought it into my kitchen, where dirty pots and pans and used bowls and coffee mugs persisted on the counters and in the sink. I made space by stacking a few bowls on top of each other. I grabbed my grandfather's silver/rust-green pen knife from my small jewelry chest and, with urgent ferocity, ripped through the packing tape. Inside, there were three layers of bubble wrap, held together on either side by a small piece of tape. I cut through it and reached for my prize. *Battlesport.* Sega Saturn. But it wasn't there. I tore through the bubble wrap. I turned the box upside down. Eventually I found a few anime trading cards and a yellow Post-it note that said "Thanks for your patronage. Please accept this small token of my appreciation." It was signed J. That was it. I checked the box again. And again. I marched outside and asked Steve and Anne if anyone suspicious had tampered with my mail.

"We've been out here all day," Steve said. "We've got eyes."

"That's why I'm asking you," I said. Maybe I said it too aggressively because Steve just cleared his throat and stared a hole right through me.

Back in the house, I studied the box for signs of tampering. I checked the shipping label.

And this is where things really started to get weird. In place of the return address on the battered, well-taped but useless Walmart box was not my address in Roll, but my old address in New York, with my own initials on top: JS. I had to look twice to make sure. It had been months since I had even seen the address in writing. Then I studied the Post-it note. Signed, J. I flipped it over and found a crude drawing of an eggplant.

I tried to keep calm. I logged into eBay to see if my address in New York was still synced with my profile. Maybe this J from Des Moines was senile and mistakenly copied my former address in place of his own. Didn't he say something about an estate sale? But would he forget to include the fucking game?

I drew in a long breath and counted to three. I clenched my fists until my fingers made red bullet points on my palms.

I opened my laptop on the kitchen counter and sent puddizzle a message.

"Hello! Thanks for shipping this so quickly. Unfortunately, there wasn't a game in the box. Only anime cards and bubble wrap."

I stopped here and gathered the cards. I spread them on the countertop where the box had been sitting. The text was Japanese. I didn't recognize the images. In one was a purple-haired girl with pointy ears against a background of polka-dots. In another was an animal of some kind, a cross between a dog and a dinosaur—big pointy teeth, tongue sticking out. Purple. They were all purple. Light purple, dark purple.

I went back to the message.

"Also, in place of a return address you listed my former mailing address in New York. Another mistake, I'm sure. Anyway, I really do want the game, so I thought I'd see if you'd be able to ship it out asap? Otherwise, I'll have to contact eBay for a prompt refund. Thanks for your attention to this matter – Josh."

I typed and erased a handful of notes about the eggplant ("Oh, and cool drawing, by the way! Is that an eggplant?" "Do all of your Post-its have eggplants on back?" "Have you ever heard of the eggplant wizard by chance?") but decided to leave it be.

His other listings were run-of-the-mill. There was nothing that signaled an elaborate scam. His writing was good, if a bit wordy, atypical of the usual Midwestern lexicon. On a 6 CD-ROM set called *Professor Teaches How to Create Web Pages*, he wrote: "The programs here may be outdated at this point, but the concepts and the HTML contained therein aren't so." The listings were clean, yet detailed. Items were tested. Contents were listed as bullet points, with certain words underlined. "As always," he signed at the bottom of every listing, "if you have any questions, feel free to message me!" His feedback rating was perfect. I closed eBay to distract myself and got started on a little bit of class planning for Tuesday.

My phone vibrated a few minutes later. It wasn't eBay. It was Natalie. Apparently, she wanted me to look over the finished article she had written and for which she had interviewed me before (finally) submitting it to class and then (also finally) PhD applications. Could I swing by her classroom and skim it tomorrow during lunch? Sure, I said. Why not? It seemed to me that it would be a way to gain some clarity. Besides, the game issue would all be settled by then, wouldn't it? In keeping with the goal of distracting myself, I recalled the framed photo of her in her underwear, from the neck down. Brandon Grey clearing his throat, closing the bedroom door behind me.

I refreshed eBay until my wrist became numb. I had a sinking feeling that something bad was about to happen, but all I could do was wait, minute to hour, hour to day, until it happened.

★

Tuesday morning, I sent puddizzle another message, but this time to his email address from Craigslist.

"Hello again. Sorry for the bother. I'm just checking to see if you received my eBay message? Just to reiterate, I didn't receive the game I paid for and on the box (which was empty except for bubble wrap and anime cards) the return address was my own. I'm attaching the eBay message for reference. I'm sure it was just a mistake. I've been shopping on eBay for a long time now, and I thought I had seen it all. I still want the game if you have it, so I hope that we can complete this transaction the right way. Please get back to me as soon as you can. Thanks —Joshua."

In Natalie's classroom, I read through her article, a compelling piece that weaved quotes from me, Meg Lemming, Steve Kirkland, and a few others to advocate for less structured learning. We talked about it for a few minutes. How, for example, one of my quotes (about service learning) was used in a way that made me sound smarter than I really am. When we finished, I sighed and craned my neck. I sat on the front desk. Natalie leaned against the chalkboard. She wasn't holding her straw. I wasn't holding mine either.

She stepped over and began rubbing my shoulders. My body tingled from my toes up to my neck.

"Is this okay?" she asked.

The tone surprised me. It was as if I were suddenly—to her, at least—someone with power, self-control.

I nodded, not knowing what else to do. Her fingers clenched my skin. The gold bangle on her wrist rolled up and down my shoulder blade. My chest was warm. It felt like I was dreaming, like when I saw Glen Gill crunching a pickle at Coney Island.

"Loosen up," she said, tapping my shoulder. "Right here. There's a lot of stress here."

"I know," I said.

"Is something bothering you?"

I closed my eyes and saw colors. Deep purple. Yellow. White. Orange. Stop sign. Her hands slid down my back and stopped abruptly. I opened my eyes, expecting to see her looking at me, waiting for my answer. But she was facing the door.

"Glen?" she said.

I turned. "What?"

A hungry and desperate Glen Gill charged at me, clutching his bendy straw. I leapt from the table and dove to the window, trying to yank the straw from my pocket. I got to it just in time and held it in front of me, as if warding off a vampire.

He just stood there and stared down both of us in silent judgment, straightening his shirt, making sure it was still tucked. He sniffed.

"He hurt his back," Natalie said.

I slouched to make it look like the running had exacerbated the pain. Gill let out a mirthless laugh and headed to the door and left. Natalie walked over and closed the door behind him.

"What a creep," she said.

"Sorry for morphing into Sonic the Hedgehog," I said. "He's taking this game way too seriously. And his Jewish fetish, that Judeophilia. It's disturbing."

"Well, good luck with that." She seemed distant again. "I should probably get back to work. I have a few things I need to get done."

"I mean. Shouldn't we talk about this?" I said.

She sighed. "Talk about what?"

"Us?"

"*Us?*" she said, flabbergasted. She stood tall and straight, hand just below her chest. "I'm married."

"I realize that."

"Do you?"

"Yeah, I do."

She slid the wedding band up and down her finger. "Then what is it that you're hoping for, Josh? Tell me."

"Nothing," I said. "For you to be happy. That's all."

"I am happy," she said. "What, because we went on a hike? Because I gave you a shoulder rub? That means I'm not happy? We're colleagues. Friends. Guys and girls can't be friends?"

"I didn't say that."

"Good."

"Then we're fine. Sorry I brought it up."

I started walking to the door, but she put a hand up. It pushed into my chest.

Her eyes were steady and piercing. Light brown like a penny. "You still didn't tell me," she said.

"Tell you what?"

"What you're hoping for?"

"Yes, I did."

"No. I mean, what you're really hoping for?"

I sighed, looking down. She took her hand off my chest and moved a few strands of hair out of her eyes. Then, her hands were on my face and we kissed. Just once. A peck. No tongue. Maybe a little tongue. A lot of tongue. I pulled back. No, she pulled back. We both did.

She was the first to speak. "I need to do work," she said, looking at the clock. "We can talk more later."

"Okay," I said.

Our eyes locked a few moments more. I wasn't sure if I should kiss her again, so I didn't. I turned to leave. But I stopped when I noticed on the wall of student portraits one that hadn't been there before. I stepped over to it, in shock. An eggplant in a robe, holding a staff and smiling against a deep purple background.

"What's this?" I asked, pointing.

"I don't know," she said. "An anthropomorphized eggplant holding a staff? Looks like the staff that goes to The Fountainhead. The one in Kirkland's office."

"The Fountainhead. The Royal Fox Society. The Eggplant Wizard."

She shook her head. "The Eggplant Wizard?"

"It's a video game character. From *Kid Icarus*. Do you know who drew this?"

"Obviously a student. I don't know which one. I don't make them sign it. Why? What's so special about it?"

"Are you sure it was a student? It doesn't look like any of the others."

"Who else would it be?" she said. "The janitor?"

"Can I take a picture of it?"

"I guess." She seemed annoyed. "Just don't go uploading it to the internet or anything."

I pulled out my phone and snapped a picture.

"What's the big deal?" she asked.

I walked out into the hallway and out the door, Splat straw in hand, someone grabbed my shoulder. It was Glen Gill.

"You and Natalie Grey are getting pretty close, huh?"

"I think you and I are getting pretty close too," I said. The breeze swept beneath my shirt. I looked across the quad for an escape route. I noticed Tyler walking circles around an elm tree.

"I'll tell you what," he said, holding up his straw like a prize. "Give me the kill and I'll say nothing."

I should have agreed to it, right? It would have made sense. I could go on to worrying about other things. Like Natalie or *Battlesport* and the fucking eggplant drawing in Natalie's room. What the hell did I care about Splat anyway? But I was really starting to resent the guy, even more than Hunter Reed, and the last thing I wanted was to give him the pleasure. I watched Tyler sit down, looking at his palms.

"That's okay," I said. "Gill. You do you."

"Then I shall," he said.

"Hey, Gill?" I said. "Do you like eggplant?"

It looked like he was really thinking about it. "Love-hate," he said, reminiscing, half-smiling. "My mother, before she died, grilled it all the time. Grew it in her garden every summer. Made us eat it year-round."

★

Back in the dining hall, Pants had just been Splatted by Meg Lemming. The dining hall was previously a Splat-free zone but had been changed recently to accommodate Splat and was quickly referred to by students as the Splatmare Massacre Café. While holding their Splat straws in one hand, those still standing, many of whom had developed celebrity-like followings, had to transfer trays and cups and consume large quantities of food, all while negotiating waves of students and staff. Even though they weren't supposed to use their straws as straws, a handful of student-players did just that. As for Pants, the story goes that he had just finished eating a plate of chicken wings and put his straw down absent-mindedly to pat his face with a napkin. As soon as he did, Meg Lemming appeared out of thin air and Splatted him. No one saw her coming. Napkin still on his face, Pants dropped his head onto the table, where he stayed for most of the period. A few students were still watching from over the partition when I got there, whispering to each other, excited.

"I got it on camera," one of them said. "Pants getting pantsed. It's totally going on 4Chan. Another casualty of the Splatmare Massacre Café. We're open late, ready to serve you Splat."

★

Wednesday came and there was still no response from puddizzle so I opened a return request on eBay, even though eBay gave sellers fourteen days to respond to such a request before taking any action. I was getting over it, or trying to, as annoying as it was, since I knew I'd get my money back eventually, but then, when clicking around on his profile for the thousandth time, I noticed a brand new listing for throw pillows. The flames were born in me again. Obviously, this puddizzle hadn't died. I went back to my email. Nothing. Messages? Nothing. I started typing. "Hello, this is my third message now. I know you're there reading this. You realize I can leave you negative feedback so bad that it would end your lovely pillow selling business. Wouldn't that be a shame." The catharsis lasted an hour or so, until I checked again and found that he had posted a new listing for an eggplant that was simply titled "eggplant." The extended description said: "see photos. You get what you get and you don't get upset. —J." The picture was of an eggplant on a wooden table. Everything behind the fruit was dark. I right-clicked the photo and did a Google image search to see if it had been ripped from elsewhere—some blog on the far reaches of the internet, or the public Flickr account of some mother in Arizona—but found nothing.

I skipped lunch so I could stare at the listing.

On the quad, while walking home, followed—as usual—by Glen Gill, I stepped in something purple. Was it eggplant? Was everything purple eggplant?

"Need a napkin?" Gill said, hovering behind me.

I dragged my foot across the grass, which didn't help, and then held up my bendy straw. "Nope, because I've got this." With a foot in the air, I dug out the shit on my shoe with my straw, and realized, quite quickly, that that's all it was: shit. And now it was covering the straw.

Gill was loving every second of it. "Looks like you got in there good," he said. "Keep digging. If you look hard enough, maybe you'll find some gold."

That night, I tried gaming—dipping in and out of various pick-me-up genres: fighters, beat-em-ups, first-person shooters—but I couldn't stop thinking about puddizzle and his eggplant. Why was he ignoring me? What the hell did I do to him?

I tried laying it all out in front of me, but I kept coming back to Glen Fucking Gill and his bendy straw, as if he were stalking my thoughts now too. I had a brutal headache.

On Thursday, puddizzle posted a few Saturn games, auction-style. I had most of them, but the starting prices were good. I clicked on *Nights into Dreams* and studied the accompanying photos. I googled the photos and found that, sure enough, they had been lifted from a marketplace listing on Amazon. I messaged him again.

"Way to rip photos from Amazon, you psychopath. You fake. Reported."

When I checked the listing a few hours later, I noticed a new, detailed description accompanying the pirated photos. It said: "Hello, eBay! Pick up this great, one-of-a-kind game while you can. I wouldn't normally sell such a beauty, but I'm kind of stuck in a rut. My wife left me (actually told people she died, if you'd believe it lol) and I managed to lie my way into a teaching position here in good ol' Iowa (actually dropped out of a PhD LOL). So, yeah. I'm kind of a bum and a douchebag, to be honest. Also, a homewrecker (but given who I am, perhaps that's one of my more endearing qualities?). So, what does that mean for you? It means I'm selling what I've got for a quick buck before they drive me out of town! Get it while the getting's good! XO EW."

There was no more staying calm. I ran into my game room to make sure *Nights into Dreams* was still there. I closed all the window shades. I went back to eBay and took a screenshot of the listing. Then I refreshed the page so many times that the screen asked me to input a captcha to make sure that I wasn't a bot. Was I waiting for the listing to disappear? Was I waiting for a laugh track to play and say, "Got ya, Joshua. Just kidding. You're only imagining this. Don't worry. You do that sometimes, don't you? Imagine?" Soon the words of the description became letters and the letters became lines. This was someone here. Someone at Fairbury. But *who*? And why? Because I had lied? Because I had tripped the Eggplant Wizard by mistake in Philadelphia? Because I had signed up for fucking Splat?

I opened my eBay messages. I opted for a more direct approach this time.

"Who are you?" I wrote. Nothing. No response.

I wrote: "I wasn't born yesterday. I can figure out your IP address. What skeletons do you have in your closet, asshole?"

After a few tense minutes, he finally wrote back, "Yours."

★

Later, the extended description was added to another one of puddizzle's game listings. After that came a third and a fourth. Even worse, one of them already had bidders. Then a second had bidders. The starting prices were fair, after all. They were, as we'd say, priced to sell.

I didn't sleep. What if Glen Gill had nothing to do with it? What if, at sixty, he didn't even know what eBay was. And what was in it for him anyway? Would he really do all this because of Splat? If not him, then who? Captain Kirk? Hunter Reed? An angry student or two? What if whoever was dressed as the Eggplant Wizard in Philadelphia invited me here just so they could make my life miserable? Sneak drawings into Natalie's classroom. Bring an eggplant costume to the school dance. Was that too far-fetched? There were other thoughts, too: like, what if it wasn't someone here at all? What if it were someone from New York *heading* here?

The only people in Roll I talked to about games were my students and occasionally Natalie. So, I asked my students the next day.

"Hey, you guys know any instructors, besides me, I mean, who are into video games?"

They didn't.

"You think you could maybe ask around?" I said. "I'm thinking of starting a gaming club."

"There already is one," one of my students said.

My heart was racing. "There is? How come I didn't know about it?"

"It's a tabletop game club."

I thought it over and decided it was close enough. "Who's in charge of that?"

"No one anymore."

"What do you mean no one?"

"It's informal."

"But someone used to run it?"

"Years ago."

"Do any of the faculty go?"

"Captain Kirk, sometimes."

I couldn't eat. I couldn't stand. I called in sick on Friday because I was puking bile (which wasn't a lie). I told the secretary I'd try to make it in for afternoon classes, but that I might need a stretcher. "I think it would be hard to negotiate that," she said, laughing. "I'll let Dr. Kirkland know that you're not well."

I made a fake eBay account with a fake address and won puddizzle's copy of *Sega Rally Championship*. I thanked the seller and asked for a PayPal receipt. The name assigned to the seller was "JS."

On Saturday, Natalie texted that she wanted to talk, to see how I was feeling. I typed and erased a few responses but didn't have the strength to send off any of them. Which made me feel like an idiot when, on Sunday, there was a knock at my door. I tiptoed to the window and saw Natalie.

"One second," I cried out. I was still in pajamas, my tattered Bugle Boy XXL sleep shirt. I hadn't changed out of it since Thursday. Think old socks and rotten eggs.

I got dressed and sprayed myself generously with an old bottle of Axe Body Spray I had buried at the bottom of my medicine chest. Then, I shoved as much trash as I could into the game room closet. I closed the door. She knocked again.

I took a deep breath and opened it. "Hi," I said. "Are you okay?"

"Are *you* okay?" she asked. "You were out Friday and I didn't see you for half of last week."

"Yeah. Just...you know."

She was wearing a North Face fleece. She looked beautiful and it made me sad. Here I was, with everything I had ever wanted, and, like usual, it was all crashing down around me.

"Are you sick?" she asked.

"You can say that," I said.

"With what?"

I pointed to my head.

"Can I come in?"

She walked into the kitchen, slowly, one foot feeling out space in front of the other, and sighed.

"Remember I wanted to teach you how to cook?"

"Yeah. I mean, did you want to do that soon?"

"I can't, can I?"

"Why can't you?"

"When would I?"

"Anytime you want."

"What would be my excuse to visit you here, Josh?"

"To teach me how to cook. Or, you know, just to play a few games."

"Yeah, that sounds perfectly normal."

"What was your excuse today?"

She faced the radiator. "To stop making the wrong decision. For myself, mostly. Brandon doesn't know I'm here."

She walked back into the living room and sat on the sofa. She drew in a long breath and adjusted her glasses. I felt a heaviness in my chest. The lights from a car outside flashed across the wall. Natalie waited for it to pass before speaking again.

"I told Brandon everything, just so you know. I can't lie to him."

"What did he say?"

"That it didn't surprise him, even though it surprised me, which means I guess he knows me better than I know myself. I'm just a predictable girl from the Midwest, easy to read."

"You know that's not true."

"But it doesn't really matter, though, does it?" she said.

It was suddenly cold. I folded my arms. The tone of her voice was making me anxious. I looked at her and wondered if I could ever love Natalie like I had loved Heloise—even if things were different, if there were no lies and no Brandon. If she could ever love me like she must have once loved him. I cleared my throat of phlegm. "Hey, do you want a drink? I have beer."

"No," she said.

"Do you mind if I grab one? I'm feeling a little...I don't know, wobbly."

She said she didn't mind, so I walked back into the kitchen to compose myself. I swiped on my phone and checked eBay. Nothing new.

She pointed to the beer when I brought it back into the living room. The thin gold bangle on her wrist slid down her hand. "You sure that's good for you right now?"

I shrugged. "We'll find out."

Her eyes fell to the floor. She was wearing brown Nikes. One of the laces was tucked into the tongue. I thought of the boots. Of my shoes. Of hers. When my crisis first started almost two years ago, just before things got *really* bad, Heloise said, *Boots are on, Josh. Laces tied.* "You know what's terrifying?" Natalie asked.

"What?"

"I thought I was pregnant last month, but then it turned out to be a false positive. That's what my intuition was saying all along, so in my gut I knew nothing was there. I could care less about cheap pregnancy tests. But Brandon was convinced. He wanted to start trying again the minute we found out it was a fake. He was really hurt. He still is."

I took a big gulp of beer. I couldn't decide if that explained anything or not. I remembered how Heloise and I tried to have kids and how relieved I was when it didn't work. "Do you want kids?" I asked.

"Why not? If it happens it happens. At least it'll seal my fate."

"I'm sorry," I said.

"Did you ever feel trapped during your marriage? Like you needed a taste of something else?"

A taste of something else? Was she talking about me? I half-nodded.

"What did you do about it?"

"I tortured myself."

"What do you mean?"

I took another sip and rubbed the cold beer bottle on my arm. I pointed to the game room, forgetting the door was closed.

"Actually. It would be hard to explain now," I said. "A lot has happened."

"I'd rather suffer than hurt the ones that I love," Natalie said sternly. "But I guess that's just me. I'm kind of numb to it these days."

"Then you should be a Jew," I said. "Suffering is in our DNA."

She let out a weak laugh. "I'm sorry," she said, turning away. "This is really hard."

"Then I'll stop."

"But that won't make things any easier. Maybe we just tell ourselves that the choices we make are right because we're the ones who made them? Because we have to live with the consequences, and so those choices have to be the right ones. Does that make sense?"

"Kind of."

She wouldn't look me in the eye. "I'm sorry," she said again. "I didn't intend on talking about me and my problems. Especially to you, Josh. That isn't why I came here."

"These are things you should be talking about. Talking is important."

"But words are just words. Like how people see me and say, *Why are you still here?* Because maybe I would have left if Brandon hadn't come along. Maybe I would have tried Colorado. Or California. Or New York. But then I remember that he and I can be really happy. And that's what I tell them. That I'm happy here. This is my home."

"That's good."

"Good?"

"If that's how you feel, yes."

"It's what I say."

"Natalie," I said. I wanted to wrap my arms around her. To smell her. To kiss her. "I think you know what I think." I toyed with a lock of my hair. She inspected her fingernails, her wedding ring. "But you already said that talking can't change anything, so…"

"You don't know what else to say?"

"There you are. Finishing my sentences again."

"Maybe you're an easy read."

"Are you sure I'm not just a new flavor?"

"You're important to me, Josh."

"Important as a friend?"

"Yes. I really do like you. I can tell you're hurting. I feel your passion. The fact that you take risks and have a sense of humor. That you can laugh at yourself. And you're great with those kids."

Did she know me at all? "Thanks," I said.

She exhaled and straightened her shoulders.

"It's also why I have to tell you this." She stepped closer and put a hand on my lower back. "You have to leave. I mean, run. You have to run."

I stepped back. "What?"

"They're closing in. He's closing in."

"Who?"

She waved her hands as if trying to make something appear. "The Eggplant Wizard."

"What?"

"The *drawing*," she said. "In my classroom. The Eggplant Wizard. That's what you called it. From the video game. It was a joke."

There were tears in my eyes. I didn't know if I could believe her. "That's a joke to you?" I cried out. I wanted to feel relief but couldn't. It was all too real. Beware the Eggplant Curse. That was it. I was cursed. Hadn't I always been cursed? I could feel her eyes waiting for me, but I still couldn't face them.

"Josh, come on. Sit up. You're scaring me. I was kidding. I thought I'd lighten the mood a bit. Change the topic. I guess not. It was a joke. Come on, sit up."

I did, reluctantly. I wanted to crawl into a corner and disappear. "What's going on? Can you talk to me? Do I need to call someone?"

I shook my head. "I need a minute."

"No one is after you, okay? No one is closing in. It was just a joke. I wanted to lighten the mood. That's all. I didn't think you'd react like this."

"Someone is after me," I said, wide-eyed.

"Who?"

"I don't know who. The Eggplant Wizard."

"That was just a drawing. A cartoon."

"No. It's real. It's someone here."

"You think someone here is an eggplant wizard?"

"Yes."

"And why would they be after you?"

"I don't want to get into it."

"Josh," she said. "Is this about Splat? About *Glen*?"

That was my out. There it was. A neat bow at the top of an empty package. This time, though, I wouldn't take it. "This is bigger than Splat," I said.

She crossed her legs. "Josh, why are you here? Why did you come here? And I don't mean that in a bad way because I'm glad you're here. You know that I am. If you weren't, then who else would I teach how to walk down a hill?"

Well, *kids*, I thought.

"People from New York—single guys, like you with almost PhDs—don't just pack up and move to Roll."

I had the sinking feeling that she was mocking me. That she was in on it all. "I came here to teach," I said. "To get out of the city. To meet you."

"Josh," she said.

"Look, I'm still, I don't know, figuring myself out. I think we all are. Sometimes we need to get away, try something new. Sometimes we make mistakes." I remembered, alas, how I had been recruited by Kirkland. Such a significant detail, but one I had ignored until now. It was all coming together, wasn't it? I felt positively sick.

"What's the truth? I want the truth."

"About us?"

"About you. Come on. You have this wall up. Yeah, sometimes you're an easy read, sometimes all of us are, but sometimes you lock up and deflect. Everyone can see it, Josh. Brandon says you aren't who you say you are, and you and he have hardly even spoken to each other. You wouldn't even show me your game room at first. Do you remember that? And that's such a big part of you. You were hiding it like you thought I'd be scared or something."

"I don't have a wall," I said.

"What was your wife's last name?"

"I think I told you that already. Schulman."

"No, Josh. Her real last name."

"I don't see why that matters."

She used both hands to steady me. "Josh, I want *your* story. I want to know the real you, not this abbreviated you."

I felt the facade slipping away. I remembered the first time I learned about the Holocaust in Hebrew School, years before I was consumed by thoughts of it, before I watched hundreds of videos, picturing myself there. Go left. Go right. At home that night, I asked my father, presently in the throes of Jewish rediscovery, why the Jews didn't just pretend they weren't Jews. You couldn't just pretend, he said. You wore it on your face like an albatross. It never left you.

"Fine," I said quietly. I couldn't go on like this. This wasn't the person I wanted to be. I smoothed the wrinkles from my shirt, took a big breath, and came right out with it. "I dropped out of my PhD. That's why I came here. I was embarrassed, and I felt like a failure. But I couldn't get over my own struggles, like usual, and I left. But then Kirkland recruited me, and it sounded like such a great chance to start over, you know? And then when I got here, he cornered me and asked about the PhD, and I just went along with it. I thought if he knew where I had come from that I'd be fired. I'm a loser. You can say it."

"You were lying this whole time?" she said.

"I'm sorry," I said.

"I mentioned your PhD in my article."

I didn't know what to say to that.

"That makes me a liar now," she said.

"I shouldn't have lied to you. I know."

"No one cares whether you have a PhD or not. That's stupid. It doesn't make you any dumber or smarter. What the hell, Josh? Weren't you the one who said that to me? Lying about it, on the other hand...well, it's unethical. And it's also kind of petty. Where did you think it would get you?"

"I don't know. Kirkland told me how excited he was to have another PhD on staff, and I was close."

"You overestimate him. He thinks he has more authority that he actually does."

"Then who does?"

"The alumni. The people who pay. The open wallets. They're the real decision-makers. You think it was Kirkland's idea to bring back Splat?" She laughed. "Brandon had a bigger part in it than Kirkland did. And Brandon hates Splat."

"I didn't realize that," I said.

"So, this is it? This is your so-called Eggplant Wizard? You're afraid you'll be found out?"

"There's also the wife thing," I said.

She cocked her head. "The wife thing?"

"We divorced. She's still in New York."

"Natalie is?"

"Heloise."

"Her name isn't Natalie?"

"No."

"And she's not dead?"

"Not technically, no."

She didn't say anything for a really long time. I asked what she was thinking.

Then she said, "Oh my God. Brandon was right."

"I get so carried away sometimes. I have walls up. I need to work on it. I know. I was scared."

"Scared of what?"

I had to really think about it. "Judgment. Shame. Facing up to who I really am."

"And who is that, Josh?"

"A failure."

"So you made up a story about your wife dying?"

"I didn't mean to."

Her eyes got large and red. She stood. "I take back what I said, Josh. Maybe this isn't the right place for you. Maybe you should leave."

I waited for her to say, yet again, that she was just kidding, that she was only trying to lighten the mood. But there was no laugh this time. We looked at each other in silence.

"Can I do anything to make it better?' I asked. "We can play a game? Go for a walk? Talk through it all? Give it some time?"

She shook her head and got up. "No," she said and left.

★

But I didn't. For one, I had nowhere to go. And two, I still needed answers. On Monday, I spent most of class time checking for account activity on eBay, thinking that it would help narrow my search down. If someone at Fairbury was behind all this, there was no chance they'd be able to maintain their ghost profile while class was in session. Then, too, was the chance I could find my way into the school's IT system and track the account activity to a specific computer.

Captain Kirk called me Monday morning to see how I was doing. I was sure that Natalie had outed me to him, so I kept the conversation brief. I told him I was fine, that I had eaten undercooked meat but had cleared most of it out. "Salmonella," I said. "Grilled a burger. Still bloody in the middle."

"That's too bad," he said. "Have a sensitive stomach myself. Did I ever tell you about the time I left half a burger in the car after a drive from Des Moines over the summer once and decided to eat it anyway? I would have bet anything that it got just cold enough at night to keep it safe. Nope. I couldn't even walk to the bathroom, Josh. I was crawling. On hands and knees. Literally crawling. Probably could have killed me. Oh well. You live and learn huh?"

The second box appeared on my front porch Tuesday afternoon, even though the address I had used for it wasn't real. This time, the return address was my parents' old house in Woodmere. I knew it was empty before opening it, but I ripped the tape off and tore the box apart anyway.

It was hard seeing my parents' address on that label. I couldn't even remember the sound of my father's voice. Linguistically, silence was the absence of speech, but, as I had tried to illustrate for my class during their silent interview activity, not of meaning and intention. I'm sure even my father would acknowledge that God was silent during human suffering. Would he call me? Never. But if I bit the bullet for both of us and called him then and there, he would have acted like nothing was wrong, as if we had been chatting all this time. How did one negotiate that kind of insincerity?

On Wednesday, I sat with a headache in front of my students and gave them some useless writing prompts. None of them had instructors-who-were-into-video-game updates.

"Choose whichever exercise you want," I said. "I'll be collecting these, so keep that in mind. Not that it should matter either way."

They wrote and I watched them hunched over their blank pages, scribbling away. One or two exchanged giggles under the breath or flashed their work to the person next to them. I watched those two closely. Tim and Marty. Two rows apart. Tim had his top button unbuttoned. Marty had his head on the desk. That was when Kirk walked in and summoned me into the hallway.

The class sat up.

He faced the students. He looked at Tim and pointed at his neck.

"Button please," he said.

I took the straw from my desk and followed Kirkland. This is it, I thought.

"Just wanted to make sure you're eating," he said. "And staying hydrated. I haven't seen you recently in the dining hall. Grab some soup when you get a chance. You can go before it opens for dinner."

"Thanks," I said.

"Did I tell you that Andy covered for you? You know Andy, yes? He left a good report. Says you've been doing some fine work in here."

"That's good," I said, shuffling my feet. "They're great kids. I really like them. Hey, do you have time to talk later?"

He was taken aback by the formality. So was I. Really, I was over it all. Throwing a huge log onto a smoldering fire, wanting for this nightmare to end. "Sure," he said. "After the final bell? I'm usually in the office until five. If the door's open, come on in."

"Perfect. Thanks, Kirk."

He stood at attention, hands at his sides. "At your service," he said. "As always."

I cocked my head. *As always.* It was the way puddizzle signed his listings. "As always, let me know if you have any questions." Kirk bowed and was gone.

One by one the students handed me their work and I added it to a pile I wouldn't touch. The bell rang and I sat at the computer and dismissed them with a weak "see you tomorrow." I loaded eBay, struck by a new idea. But when I stood to get it started, Tyler from Wisconsin appeared in the doorframe.

"Oh, hey," I said, sinking back into my seat. "Looking for me?" It had been five periods since I saw him. He was one of my morning students. "Or something you left?"

He balanced his straw between his fingers. He was one of only a handful of kids who hadn't been Splatted yet. As of that morning, the master list had been cut by more than three-quarters. It was slow going, but most would say that was the way the game should be played. A torturous marathon, the point of which was to wear the players down and punish them slowly.

"I was just wondering about the writing activities in class today." Tyler paused. "When do you think it's not okay to write about something?"

"*Not* okay?"

"When something is hard. Like, something that can make people uncomfortable. When is it a bad idea to write about it? Or when is it a good idea not to write about it?"

"Here's the thing. I actually think it's important to write about things that make people uncomfortable. Even if it's hard. Because it's still a reality for thousands of people. You know what I mean? Even more than that sometimes. Hundreds of thousands. Millions. I don't know. Writing gives voice and meaning to that kind of stuff. It legitimizes it. Makes it real. Especially when something is uncomfortable, we need writing about it. We need someone to explore those things. Otherwise we just run from them." I looked down at the floor, thinking over my answer. So many wasted opportunities, I realized. I was such a fake. "Does that make sense?"

He nodded.

"What were you writing about?"

"Just bad thoughts I had."

"Like what?"

"I don't know. I don't want to *talk* about it really. I prefer writing."

"And that's okay. That kind of energy can really fuel your writing. Give it a boost."

He scratched the back of his neck with his Splat straw and then rubbed his face. There was a white pimple at the bottom of his chin that looked like it was about to pop.

"You didn't like writing before, did you?"

"No," he said. "But I've been trying it here and there."

I felt a pang of pride when I realized it was me who had instilled that in him. "Do you often have bad thoughts?" I asked.

"Um." He swayed and turned to the window. It was cloudy and cool. Typical October in Iowa. At first the brown didn't bother me. Now I found it borderline oppressive.

"You just don't want to talk about it?" I said.

He nodded.

"Do you want to talk to someone else about it?"

He shrugged in a way that looked more like a no than a yes.

"It's good to talk, too," I said. "It can really help." Okay, so I knew what a hypocrite I was, but generally I found it easy to be rational when dealing with someone else's problems. It was that curse again. I was a teacher who couldn't learn. I studied language but avoided language. When things got tough, I took solace in something new. Every time. Walls. Walls. Walls. Big, beautiful walls.

★

I went back to eBay. I sent a message to puddizzle from my fake account complaining about how unsatisfied I was with my recent purchase of *Sega Rally Championship*.

With trembling hands, I bought another one of his items using yet another account, his "Support Now" T-shirt for $9.99, and sent the same message even though that item hadn't been shipped yet. I read the description. *As always, let me know if you have any questions.*

I made another fake account and bought a harmonica. I

sent another message, but this time I wrote only, "Hey, I have a question. It's an emergency." I erased the chalkboard. I checked all three accounts. I logged out and logged in. I opened the first of my return requests to check its status but instead was greeted with a notification from eBay that puddizzle had deactivated his account.

I sprinted out the door and across the quad to the Admin building to see if Kirkland was there, but he wasn't. Then I ran back to Academic I, worried that time was fleeting, and barreled down the long corridor. Hunter Reed's room was locked and dark. So was the computer lab. Meg Lemming was in her office, at her computer, but that didn't sound any alarms within me. I went upstairs. Steve from Poli Sci. Lights off. Natalie's door was closed, lights on. I peered through the small window but could only make out the upper rim of the chalkboard. I knocked and turned the doorknob. It was locked. The door opened, and Brandon Grey was standing in front of me.

"Joshua Schulman," he said. "What a sweet surprise. I didn't expect to see you again. At least not in person."

"Oh, hi, Brandon." I thought quickly. "Sorry, I thought I heard a noise. Wanted to make sure it didn't come from up here."

He raised an eyebrow.

I tried looking over his shoulder but couldn't see much. "It was like a bang. Is Natalie here?"

"Nope. No Natalie here," he said, smiling, sounding boastful.

"Well, I should probably be going then."

"I don't disagree with that," he said. Then, "Hey, before I forget. How are your games? Play anything fun recently?"

Sweat pooled in my armpits. "Wait, what was the question?"

Forget it," he said, waving a hand. "I wouldn't want to bore you. You've got places to be, right?"

"Kind of."

He curled his lips and made a grunting sound. "You're really getting around for a new guy. Good for you."

I pretended that I didn't know what he was talking about. "I really should go," I said.

"Right," he said. "Go. But here's just a quick tip for next time, if you can spare a minute from your Magical Mystery Tour. This isn't one of your little games, okay? Maybe someone never told you that. I don't know. Or maybe you just weren't raised right. Maybe you think you walk on water. Like Jesus."

I wiped my forehead. "Okay," I said. "I know. I'm sorry. It's over. It was just a misunderstanding."

"No, Josh. It wasn't a misunderstanding. Gaslighting isn't going to work on me because guess what? I can see right through you. I've got you read like a Polaroid."

"What are you talking about?"

"I'm talking about the fact that you think you're some kind of free agent in the moral universe. That you think nothing is off limits. Not to Joshua Schulman. Mr. Almost PhD."

"You've got it all wrong," I said. It wasn't all wrong. Obviously, Natalie had told him everything. What excuse did I have? I was different? I wasn't from around here? I knew it was a bad idea pursuing Natalie, but I did it anyway. I couldn't avoid it. It was my burden, my fate. I was pathetic.

Then it started coming together. It wouldn't have been hard for Brandon to find the video of me tripping the Eggplant Wizard at the gaming convention near Philadelphia. It more or less went viral, even if in a relatively exclusive circle. And the games? *Battlesport*. eBay. I opened that door for Natalie. I let her inside. I trusted her as she trusted me.

The Almost-PhD. Heloise. They were a part of my history. I could delete what I wanted from the internet, but I couldn't delete my own history. All it took was someone willing to put in the legwork, the time to uncover it.

Brandon knew everything. And he, above everyone else, had a reason to hate me.

The hall was spinning. "Hey, Brandon. What do you know about eggplant?"

The Eggplant Curse and the Warp Zone 201

He closed the door slowly before catching it with his foot. "So that was your question? Some emergency."

The door slammed shut.

★

In a daze, I drifted down the stairs and then across the quad to Academic 2 where I found, sure enough, Glen Gill, locking his science lab, his face flushed. He was still carrying his Splat straw. As soon as I saw him, I had a feeling that whatever this was, he was in on it.

"Hey, Gill," I said. "Fancy seeing you here."

"This is my classroom," he said. "What affords me the pleasure?"

"Heading out to see Brandon Grey?" I asked.

He looked at my waist. I didn't have my straw. He smiled.

"Shit," I said.

"Gotcha," he said, tapping his straw against my arm. "Splat! I gotta say, you were a noble target, Schulman. Especially for a newbie. Thanks for the chase. It was well earned. You sure didn't make it easy." He whistled. His eyes widened and he laughed. "I hope we can still talk, though, now that you've officially been Splatted and all. Say, who was your target? Time to move on to victim numero dos."

"Fuck off."

"Excuse me," he said, leaning an ear closer, sniffing. "What was that?"

"You think I don't know it was you. You and Brandon Grey. Who else was involved, huh? You think it's all so funny? Teaming up on the new guy? Waiting for me to slip up?"

"What was me?"

"Don't play stupid."

"The Natalie Grey thing? Low tactic, yeah, but that's the game, man. I didn't actually tell anyone. Just trying to be creative. Make you break. Didn't you read the rule book?"

I pointed to the classroom. "Open the door then. Let me see your computer."

"For what?"

"For harassment. Deceit. Impersonation. The Eggplant Wizard?"

"What in the hell are you talking about?"

I chuckled. "Don't play coy. I'm from New York. You're from what? Iowa? Give me a break, you loser. You wannabe Jew."

A student appeared in the hallway, pretending not to see or hear us.

Gill scoffed. "First of all, I'm from Kansas."

"Same difference."

"Second of all, I'd make a better Jew than you, Mr. Schulman." He checked to make sure his door was locked. Once, then twice. "I'll be reporting this."

"As will I," I said. "As I shall."

★

My entire body was hurting.

But the truth was this: I couldn't actually be mad at Brandon Grey. I wanted to punch him in the face, but if the roles were reversed, how would I have felt?

Kirkland walked past and told me he'd be just a minute. Then he talked on the phone just out of earshot. Maybe he was talking to Brandon or Natalie. It was he who insisted I spend my second night in Roll at the Grey's Cape Cod style house.

When he called me inside his office, he said first that his invitee for the speaker series might have fallen through. "Family conflict," he said, with clenched fists. "This happened last year too. Very frustrating. Feel like you can't catch a break. What are the chances you'll be able to persuade one of your guys in New York after all? I'm afraid we're running out of time. The last thing we can do is cancel this." His chair squeaked as he sat up.

"At this point, not super likely," I said.

"Hm. Well, I'd like you to try," he said. "Money talks. We'll spare no expense."

"Okay," I said.

"You're a good man," he said. "What did you want to talk about? Did you manage to get that soup from the cafeteria?"

I checked behind me and launched, suddenly, into an impassioned speech about Brandon Grey and his disturbing tricks on eBay and again about Glen Gill and his Splat tactics. I was careful not to give too many details so I could get a sense of how much he already knew. As I talked, he scratched at his red beard, finally putting up a hand to slow me down.

"Why are you telling me all this, Josh?"

"You don't seem surprised."

"I'm confused."

"I just want to know if you were in on this too, Dr. Kirkland. Please be honest with me. I can't take much more of this."

His eyes widened. He leaned back. "Pardon?"

"Is that why you brought me here? So these nutjobs could have their fun with me? Or was it to save face?"

He shook his head and sat up. "Josh, quite frankly, I'm shocked that you'd insinuate such a thing." He spoke calmly, as if I were a child being scolded. "Hold on." He stood and fetched me a cup of water. I pushed it away.

"Please just admit it. I want to know. I need to know. That's why you brought me here, isn't it? That's why you bypassed everybody else, to have a little fun as I suffered. That article I wrote three years ago. Your so-called diversity hire. None of it makes sense."

"What? No, Josh, I saw that article and you know what I thought? I thought: 'now here's a smart guy.' Someone who appreciates the tradition of language, when sometimes it feels like we're losing it. You hear the way kinds talk these days. Someone who knows a bit about theatre too."

"Come on," I said.

"And I needed a teacher and thought I'd give you another chance."

"Another chance?"

"A smart guy like you without an academic appointment, yeah. We all mess up sometimes."

"Who said anything about messing up?"

"You did. Before we hired you. When students correct you, sometimes mid-sentence? When you mess up, as you said you often do. What was the Yiddish word again?"

"Meyven."

"Meyven," he said, sounding it out. "A great word. I really appreciated that moment of vulnerability. Those are the kind of teachers we need. Look, Josh. I knew the transition wouldn't be easy. It wasn't easy for me either. But frankly, I'm shocked by all this. No, that's not even the right word. I'm hurt. I'm really hurt. Annoyed, too, if I'm being honest. As for Gill, well, yeah, he is one of our best Splat players. No one's arguing that. He had quite a streak the last time we played. I don't know his in-game strategies, but I do know that he's a consummate professional. Personally, I wouldn't have put him on a first-year. But sometimes those are the cards you're dealt. Why would he lie about it? Under the cover of the game, no less? You've been Splatted, haven't you?"

I felt like I had weakened my case by talking about Gill. "This is really about Brandon Grey," I said.

"Whoever it's about," he said. "There's no point arguing semantics."

"Well, sometimes there are people who want to bring others down."

"They're out to bring you down?"

"Seems so."

"And why is that?"

And I paused because, finally, this was the very question I could answer. It wasn't because I had tripped an eggplant in Philadelphia. It wasn't because of Splat. It wasn't even because I had lied about who I was or came into town a *certain* way. No. It was actually *because* of who I was. And the only one in control of that was me.

"I kissed Natalie," I said.

"Natalie Grey?"

"Yes."

"Why are you telling me that?"

"I just thought you should know."

"I don't see how that's any of my business," he said. "As long as it was consensual."

"It was."

"Okay. Look, Josh, I'm sorry but I have to cut this short. I have a parent who's waiting for my call. One of your students, actually. Tyler. Is there anything else that's urgent?"

And that was when it really hit me. When I realized who I had truly failed. My students. The real reason I was here. Tyler was disturbed by something he wrote, something he handed in to me, but had I read it? No.

"Is he okay?"

"He's fine. He likes your class, by the way. Just take a break for a bit, all right? Work on your dissertation if you have to. Why can't you just focus all this energy on that? For God's sake."

★

After that, I sat on a rock overlooking the south side of the lake. It was chilly, but it wasn't cold. The sun was low in the sky but still caught parts of the water. I thought about calling Thiago. I thought about calling Heloise. I thought about calling my father.

I didn't know what to do next.

I never knew what to do next.

I just knew that I didn't want to leave.

But I also knew that maybe I would have to.

I watched a swarm of birds lap the horizon, mirroring each

other. Sometimes I wished I were a bird. Like my "reincarnated" mother—a cardinal perched on the neighbor's fence, flying, flying.

A figure emerged a few yards away, out of the brush. He stood at the water's edge, looking pensively at the lake in front of him. He pulled his shirt off and appeared to step out of his pants. I couldn't see his face. The wind picked up and he seemed to hesitate. Then, he dove into the water. Iowans have a good tolerance for that kind of thing. An early October swim in a cold lake. It wasn't on my bucket list. I kept waiting to see him emerge but instead the water was still.

I walked to his clothes, suddenly struck by curiosity. There are some things I would never know, I reasoned, but others I would. I realized, when I got there, that they were Fairbury clothes. I checked the lanyard. It was Tyler's.

I still couldn't see him out there, so I yelled for him. There wasn't an answer. Then I did the only thing I could think to do. I jumped.

The water was cold but when you're running on adrenaline like that you don't care. I swam as fast as I could, though my clothes were weighing me down, until suddenly he emerged from the water beside me, at peace. When he saw me, he flipped over and began dog paddling, coughing gulps of water into and out of his mouth.

"Tyler," I yelled. "Are you okay? What are you doing out here?"

He ducked his head under water and emerged again. He shook his head and water sprayed from his hair.

"I was going for a swim," he said. "I was only swimming."

"You're not allowed out here alone," I said. The water formed massive bubbles beneath my shirt which I pushed down with a fist.

"I know. I'm sorry."

"So then why are you here?"

"Because I like it here. It's relaxing."

"But it's against the rules."

My arms and legs were getting tired, so I motioned with my head to the shore. We swam together, the wind intensifying around us, seeming to change direction mid-gust.

On shore, he lifted a towel from beneath his pile of clothes. I let him dry off with it before sitting next to him on a rock, trying to catch my breath. He was wearing only a pair of boxers. He had a few strands of hair on his chest.

"What activity are you supposed to be in right now?" I asked.

"Silent reading," he said. I could hear in his voice that he was shivering.

"What's the real reason you're here?" I asked.

"I told you," he said. "Because I like it here. It's my secret place. It makes me feel small. I mean, I am small. But I mean, really small. It makes me feel really small. Like I have control. Did you know if you cry in space the tears just stick to your face? Did you know that?"

"I didn't know that," I said.

"I just thought it was interesting."

"You should get back to campus before someone realizes you're gone, okay? I'll keep this between you and me. But you have to promise me that you won't do it again. Not alone. Not unless you tell somebody. You have to remember that people here care about you. Tyler, I care about you. You're important. You're special. Don't be anything less than you are, okay? If you can help it. What you are is okay. Don't be what someone else thinks you should be. Or wants you to be. Or even what you think you should be. Don't be you in secret. I wish someone would have told me that even two, three months ago."

"Okay." He stood and handed me his towel. I dried off my hair with it. "Thanks, Almost Dr. J."

"Josh," I said, handing the towel back. "Just call me Josh."

He looked confused, but started to run off. Then, he stopped and turned to face me again. "Are you doing okay, Josh?"

I pointed at myself. "What do you mean?"

"I mean, do you like it here? Do you want to stay at Fairbury?"

"I do, but there are things I really miss at home too."

"Like what?"

"People, mostly."

"Me too," he said. He headed back toward the school.

Alone again, I faced the water. The sun was starting to set. Then I saw the Eggplant Wizard, walking in the center of the lake, away from me. One foot in front of the next. I went in after him. The water was even colder this time. I swam only about fifteen yards before he was gone, so I just waited there. I heard the sound of a car in the distance, but everything else was still. In a way, I felt at peace with it all. I let it slide off my shoulders. I took all the time I needed before swimming back to shore.

IX: INSERT SECOND DISC NOW

THE LISTINGS KEPT COMING from dozens of new profiles, flooding the fantastical world of eBay with my abridged biography, a character study of some shmuck from Long Island, slowly altering the efficacy of my own gaming collection to do as my other fixations once did: distract, avoid. Until, the games I owned, played, and 100-percented, the games I held sacred and kept safe, the games who drove Heloise away, who drove me, in one way or another, to Iowa, were no longer mine.

Finally, it was time. I listed my collection as a handful of massive lots, auction-style. The bids came. They were selling.

At school, I cornered Natalie at lunch. I brought a warm cinnamon roll to her table.

"Thanks for not saying anything to Kirkland," I said.

There was pity in her eyes. I held the cinnamon roll out, but she wouldn't take it.

"Thanks," I said again.

"I don't know why you're thanking me, Josh."

And she got up and left.

I went out the door after her, biting off chunks of the roll. I tossed what was left in the trash and wandered aimlessly around the Fairbury grounds, zigzagging past the cluster of academic buildings and the courtyard between the student barracks until I was at the parking lot where I had first parked my U-Haul. The sun was pounding against the pavement. Only a few cars were there. I recognized Kirkland's green MINI Cooper and I thought back to Natalie's self-portrait exercise and wondered how Kirkland might have drawn me, his new instructor. Someone respectable, deserving. Yet this was how I repaid him. My mother would have been disgusted.

He'd find out sooner or later. Better he heard it from me than from someone else. At least I owed him that. At least I could show him some decency.

I found him just outside the admin building, sipping a coffee while chatting with someone from the maintenance crew about floodlights. I walked up next to them and their conversation went on as if I weren't there. I wondered if he already knew, if I was too late.

"Hey, I need to talk to you again," I whispered.

Finally, he looked at me. "Can it wait? Dom and I have a few more stops on the great light tour."

"It really can't."

He thought it over. "I'll be right back, Dom." I followed him to a metal bench nearby. "What's going on? Is this about Natalie?"

"No," I said. I buried my head in my hands.

"Josh," Kirkland said. It was the kindness of his voice that ripped me.

I told him that I had lied, that it was all a lie, that I wasn't who I said I was. "The PhD," I said. "My dead wife. All of it was a lie. I dropped out of the program. My wife left me."

He put the coffee on the ground at his feet. Now he was the one who didn't look well. "But you do have your Master's?"

"I do."

"So why lie?"

I told him about my parents. I told him about my games. I told him about the Eggplant Wizard. I told him how badly I wanted to fit in.

"The Eggplant Wizard?"

"If you want me to leave, I'd understand," I said. "Even though I don't have anywhere to go. You'll never hear from me again. I promise."

He rolled his eyes. "Josh, look, this is indefensible and I'm gonna need some time to think on it, but you're a good teacher and the kids like you."

"I do love the kids," I said.

"And to be honest, I don't have anyone to cover your classes right now. I'll let you know what I decide."

He picked up his coffee, tossed it in the trash, and left.

★

By the end of the week, everyone at Fairbury knew I had lied. My students passed notes and interrupted my lectures with questions about morality and justice. In the hallways, Pants and Pomm and Timmer and Jane ignored me. Hunter Green smiled whenever we saw each other, which really got under my skin. During lunch, there was nowhere to sit except next to Glen Gill. "You're lucky you're Jewish," he told me, "Or this seat would be reserved." By the end of the week we got to chatting about my bar mitzvah, how I had fallen off the chair during the hora because one of my cousins thought he was a lot stronger than he actually was. He laughed so hard he almost spit out his milk.

All my games sold for a pretty penny. I packed them into boxes and stuffed the empty space with bubble wrap. I brought them to the post office just before they closed for the weekend. I made sure the teller marked them as fragile and watched as she took them away. Then I deleted my eBay profile and removed the app from all my devices.

At home, I sat on my beanbag chair in the game room, staring blankly at the empty shelves. Look on the bright side, I thought, maybe this was the push I needed to get into something that could be more productive, that could help make me respectable. I thought of all the things that could fill those shelves: movies, books, records, souvenirs from faraway places. I wouldn't have any of it. I lifted the shelves onto my back and threw them into a big pile in the alley behind the house. Inside, I took my clothes off and collapsed onto the floor of the empty room, listening to the sound of my heart trying to slow down. Maybe Therapist Number One had been right. Maybe those games didn't make me happy. But then why, lying there in that room stripped bare, did I feel so fucking miserable?

★

On Monday morning, Dr. Kirkland called me into his office. I was already preparing to be fired. I had imagined cleaning out my desk and spending the afternoon at Twin Oaks searching for teaching jobs and then applying to be a barista if I got frustrated.

In the crimson glow of his office, Kirk, with great flair, pushed the door closed behind me to reveal a purple robe hanging on a coat hanger that was pinned to the back of the door. With it was a giant purple one-piece and a big green helmet drawn like an eye with a half-open mouth.

"Look familiar?" he said. "Say hello to your new outfit. Mondays only. Made it myself. Bet you didn't know I can sew? We all have identities here, Josh. If you aren't Almost Dr. J, then maybe you can be this so-called Eggplant Wizard instead."

"You don't seriously expect me to wear that?"

"Not just wear it, teach in it."

"Dr. Kirkland, I…"

He put a hand on my shoulder. "Josh, you will be the new head of the Eggplant Wizard Society. I already got approval from the powers that be. Picture it one day in the Fairbury Bible, right there between The Caloian Rain Ritual, The Holder of the Duck, and Splat. Let's just say these are big shoes to fill, but I know you have it in you. I always knew that you did. Now come on, try it on."

He took the costume into his arms and held it out for me. I didn't know what else to do but take it.

"This is crazy," I managed.

"You can change in my bathroom," he said. He pulled the long wooden staff from the Fountainhead, the Royal Fox Society and pointed to the hallway. In a daze, I started walking, but then the staff swept beneath my feet and I fell face-first onto the tile.

When I came to, Kirk was standing over me, apologizing.

"It was the staff," he said.

"I'm okay," I said.

I waited for him to hold out an arm to help me up, but instead he drew a rainbow with his hands. "Beware the Eggplant Curse," he said, laughing. "Oh, this will be fun. You know what I was just thinking: maybe you can make it a video game club. You collect games, don't you?"

ACKNOWLEDGEMENTS

With thanks to the faculty who have guided me for years, especially during my tenure in the MFA program at the University of Idaho and the PhD program at the University of Nebraska-Lincoln. And to the writers and friends in those programs with whom I've shared workshops and offices and printers and drinks and Mets games and road trips.

With thanks to Laura Stanfill and the students in her publishing seminar at Portland State University, where this book was assigned, for the feedback letters and copy edits during a critical stage of my revision.

To Leland Cheuk, the editor I never knew I needed. Thanks for giving this book a home and for welcoming me to the 7.13 Community, a brave, badass group of writers. If you're reading this, support these writers and buy some more books.

To my family. My parents for their unending support. My brothers for pushing me to be better. My grandmother for always believing in me. Aunts, uncles, cousins. You've always had my back and I'll always have yours.

To Ellie, above all. My best reader. My rock. This exists because of you.

ABOUT THE AUTHOR

Shawn Rubenfeld has had short fiction appear in journals such as *Permafrost*, *Columbia Journal* and *Portland Review*. He has a Ph.D. in English and Creative Writing from the University of Nebraska-Lincoln, where he is currently a lecturer. He lives in Omaha.

7.13BOOKS

CPSIA information can be obtained
at www.ICGtesting.com
Printed in the USA
FSHW011252200521
81663FS

9 781733 367288